THE KILLING SITE

A Liberty Lane Mystery

Caro Peacock

Severn House Large Print
London & New York

This first large print edition published 2019
in Great Britain and the USA by
SEVERN HOUSE PUBLISHERS LTD of
Eardley House, 4 Uxbridge Street, London W8 7SY.
First world regular print edition published 2018 by
Severn House Publishers Ltd.

British Library Cataloguing in Publication Data
A CIP catalogue record for this title is available from the British Library.

ISBN-13: 9780727829559

Severn House Publishers support the Forest Stewardship Council™
[FSC™], the leading international forest certification organisation. All
our titles that are printed on FSC certified paper carry the FSC logo.

MIX
Paper from
responsible sources
FSC
www.fsc.org   FSC® C013056

Typeset by Palimpsest Book Production Ltd.,
Falkirk, Stirlingshire, Scotland.
Printed and bound in Great Britain by
T J International, Padstow, Cornwall.

One

'Dearest Robert, I am alive . . .'

My head was throbbing, my pulse hammering in the bulge behind the top of my left ear. If I touched it, the area felt as hard as a tortoise's shell, a mass of dried blood and hair. How long had it taken to dry out and harden? One day, two? The iron taste of blood was still in my mouth, or perhaps only a memory of it. This was like trying to set up signposts in the sea – a dark sea and blank signposts.

'It's implied. I'd hardly be writing if I weren't alive.'

My voice seemed to be from another life – controlled, almost amused. I'd protested, just to hear myself say it, though I knew it would be no use.

'Write what I tell you.'

A woman's voice, authoritative and deep, but not ladylike. The sort of voice you might expect in a prison wardress. Forty or older. They'd had to bring in a candle so that I could write, so I could see more of her than before. She wore a black wool dress and an outdoor bonnet with a thick veil coming down over her face. The candle was a cheap one in an enamel holder and, after the near dark, the light of it was hurting my eyes, making my head throb more. It was beside me on the table where I was writing, with the

1

sheet of paper on an old blotter. The woman and a man had carried in a small table and chair for me to write. Until then, the only furniture in the room had been a thin pallet by the wall. The chair was hard through my petticoat and my back ached. How long had I been curled on the pallet, unconscious or drifting in a semi-conscious haze, before they came and made me stand up? I had no idea. The woman stood just behind my shoulder. I turned suddenly, sending pain jabbing through my head, but managed to see a gleam of eyes through the veil, as intent as a robin's on a worm. Her smell was old sweat, onions and a naphtha whiff of mothballs. So the black wool dress had been brought out of storage – it wasn't her everyday wear. She might even be a man in disguise. She was tall and heavy enough, and the voice might have been put on. When I thought about it, the sweat had the sweetish candlewax smell of a man's sweat. Or perhaps that really was the candlewax, or from the man standing behind my chair. I'd caught a glimpse of him in the candlelight before he moved behind me – younger than the woman, long black hair, a pale, intense face that might have been appropriate on a poet, and arched eyebrows. His boots squeaked, and the leather looked cheap and yellowish. New boots. In spite of myself, my mind was trying to get back to its own skills, but feebly and not usefully. The woman shifted to one side of me when she saw my eyes were on her, but I caught an impression of a forehead that bulged out like Minerva's in a helmet on a statue. She went on dictating.

2

'*If you wish to see me again, tell nobody. You will be contacted by people who will tell you what to do.*'

'If you're thinking of a ransom, you've chosen the wrong people,' I said. 'We're not rich.'

Robert would pay every last penny we had, I knew that. Raise more from his brothers if necessary. Perhaps by some people's standards we might even be considered quite rich, but not enough to make us victims of a simple kidnapping.

'Write.'

I wrote. My left wrist, holding down the paper, was hurting. It must have been sprained when they attacked me. Did I have a memory of somebody grabbing it before the blow came? I couldn't distinguish between real memory and my mind's desperate attempts to put anything in place of the great blank. Unconnected scenes or bits of conversation had swum up to me when I was half-conscious, like fish behind glass, mouthing then finning away.

'. . . Stood to reason, railway shares wouldn't go on rising forever . . .'

A woman's lower arm, white out of green silk. 'More syllabub? The cream's from the dearest little Jersey. Cook keeps her in the garden.' Not a young arm; there were some faint brown age spots on the white.

Then a child's face, pink and tearful. 'Going out again. Always going out.'

Of course, we weren't. It was our first evening out for ten days. I remembered counting with him. Harry could get up to ten, usually, but it didn't pacify him.

The smell of leather. Where did that come from? No leather in this room. Was it leather upholstery in a coach they'd used to carry me away? I had a sudden memory of new red leather – a lot of it – but that couldn't be anything to do with it, because how would I have known the colour? Insensible. Before they hit me, the man had said Harry had been taken ill. A lie to get me out of the house; I was sure now that he'd been lying. I'd had to ask him to repeat what he'd said because of the noise of dogs barking, several of them at the back of the house, and voices shouting. Then the blow and instant darkness, not even the sensation of falling, though I surely must have fallen.

'Then sign it as you'd usually sign a letter to him.'

The voice had a strained quality. I hesitated. There were so many ways we signed off our letters – lovingly, jokingly, in haste. I wrote: *With all my love, Libby.* I could feel her eyes on me, then her hand came over, picked up the thin sheet of paper, pressed it face down on the blotter and snatched it away. Minerva, I'd call her. She went, taking the candle, and the poet followed her. They shut the door and one of them turned a key in the padlock. I knew it must be a padlock because it thumped back against the door once the key had been turned. They left me the table and chair. The two pairs of steps went only a short distance away, then another door opened. They weren't far off. I could hear them moving about, just on the other side of the wall, a plain wall of vertical planks, roughly whitewashed. With the candle gone, I could just make out the colour of it, so a little light must be coming from somewhere, from up above me, I thought, but it hurt my head too much to look up. They might at least have helped me back on to the pallet so that I could curl up again and sleep. I had to do it myself with shaky legs, supporting my weight with a hand on the table, then something between a stagger and a fall on to the pallet. I was more feeble than a day-old pup. Helena and Harry kept bothering us for a puppy. I could think of them, imagine every detail of their faces down to the last hair of an eyebrow, but trying to remember anything else was like heaving a load up a hill. Perhaps I was in a basement. This wasn't a large place, by the sound of it. I'd noticed a whiff of damp and bad drains, so perhaps it was a rented place that had stood empty and had been taken by Minerva and friends for this. A cheap place, judging by the thin wall. But where was it? If I knew how long I'd been unconscious, I might have some idea. Westminster was where it started, I knew that much, but I could have been taken anywhere. It took the Royal Mail one day and nineteen hours to get from London to Edinburgh. How could I remember that when there was so much I couldn't remember? Could I have stayed unconscious for nearly two days in somebody's fast coach? Perhaps, yes, if I'd been drugged, which might explain why my mind was so much at odds. I pulled the damp and uneven blanket up over me, cried and slept again.

Two

'It's been nearly two days now.'

Miles Brinkburn was perched on the edge of an old armchair by the bookcase, anxiety sitting uneasily on a face made for cheerfulness.

'Forty-one hours.'

His half-brother, Robert Carmichael, spoke without emotion, as if reciting a scientific fact, but his thin face was ghostly and his eyes dark-rimmed. After a first glance when they arrived, Miles couldn't bear to look at him. He stood leaning against the mantel-piece, the fire unlit in the July heat.

'And still nothing from the police?'

This from Miles' elder brother, Stephen, picking up from Robert's apparently calm tone. He was Lord Brinkburn, on many committees, and had a politician's habit of speaking as if anything that had happened was the other man's fault, though he was as shaken as any of them.

Robert shook his head. 'Sergeant Bevan said he'd send a messenger directly when he heard anything. That was yesterday morning. There's been nothing since.'

'Bevan. I've heard the name, haven't I?'

'A rising man, or so Libby gathered. I suppose he's a friend of hers, after a fashion, as far as anybody in the force is. He's been involved in several of her cases. That's why I asked for him particularly.'

'And what did he say when you spoke to him?'

'He wanted to know what she was working on at present.'

Stephen leaned forward. 'And what did you tell him?'

'The truth, as I've told you. She's working on nothing at the moment and nothing all this year. This can't be connected with a case of hers because there isn't a case.'

'I thought she'd finish with that anyway,' Stephen said. 'Once you were married, and especially after the children came along, it was totally inappropriate.'

Robert's lips turned up in something that might have been intended as a smile. 'We thought so too, but you know that line of Milton: *one talent which is death to hide.* Now and again, there'd be somebody appealing for help and, either out of pity or curiosity, she'd be in there again.'

'And sometimes doing things Disraeli wanted her to do,' Stephen said, his low opinion of the MP in his voice. 'Does he know?'

Robert's own early suspicion of Disraeli had mellowed. 'No, he doesn't know. Apart from Bevan and whoever he's consulted, the family and the Maynards, nobody knows.'

'And several dozen servants,' Miles broke in. 'Don't look at me like that, Stephen. It's what Libby would have said herself. Probably half the kitchens in Mayfair know she's missing.'

'There's the maid that brought in the message for a start,' Robert said. 'She's the only person we know who saw one of the men involved, not that she was able to tell us much. It was dark on

7

the step and she was dazzled by the candles inside. Just an ordinary man, not tall, with his collar turned up, saying he had a message for Mrs Carmichael that her son was ill.'

'So the maid took in the message and Liberty went rushing out,' Miles said.

Robert nodded. 'I blame myself for that. I should have gone out with her. I wanted to, but we were talking to Maynard about that confounded hospital donation and I didn't think it was anything too serious. Mrs Martley does panic about Harry sometimes. I followed her just a few minutes later, but then it was too late.' He closed his eyes, remembering those first few panicking minutes, calling for Liberty more and more urgently. For a while, he'd turned from a scientific into a superstitious man, and thought the gods had somehow snatched her up.

'So the maid still can't remember anything else?' Miles said.

'No. She doesn't seem to be a very intelligent girl, or perhaps she was just scared out of her wits by all the panic. She opened the front door because the butler was occupied elsewhere.'

'And those dogs,' Miles said. 'That didn't help.'

'Dogs?'

'You didn't hear them? Their bitch had got loose, so all the dogs in the neighbourhood were yapping and yowling in their gardens. Half the servants were out in the garden trying to get her in when they should have been looking for Liberty. By the by, I think we should ask Legge to come up.'

'Legge the groom?' Stephen said.

8

'Amos Legge, our friend,' Robert said. 'He's here?'

'Down in the yard. You want me to fetch him up?'

Robert nodded and Miles ran off downstairs. They were meeting in Liberty's old lodgings at Abel Yard, because Robert had spent most of the last two days there in the belief that any news about her would come to the yard rather than their house a few streets away, where Mrs Martley was looking after the children. They'd kept the lodgings on partly as a repository for his books. Amos Legge followed Miles back in, bending his head to get through the doorway. Robert was tall but Legge overtopped him by six inches. His breeches and jacket were as neat as when he rode out in the park with his customers from the livery stables he part-owned. He carried his brown top hat with the gold rosette but his face was almost as grim as Robert's. The two of them exchanged a look.

'Nothing?'

'Nothing, sir. I reckon I've accounted for every cart or carriage that stopped anywhere near that house all evening up to past midnight, and nothing.'

'Suppose she went on foot,' Miles said. 'She comes out of the Maynards' house and starts making for home.'

'But she wouldn't, not without telling me.'

'In any case, somebody would have seen her.'

'Not necessarily. It was dark by then, and . . .'

Stephen held up his hand. 'Let's go over it all again, the whole evening. Who knew you'd be

9

dining with the Maynards? Robert and Miles, you were there and I wasn't. Let's start from who organized it and why.'

'I suppose I did,' Miles said. 'Robert and I were discussing raising funds for the eye hospital. I mentioned that Godrich Maynard had millions from his coal mines and eased his conscience sometimes by giving some of it away to good causes, and Rosa and I occasionally had dinner with him and his wife. Robert was interested and I got Maynard to invite the four of us on Monday – Robert and Libby and Rosa and me. They have a house just off Millbank, near St John's Church. Rosa and I picked up Libby and Robert in our carriage and off we went.'

'And Libby seemed perfectly normal?' Stephen asked.

'Good heavens, yes, in fine form. In fact, it struck me she was looking particularly well. Blue dress – new, Rosa said . . .'

Robert nodded.

'And that dragonfly thing of hers in her hair. She and Rosa were chattering happily on the way about the children. At dinner, she was sitting on Maynard's left, with Rosa on his right. There were only the six of us so the conversation was pretty general. I can't remember anything of significance.'

'Railways,' Robert said. 'Maynard's part of a group promoting a new line in south Wales. Your story about the young horses and your carriage being run away with, Miles. And whether the Maynards should move house.'

'Yes, he did rather harp on about problems from

the rebuilding of Parliament,' Miles said. 'Of course, it's difficult for them, living in Westminster with all the carts coming and going and the noise and mud and so on, and it has been going on for ten years or more. Still, it's got to end sometime, and I thought they should hang on.'

'And Liberty was joining in the conversation?' Stephen asked.

'She certainly was,' Miles said. 'Libby's never been one for womanly silence and she fairly quizzed him about mining casualties, though not to the point of being offensive. But I can't remember a single thing said that seemed to strike her particularly.'

'I agree,' Robert said. 'It was just a perfectly normal dinner table conversation.'

'Did you talk about your eye hospital?'

'It's hardly my hospital. Yes, the three of us talked about it after the ladies withdrew. Miles and I both had the impression that Maynard was likely to subscribe. Of course, we don't know what the ladies talked about on their own.'

'I do,' Miles said. 'Rosa told me it was almost entirely about dogs. Mrs Maynard breeds King Charles spaniels. Rosa thought there was a limit to what could be said about spaniels but Libby kept the conversation going, as she does. In any case, the ladies weren't on their own for long. We joined them in about twenty minutes or so, there was more general conversation, then the message arrived.'

All the time, Amos Legge had been standing just inside the doorway, hat in his hand. Robert turned to him.

'You're certain she didn't go off in a vehicle, Amos?'

'As certain as I can be. I've made a list I'll give you of every vehicle that stopped in that street or round the corner from early Monday evening until after midnight. There were eleven of them – everything from carriages to the rag-picker's donkey cart. They're all accounted for, with a reason to be there, and none of the drivers saw any sign of a lady answering her description.'

'It might not have stopped,' Miles said. 'If it just drove past and somebody jumped out and snatched her up . . .'

'There's something else, isn't there, Amos?' Robert said.

Amos nodded and slid a hand into the deep pocket of his jacket, looking as guilty as if he were producing a stolen thing. The hand came out holding something blue and dust-covered. Robert closed his eyes and rocked forward, then opened them and took the thing from him.

'It is, isn't it?' Amos's voice was low.

Robert nodded. 'Her shoe.' An evening pump, not intended for much walking, blue satin lined with white kid, soiled as if a cart wheel had gone over it. A jagged tear ripped across the toe. 'The buckle's gone.'

'Somebody'd have torn that off to sell,' Amos said. 'There was no buckle on when Tabby got it off the boy.'

'So Tabby knows,' Miles said.

Amos turned to him. ''Course she does. She's spent every waking hour and some sleeping ones round that house where you had dinner. This morning, some urchin came up to her with this. He said he'd found it in the gutter and she reckons he's telling the truth.'

Silence, broken by Miles. 'So she was taken against her will. She didn't just walk away.'

Robert was still looking down at the shoe. 'Toothmarks on it. A dog's, I think.'

'They'd fight over it if it was lying in the gutter. It doesn't mean anything.' Miles was still trying to make things better, smoothing away the picture of Libby being attacked by dogs. 'Shall you give it to Sergeant Bevan?'

Robert nodded and put it in his pocket. It was shallower than Legge's, and part of the shoe stuck out over the top.

Miles went on with his story of the night. 'Robert went out and came back in saying Liberty had disappeared. Somebody was sent running for the police and Robert and I went up and down the street and all the side streets calling for her. Then our carriage arrived and we sent Rosa off, to see if maybe Libby had gone home by cab, though goodness knows why she would have. After that we came and woke you up, Stephen, just on the off-chance she'd gone to you.'

Amos Legge stood like a statue. 'I'll go on trying, sir,' he said to Robert. 'All the cab drivers, carriage hirers, everything.'

Robert nodded his thanks and Amos turned and went slowly down the stairs, leaving the three brothers looking at each other as if one of them, against all probability, could come up with an answer.

Tabby was waiting down in the yard by the mounting block. She wore a brown skirt, a long jacket like a man's and no hat, her pale brown hair, none too clean, caught up in an untidy knot at the back. Her feet, in brown boots, were scuffing the straw between the cobbles. She was probably in her early twenties but had never known the date of her birthday, the name of her father or very much about her mother, beyond the fact that she'd been a prostitute and had died when Tabby was a child. From an alliance a long way back, she'd become Liberty's assistant, and was now the guardian of Abel Yard, living in a cabin halfway between the gates on to Adam's Mews and the cow byres at the far end. In the years following Liberty's marriage to Robert, when she'd done less investigating, Tabby had set up on her own.

'Well?'

'Yes, it's hers,' Amos said.

'Knew it was. Did he say anything?'

'Not much. He's like a bull that's run into a stone wall, plain moithered. They all are.'

The noise Tabby made was somewhere between impatience and contempt. Amos looked down at her. 'We're not doing any better, are we?'

'Depends. That shoe means something, two days after.'

'Yes, it means she didn't walk off on her own accord, not in one shoe. But that's what we thought.' She gave him a look, not much more polite than the sound she'd made. 'Are you saying we're missing something?'

'The boy came up with it this morning, so it's been lying in the gutter all yesterday, has it?'

14

'Seems so.'

'You wouldn't get an old seg off a boot sole lying there that long – somebody would have it. And somebody did have it to take the buckle off, but even with the buckle off, it's worth something with a lining that was new kid. So why didn't somebody pick it up before?'

'What are you thinking?' Amos said.

'That it wasn't there in the gutter until sometime after she went. So where was it?'

'Somewhere a dog chewed it.'

'I've been talking to a maid in the house where they went to dinner. She reckons the bitch had never got out before that night. When she's in season, they keep her shut up in an old pantry, nice and comfortable with a basket and cushion, and the maid takes her meals on a plate. It's more than the maid's job's worth to let her out and she swears she never did, but she got out – the door was unbolted.'

'So there were all the dogs yapping and yowling out in the gardens. They said that upstairs, but I don't see . . .'

'With all the noise out in the garden, people wouldn't know what was going on out front.'

Amos frowned. 'You're saying somebody in the house let the bitch out on purpose?'

A nod from Tabby.

'And whoever it was did it because they wanted to help whoever was getting her away?'

Another nod.

'But how would they know she was going to dinner there in the first place?'

'The butler and housekeeper would know who

15

was coming, and if they did, somebody else could.'

'It seems far-fetched to me.'

'It's far-fetched that she vanished from under their noses and you can't find out how she was taken away.'

He thought about it, head bowed. Then, 'So what do we do?'

'I don't know what you're going to do. I'm going to keep as close to that house as a maggot in meat.'

With nothing else to say, he wished her goodbye, unhitched his patient cob from the ring beside the mounting block and swung into the saddle.

'You'll get word to me if you find out anything?'

She didn't bother to reply.

Upstairs, the three men were finding that they had nothing else to say. They'd discussed so many possibilities and theories but were no closer to finding her than Robert and Miles had been in those first disbelieving minutes outside the Maynards' house. Stephen had a meeting to go to and Miles got up to leave with him. At the door, Stephen turned back to Robert.

'If it had been a simple kidnapping for money, you'd surely have heard by now. And you haven't?'

Robert had been looking down at the carpet, but he raised his head and looked up at Stephen.

'I've heard nothing.'

With more assurances about coming back as soon as there were any developments, Miles and Stephen went away downstairs.

* * *

16

Amos Legge thought about what Tabby had said on his way back to the stables. He checked the tack cleaning, supervised the evening round of feeding and watering, spread ointment of his own making on a kick injury on a carriage horse's hock. None of the lads who jumped to it when he noticed a bucket or a blanket strap out of place guessed that most of his mind was elsewhere. He decided that it would make sense to discuss Tabby's theory with Mr Carmichael. By then, the horses were rugged up and eating their feed, so he walked for once, across the park towards Abel Yard. He was about to turn into Adam's Mews when he saw Robert Carmichael about two hundred yards away, walking down Audley Street towards Piccadilly. It would be unthinkable to shout out after a gentleman like a tinker calling his dog, so Amos followed him, confident of catching up. But Mr Carmichael was striding out like a man in a hurry and Amos was hardly gaining on him. Amos noticed that he was carrying a canvas satchel, and it struck him suddenly that Mr Carmichael had heard from the kidnappers and was going to pay a ransom. This put a different complexion on things and meant that Mr Carmichael would not welcome company. If that was what he was going to do, Amos didn't blame him. In the circumstances, he'd probably have done the same thing. But he'd be taking a big risk. What was to stop the kidnappers snatching the bag and running off without delivering? What if they weren't the kidnappers at all, only sneak thieves who'd somehow heard she was missing and were taking advantage? Mr Carmichael, in his anxiety, wouldn't have thought of that, so it was Amos's business to be there when the money exchanged hands and do what he could to protect him. Once he'd decided that, he simply kept pace with him and followed him from a distance into Piccadilly. At this time in the early evening, it was particularly crowded, with carriages jammed in the street, gentlemen coming from clubs and couples sauntering. Amos collided with a young lady under a sunshade and nearly bowled her over. His red-faced apologies and a diatribe from the older woman with her meant that by the time he could look out for him, Mr Carmichael was out of sight. Crestfallen, he walked on eastwards, surprised that any criminal should choose such a public place to meet his victim. Then, just before Haymarket, he saw Mr Carmichael again, still a couple of hundred yards ahead. Amos zigzagged through the crowds, getting closer, just in time to see him turn into the yard of the White Bear inn.

Amos slowed down, near familiar territory now. The White Bear was one of the main starting points for stage coaches. He'd sold horses to them and knew dozens of the grooms, drivers and ostlers. It struck him that the kidnappers might be playing a clever game – grab the money then get away behind four fast horses on a stage coach. If so, they'd miscalculated. Amos could take the best horse from the yard and follow. For now, though, some caution was needed. Mr Carmichael would not want to see him there. With Amos's height and breadth of shoulder, it was hard for him to be inconspicuous, but he did his best, keeping his head bent so as not to catch the eye of anybody he knew, mounting the outside stairs that led to the balcony of the inn over-looking the yard. Mr Carmichael went inside the inn, then came out again a few minutes later with the satchel as plump as when he'd gone in. He didn't look up to the balcony. A coach was standing in the yard, horses harnessed, passengers inside, a few on top and ostlers loading luggage. No driver was on the box yet, but apart from that it was almost ready to go. Amos had the time-tables of most of the coaches from this part of London in his head. This was 'The Union', an overnight coach for Dover via Rochester and Canterbury, arriving at the port around dawn. Mr Carmichael was talking to one of the ostlers, handing him something – certainly not a fat wedge of money, just a folded sheet of paper, by the look of it. The driver had come out of the inn and was getting up on the box, the horses stirring as he took the reins in his hand, wheels grinding on the cobbles. If a handover of money was to happen, this was the moment for it. The ostler nodded and put the folded paper in his pocket. Mr Carmichael ran to the coach just as it was moving and swung himself up the steps to the seats on top. As he plumped down on to a seat, still with the satchel, his head was just under Amos's feet. Thinking about it afterwards, Amos blamed himself for not vaulting over the balcony rail and joining him on top of the coach, but at the time he was too surprised by the speed of events. He watched as the coach turned out of the yard into the street and broke into a trot, then was lost in the press of traffic. The ostler was still in the yard, sweeping straw. Amos knew him by sight, and his offer of a drink was happily accepted. He went inside, ordered two pints, and was halfway down his by the time the ostler joined him. Amos explained that he was there to see off a gentleman on 'The Union'. The ostler swallowed the pint pretty well at a gulp and Amos ordered two more.

'Was that a letter he gave you?'

The ostler nodded. Amos was an important man in the horse world and being treated by him was an honour.

'I expect he'd have given it to me, only I was up on the balcony and he was in too much of a hurry,' Amos said. He had an air of authority about him, especially in the stables. 'I'll take it and deliver it for you, and you can keep the shilling.'

Something in the ostler's expression told Amos it had probably been nearer half a crown. 'The gentleman said I was to deliver it tomorrow afternoon.'

'I'll see to that.'

The ostler produced a letter from inside his tunic and handed it over. Amos finished his pint and took it back to his room at the stables. It was a single sheet of paper, folded double, addressed to Miles Brinkburn Esq., at his home in Knightsbridge. If the fold had been sealed, Amos might have been reluctant to break it, but it was simply secured with a smaller triangular fold at one corner. He was feeling pretty close to anger. Mr Carmichael had chosen not to confide in him.

He and his brothers were planning some rescue and wouldn't trust Liberty's oldest friend, who'd been with her in tight places before she even knew they existed. If he thought they'd manage it without him he might just have tolerated it, but she'd need him, he was sure of that. So, without any particular feeling of guilt, he undid the triangular fold and read.

Dear Miles,

By the time you read this, I should be some considerable distance away. I have some information which I'm afraid I am not free to share with you and Stephen without a great risk to Liberty's life. I shall be in touch with you as soon as possible but do not know when that will be. It will certainly be some days. Meanwhile, you should continue by all means to look for her and encourage the police to do so. She may yet be found by methods other than the one I have had to adopt. With all my heart, I hope so. In haste, and with kindest thoughts of you all whatever happens, your brother, Robert.

He read it through twice, a little consoled that the brothers were as much in the dark as he was, but puzzled. If Mr Carmichael had picked up some clue, why shouldn't he have included them all in the search? His first thought was that he should deliver the letter to Miles straight away. But then, if Mr Carmichael really did have good information, why take the risk of hindering him? On balance, he'd keep the letter till tomorrow afternoon. It was a hard decision, because every muscle in his body was tense with a wish to be on a fast horse, following Robert into goodness knew what.

I hope you know what you're doing. He said it in his head to Robert, without much belief in his heart.

Three

I woke up and something was different. It wasn't anything to do with the room. That was so dark that it was probably night outside. The change was in my mind. My head was still sore, though not as bad as it had been, but my mind had started to work again. It was my trade, after all, finding answers to questions, looking for facts then drawing conclusions from them. So, I started with what I knew, which was this room. If I couldn't remember what had happened, I'd work back from when I'd first woken up here. Never mind how many days ago that was, just think. Even after I'd woken up, I'd kept my eyes closed, probably for a long time, because of the throbbing in my head. The pallet was lumpy under me, and when my hand slid off it I felt bare boards against my knuckles. Grittiness, too, as if somebody had sprinkled the boards with coarse sand. I was on the floor, then. I'd opened my eyes, then closed them again, but after a while I'd managed to open them long enough to look around me. At first, the darkness had seemed total, but gradually it had given way enough for me to make out a gleam of something white, by far the brightest thing in the room. It had taken me some time to realize that it was a chamber pot and my bladder was almost bursting. I'd managed to roll myself out of bed, crying at the effort, and crawl across the floor to it. As I'd crawled, I'd been aware that I was in my underthings – chemise and stays, petticoat and stockings. In the strange way that things take you, I'd registered that they were one of my best pairs of stockings and they'd never be the same again. The garters had slipped down to below my knees. When I'd used the chamber pot I'd tried to stand upright, but the whole room seemed to be rocking from side to side, so I'd got down on my hands and knees again and crawled back to the pallet. The rocking seemed to go on a long time and I'd slept again. Sometime after that – days or hours, I didn't know – Minerva and the poet had come in and made me write the letter. Before I'd started writing, I'd complained I was thirsty. Minerva had nodded to the poet, and he'd gone out and returned with a willow-pattern cup, coarse stuff of the kind you get on market stalls. The water had tasted bitter, I'd thought, probably from the lingering taste of blood in my mouth, but I'd drained it.

Laudanum. I'm sure they put it in the water, or else why should I sleep so much? At least, I think I'm sleeping so much, or perhaps that's an illusion. Perhaps I'm only sleeping for a few minutes at a time and not the hours I imagine. It's even worse to lose track of time than of place, but I don't know how to find my way back. I've only ever had laudanum once before in my life, and that was when I was fifteen or so, not able to sleep from toothache. It had been, I'm sure, greatly diluted, but even so, my father had been angry when he'd heard about it. I can remember my father. He's dead. I don't think about that – I concentrate on where I am. A strangely shaped house, specially rented probably. At least two people in it, possibly more. It's certainly somewhere quiet, because I have no memory of hearing voices or vehicles from outside, except once, in a half dream, some distant shouts. Thinking about them, they had not been alarmed shouts, more like men working together – carters or builders. Possibly near a building site, in a place that might be London but might equally be anywhere else in the country. It was not much to go on, and my mind refuses to be pushed any further for now. The room seems to be rocking again, not a good sign.

Later and now, not memory. They've decided to feed me and there must be at least one other person in the house, or maybe half a person because he's so small. Minerva came in carrying a china bowl giving off a meaty smell and a spoon, and stood over the pallet. Not wasting words, she signed with a jerk of her chin that I should get up and sit at the table. As I moved stiffly, I was aware of another person behind her, probably barefoot or I'd have heard him. He was no more than a boy, perhaps ten or eleven years old, and so desperately thin his pale face looked almost transparent, wispy fair hair straggling down to his jaw. His eyes were large and scared. He carried the willow-pattern cup in one hand and a candle in a holder in the other. His hands looked almost as fleshless as anatomical drawings. At another nod from her, he set candle and cup on the table. I sipped and tasted the bitterness again, but I was too thirsty not to drink. The contents of the bowl were a kind of beef stew, stringy and salty. I could only manage a few spoonfuls. Minerva left the room, leaving the boy with me. His eyes were fixed on the bowl.

'Do you want some?' I said. It was a relief to hear my own voice, though it felt as if it were coming from somebody else. His eyes looked like an obedient dog's, desiring the biscuit but not daring to go against his master's command. I handed the bowl and spoon to him and, after one more disbelieving stare, he ate the remains of the stew as quickly as a pike taking a minnow. He finished as we heard Minerva's steps outside the door, panic on his face. I took the spoon and bowl from him so that I seemed to be eating the last morsel as she came in.

She nodded at the boy, then towards the chamber pot. He picked it up and carried it out with some difficulty as it was nearly full – surely that means I've been here several days – then returned with it empty. She stood beside me, almost touching.

'Aren't you going to finish your water?'

I wondered whether to tell her that I prefer it without laudanum, but decided against it and just shook my head. She picked up the candle, waited for the boy to gather up the bowl, cup and spoon, then they both left.

The laudanum's left me muzzy-headed, but it's not so bad as it would have been if I'd drunk it all, so I think about the kidnap. A dinner table and a woman's voice: *'They've even managed to cut off the pipeline to our well, so we're having water brought in.*' That wasn't long ago; it was so close I could almost stretch out my hand to the crystal glass. A glass of red wine was beside it but now I'd prefer the water. Then a maid brought in the message. My left wrist is the one aching, so if the person who grabbed me were right-handed, he'd be facing me. I can't remember a face, but perhaps a blackness where there should have been a face. A mask? There must have been more than one of them attacking me, because something came across my mouth from behind. An arm, I think, and a jacket of some rough material. A smell came from it but, curiously, not a bad smell. It's nagging at my memory as a smell associated with some pleasure or even excitement, a long way back, perhaps even in childhood. They didn't say anything, not a word, then there's nothing but blackness until I woke up here, wherever it is. When they made me write the letter to Robert, they didn't ask what address to send it to, so they know where I live. I've made enemies, of course. If you work as an investigator, you can reckon on at least one new enemy with every case. But the fact was there'd been few new cases in the past two or three years and no enemy I can think of so bitter as to go to all this trouble. It's getting dark now; what little light there is seeping away. There's a round window in the ceiling above me but I think it must be covered from outside as there's so little difference between day and night. In summer it won't be completely dark outside until well after ten o'clock. How do I know it's summer? Most of the time, I'm not cold. Now it's probably night

27

there's enough chill in the room to make me wrap myself in this rough blanket. It's very rough, too. It smells of tar and has raised patches on it that might be tar itself, or gouts of my dried blood, or anything. Also, these are my summer petticoats. If, in my underthings, I'm not cold in what passes for day, then summer it probably is.

I must have slept again because, the next thing I knew, light was filtering in. Sometime afterwards, Minerva and the boy arrived with what was probably breakfast, the same bowl but this time with gritty porridge in it, and the same willow-pattern cup of water. I drank half of it because I had to from thirst. While I was eating, the boy picked up the chamber pot and left. She stayed, her back to the door. I spooned some of the porridge up, making a show of eating but not taking much. Thirst left me with very little appetite. I put a hand to my stomach and groaned.

'It hurts.'

'You shouldn't have eaten so quickly.'

I went over to the pallet and flopped down. She came and stood over me.

'We're not fetching you a doctor, if that's what you're thinking.'

The boy came back with the empty chamber pot. As he was putting it down, I caught his eye and looked towards the table with the bowl on it. He was there in a second, eating with his eyes fixed on Minerva's back. I did some writhing so that her eyes stayed on me.

'You're not convincing me.'

'Perhaps if you let me walk around outside . . .'

I only got a laugh at that. Besides, how could I, in stockinged feet and petticoat? 'Water, then.'

The boy had finished and was standing by the table, empty bowl in hand, as if he'd only gone there to pick it up. It suited her that I should drink the laudanum-laced water, so she brought it to me. I managed to spill a fair bit of it but still had to drink some. It tasted more bitter than ever. She took the cup from me and left, followed by the boy. He looked at me from the door with curiosity rather than gratitude in his eyes. So he wasn't stupid and knew I was giving him an opportunity to eat but didn't know why. I took a chance and mimed drinking a cup of water. He blinked and left hastily. Minerva must have been waiting in the corridor to lock the padlock because it banged back against the door. I stayed on the pallet and gave in to the dreamlike feeling the laudanum produced, but with just the smallest feeling of satisfaction at having done something to fight back. I didn't have much to give in the way of bribes, but I'd used what there was and would have to wait for the result.

Much later, in the afternoon, I think, when I was half asleep, the boy came back, so quietly that he was in the room before I knew it. He carried the willow-pattern cup but the water in it, blessedly, tasted of nothing but water. I drank it to the last drop and mimed my thanks. He looked terrified, grabbed the empty cup and left. That night, Minerva left the room after the bowl of fibrous meat had been delivered, so it was easy to give the whole of it to the boy. I'd never seen anybody eat so fast. They must have been starving him. I sipped the water but there was the bitter taste again, so, under his eyes, I emptied it into the chamber pot. I'd be thirsty by morning but it might be worth it to feel clear-headed. As it happened, I slept fitfully, perhaps missing the drug. When I slept or half slept, pictures of Robert, Helena and Harry came that were as vivid as if they were standing there, quite unlike the things I couldn't remember at all.

It's beginning to get light, just a little of it creeping past the ill-fitting cover over the round window. I can hear somebody moving, from the sound just on the other side of the wall, but higher up. Then the murmur of a voice – Minerva's, I think – presumably talking to the man, though I can't make out what she's saying. This room I'm in is a long rectangle, the shorter side dividing it from what must be Minerva's and the poet's living quarters. I've run my hands over all the walls and they feel like planking rather than bricks or stone. I try to take my mind off the thirst by standing up and taking a few steps. I seem as unsteady as ever, if not worse, and the room is rocking more. Curious. I sit down at the table and think about something I remember all too clearly – that letter to Robert. Should I have refused to write it? Possibly, yes, because if the people holding me wanted it, then it must be for some bad purpose. But surely, above all, Robert would want to know that I was alive. *You will be contacted by people who will tell you what to do.* Did that mean money? If so, I knew he'd pay it somehow and I wasn't sorry. It's all very fine to say, when you're free and healthy, that it's wrong to pay ransoms to kidnappers. I'd said so myself, once when I was employed on a case. It's alarming how easily your opinions change when you're helpless and in the near dark. And yet, deep down, I didn't think it was about a ransom.

I hear Minerva's brisk steps, and the soft padding of the boy's. I go as quickly as I can over to the pallet and roll myself up in the blanket. If she expects me to be drugged, that's one small advantage I have over them. She has the porridge bowl, he the cup. As Minerva advances the few steps from the door, something happens. She loses her balance for a moment and some of the porridge slops on to the floor. For a second, the boy looks unsteady too, but manages better. Minerva rights herself, slams down the bowl on the table. Then she picks up the chamber pot and carries it out, moving cautiously. I push myself upright, feeling the floor unsteady under my feet still, but this time having to hide my triumph because they are unsteady too and the room really is rocking. I am on a boat. I think about it as I'm watching the boy eating the porridge, waiting for Minerva to come back. The water is drugged again. I sip a little and pour the rest of it away in a corner, nudging some of the grit on the floor with my toes to soak it up, and sign to the boy as urgently as I can to bring me some proper water later.

When they've gone, I run my hand down the wall again and, sure enough, it curves slightly inwards. If I'd noticed that before, I'd have put it down to being drugged, but now it's obvious.

With no sense of moving forward, the boat's moored or, more probably from the movement, at anchor. The rocking must come from the tides or perhaps other boats passing, which might account for the shouts I'd heard. The triumph of finding out something doesn't last for long, though. For one thing, I'm no nearer knowing where in the world I've been taken. I sense, and I can't say how, that we're still somewhere in the kingdom. Perhaps there's some familiarity in the smells or the light, however limited, that tells me we haven't crossed the Channel. But apart from that, we could be anywhere in the country that has a sea coast. A boat, running before the wind, can travel as fast or faster than a coach. We might be anchored in the Firth of Forth, the Solway, Dublin Bay, anywhere. For another thing, escaping from a boat will be even harder than from a house. That stops my thoughts in their tracks, because it's the first time I'd even thought of escaping. So far, I've been as passive as a baby, waiting for things to be done to me, but seeing Minerva stumble has woken just the slightest feeling of independence. Yes, it's harder to escape from a boat, but a boat limits the number of people against me because they can't easily call in reinforcements. Two-and-a-half people. Are there others? They'd need more to sail a boat, but if it's at anchor the two and a half might be all there are. That note to Robert would have had to be sent ashore. Had a rowing boat come for it or are we tied up to a jetty after all? I sit there, trying to answer the question, noting every movement of the boat. Now that I am aware of it, I can feel it shifting and rocking all the time, mostly quite gently but now and then the move-ment is stronger – probably the wake of other boats passing, though not very close. There's nothing in the way of heavy waves, though, so we are in a sheltered place. Which almost makes me smile, because I've seldom felt less sheltered than now.

Four

Once, when Tabby was ten years old or so, she'd stood in the crowds on Westminster Bridge with what seemed like most of the rest of London and watched the Houses of Parliament burn down. At that time, she didn't know they were the Houses of Parliament, they were just some of the big buildings of London that were as remote from her life as the man on the moon. She'd gone there on business, because where there were crowds there were pockets to be picked, but became as interested as anybody in the sheer size of the fire that filled the sky and lit up the river so that the flames in the air and the flames on the water seemed to merge into one, with flakes of ash snowing down on the crowds and a crackling like the Devil's laughter. That had been thirteen years ago, and Parliament was still only half rebuilt. As Tabby walked past it to the Maynards' house, with a small bundle of clothes under her arm, she craned her head to see up to the top of a new tower, with small stick figures of stone masons working on what looked like precarious scaffolding. It was quite a lot higher than the last time she'd been there, but that had been a while ago. Westminster was not one of her usual haunts, but it had one building that had a far deeper place in her mind than Parliament or the abbey: Millbank Penitentiary. Just upriver

34

from Parliament on the bank of the Thames, six huge brick cliffs met in a central watchtower and housed the criminals who were to be transported to Australia. She'd grown up with the idea that being sent to Millbank was only a small step better than being hanged, and perhaps not even that. A man from her old gang was in there at present – Drubbin, a fairly successful pickpocket who'd tried to graduate to burglary and failed miserably. He'd been sentenced to seven years in Van Diemen's Land – though some of those who were meant to be away seven years never made it back again – and due to sail any day. She hadn't been particularly fond of Drubbin, but yesterday she'd stood staring at the prison, thinking of him inside. That had been a diversion from the job she'd set herself – getting to know the Maynards' house. Convinced from the start that somebody in there knew what had caused Liberty's disappearance, and not trusting the police to investigate the quality, she knew that if she waited and watched, she'd find something. Nobody was better at waiting and watching than Tabby, and no one could melt into the background like she could. She was wearing her grey dress, so at first glance she might be taken for a not-very-satisfactory servant from a not-very-particular household. Nobody gave her a second glance.

She stepped aside to avoid being crushed by a four-horse vehicle carrying great planks of wood, and walked on with Westminster Abbey on her right. The Maynards lived in a three-storey house close to St John's Church in Smith Square, off Millbank but not as far along as the prison. Its closeness to the abbey and Parliament had once been an advantage, but for the past ten years it had been on the edge of the largest building site in the world, with no sign of an end to the work. She'd been watching the house for the first day from the front, then from the side entrance by the coach house and, in the late evening, from the large back garden. Now she'd decided to move in – or, rather, to set up a camp for herself nearby so she could watch it day and night. It shouldn't be too difficult. It was one of those rich, busy houses with visitors, servants and tradespeople coming and going all the time. The white stone church with its four towers in the middle of the square attracted its own share of visitors. Tabby walked into the church, fairly confident of finding it empty in mid-morning. A woman was polishing a candlestick up at the far end but she had her back turned and didn't notice as Tabby entered, soft-footed, and made her way to a small side room near the entrance that she'd reconnoitred the day before. It was more a large cupboard than a room, piled with dozens of dog-eared books, musty folded curtains and some of those square things people knelt on that the moths had been at. By the smell of it, nobody had been inside for months. She stowed her bundle behind some of the books and partly unfolded one of the curtains, just for the pleasure of seeing what a good bed it would make. Luxury, this was, compared to the alleys and doorways where she usually found herself keeping watch. The woman was still polishing the candlestick, or perhaps another one, so Tabby strolled out unobserved into the sunlight of the square and to the front entrance of the Maynards' house, with its white marble steps and columns with ferns carved on top on either side of the door. She turned down the side of the white-painted garden wall into the wide cul-de-sac that ran alongside the coach house. The large doors over the arched coach entrance were closed. On the far side of the coach house was the small door into the garden. She'd used it the day before when she'd done her evening watch on the house. Now she lifted the latch, pushed back the door and walked inside. The garden was quite a large one for a town dwelling, around an acre, with the house closing off one side and high walls the rest. A glasshouse stood against the south wall and a miniature orchard of half-a-dozen apples and pears took up one corner, closed in by wooden rails so that the small Jersey cow could graze inside. The cow had her own little shelter in the corner that looked more like a summerhouse, freshly painted with fretted woodwork round the eaves. Near the glasshouse, a gardener and a boy were picking gooseberries. At first, all Tabby could see of the gardener was the tightly stretched seat of his corduroy trousers as he bent over the bush. The boy, standing beside him and holding a trug, was the first to see Tabby. He caught her eye and grinned. Grinning back, she sketched a kick towards the gardener's backside, though too far away to connect. The boy snorted with laughter and the trug tilted, scattering gooseberries. The gardener straightened up and cuffed the boy round the head, not particularly hard and almost automatically, as if he'd

37

done it many times. He was an old man, grey-bearded, with thin strands of grey hair escaping from under a low-crowned hat.

'So who might you be?' he said to Tabby.

'Mary's sister, come to help with the wash.'

Tabby knew it was hardly a risk at all. In any household of a dozen or so – and from the size of this house, there'd be at least a dozen servants – somebody would be called Mary and there was always some stage of washing.

'Big Mary or little Mary?'

'Little Mary.'

'So why aren't you helping?'

'They don't need me this minute.'

He grunted and went back to the gooseberries. The boy was taking his time picking up the spilt ones. He saw Tabby's eyes on him and made a face. She made a face back. She strolled over to the rail round the fruit trees, looking at the back of the house. A window on the upper floor was open with an eiderdown spread over the sill to air. A woman in a black dress and long apron came out of a back door on the left with a bucket of peelings for the pig bin. Saucepans clashed inside. After some time, the gardener took the trug of gooseberries from the boy and walked stiffly towards the back door, not glancing towards Tabby. She went over to the boy, who was sitting on the grass eating gooseberries he'd probably squirreled away from the spill.

'You'll catch it,' she said.

'No, I won't. 'E'll stay there 'alf an 'our by the church clock. She gives 'im a glass of beer and cheese. Want one?'

She nodded and he handed her a gooseberry, big as a bantam's egg and warm from the sun. She squatted down beside him.

'You're not little Mary's sister, are you?' he said.

'Who says?'

'I've seen her sister. She's a long streak of misery. Are you a burglar?'

'What if I was?'

'You should let me in on it. I knows where they keeps the silver, everything.'

'I bet you've never been inside the house.'

'I 'ave so. I go in there sometimes when I walk the dogs.'

'Just into the scullery?'

'I went into the passage once, when one of the dogs got free.'

'Do that a lot, do they?'

He pushed the last gooseberry into his mouth and shook his head. 'So are you or ain't you?'

'That 'ud be telling, wouldn't it? What I'm doing now is I'm looking for a friend.'

He looked disappointed. 'Yer young man run off, 'as he?'

'A lady. She came to dinner here three days ago.'

'Quality, you mean?'

'Yes.'

'But you're not quality.'

'Do you remember any talk about a lady gone missing?'

'Jane said summat about a fuss over a lady that 'ad run off and left her 'usband, only I reckons they're always doing that. I don't pay much notice to what goes on inside.'

'I thought you knew where the silver was. Who's Jane?'

'Scullery maid and she does some of the fires, downstairs mostly.'

'How many servants are there here?'

He thought about it, then counted on his fingers. 'Madam's maid, bedroom maid who does the upstairs cleaning, parlour maid, Sukey does the downstairs rooms, Jane in the scullery and little Mary, who mostly does the washing. Then there's the cook and the kitchen maid, big Mary and the boy that does the boots and brings in the coal. That's nine if you count the boy.'

'Don't they have a housekeeper and butler?'

'They don't count as proper servants. Then outside there's me and Dismal Joe for the garden, the coachman, Mr Daniel, and the stable boy. That's about it.'

'How often do you walk the dogs?'

'When the stable boy's out riding postilion on the coach early. Once every two weeks, maybe.'

'Who brings them to you?'

'Jane, usually. They know her because she's the one who feeds 'em.'

'A bitch got out, didn't she, the night the lady disappeared?'

He looked at her, sideways on. 'You know a lot more than you're letting on, don't you?'

'You heard about it?'

'I saw it. I sleeps in there.' He glanced over his shoulder at the greenhouse. 'Under the staging. Don't tell Dismal Joe. I'm supposed to live out and they'd dock it off my pay if they thought I was living in. But it's more comfortable than at home. I got some sacks and an old pillow they threw out.'

'So what exactly did you see?'

'First thing was 'earing it. Yelping, yapping, barking – sounded as if all the dogs in Westminster had got in the garden. And Jane at the scullery door yelling for the bitch to come in, only she might as well have shouted for the river to run backwards and you could 'ardly 'ear her over the noise. So I went out. It was after ten, dark. I fell over a couple of dogs, barked my shin – look, it's still sore. Stable boy fell over me and Mr Daniel swore at both of us. They'd come out from the coach house. Then the cook and big Mary were at the scullery door, throwing out great panfuls of water, only I reckons they missed most of the dogs and got Mr Daniel, so 'e started swearing again. In the end, me and the stable boy grabbed the bitch, more by luck than anything, and threw 'er to Jane inside the scullery. I 'ad to make myself scarce before anybody started asking 'ow come I was so 'andy on the scene.'

'And Mr and Mrs Maynard didn't come out?'

'Well, they couldn't, could they? Not if they was entertaining.'

'Whose fault was it the bitch got out?'

A pause. 'Well, Jane's, I suppose, if she hadn't done up the door properly after she took her supper into her.'

'What does Jane say about it?'

'Dunno. I 'aven't spoken to her since. I reckons she's in disgrace.'

'I'd like to speak to Jane. Could you get her to come out?'

'Why? About the burglary?'

'I'm not planning on burgling just at the moment. Would this help?' Tabby held out a half-crown coin on her gloveless palm.

The boy looked at it hungrily.

'And the other half after I've spoken to her.'

He scooped up the coin, bit it and put it in his pocket. 'She might, she might not.'

'Try.'

He stood up. 'It'll 'ave to wait till tomorrow, if she does. You'd better go. Dismal Joe will be back any minute.'

'While you were all chasing the dogs around, you didn't know what was happening at the front of the house?'

'Not a chance. The lady 'asn't come back then?'

'No.' Tabby stood up and looked back at the house. A low terrace ran along it, three-quarters of it obviously for the family's use, screened from the kitchen door on the left by a trellis covered with passion flowers. Beside the trellis, a lean-to summerhouse, made of picturesque gnarled and twisted boughs, looked designed for taking tea on a summer afternoon. The church clock was whirring and the boy was fidgeting. 'What's your name?'

'Toby.'

'This time tomorrow, then.'

She went through the door to the side street just as the clock was striking. She'd been tempted for a moment to go into the house and talk to the scullery maid then and there, but she'd learned to be patient and wait.

*   *   *

42

When 'The Union' got back to the White Bear in Piccadilly at half past five the day after it had set out, Amos was in the yard, waiting for it. He'd delivered Robert's letter without letting on that he'd read it, but Miles had shown it to him anyway, every bit as worried and puzzled as he was. When Amos left him, he was on the verge of going round to show it to Stephen, without much hope that he'd learn any more from it. Even before all the passengers were off, the coachman had swung down from the box and was on his way into the public house. Amos followed him and watched as he downed in one gulp the pint that the publican had drawn for him as soon as he heard the coach arrive. Amos's offer of a second one was accepted with a nod, and before he was halfway down it they'd discovered they had coaching friends in common. The man's assistant joined them, thirsty from dealing with the passengers and their luggage, and Amos bought him a pint too. After a while, he turned the conversation to their journey down to Dover. Did they remember a gentleman on his own, travelling outside, only a satchel for luggage, tall and brown-haired, fortyish? They both remembered him well because he'd tipped generously, though hurriedly.

'The steamer was just going out and he was in a hurry to get on it. Yes, it will have been going to Calais, as most of them do, but we've got no notion where he was going on afterwards. He didn't say much beyond thank you.'

Amos drank another pint with them but got no further. As he walked back to the stables, a line from Robert's letter kept running around in his mind: *She may yet be found by methods other than the one I have had to adopt.* He hoped so, but he didn't see how.

Five

Five meals I've counted – that's two-and-a-half days, I think. I'm nearly sure from the patterns of light and dark around the window, or the porthole as I suppose I should call it now. But I still can't guess how long I was unconscious. The great discovery that I'm on a boat, with my senses more alert now I'm drinking less laudanum, makes it possible to put more things together. I've managed to see that the boy has had something to eat from my bowl on three visits and he's crept in twice with a cup of water. I think that where I'm being kept is a storage hold with part of it raised up above the deck, which is where the porthole is, no more than seven feet above my head. I suppose it is there for people to look down at the cargo, rather than for anybody inside to look up. There may be more than one hold, because this one seems not so very large, maybe about twice the dimensions of our drawing room at home. If I stand up with my arms at full stretch, I can almost touch the ceiling, or rather the hold cover. A merchant ship, then. I've been wondering, to no great purpose, what it carried. Not coal or hay, because it would surely smell of them. Probably not wood either, though the smell would depend on what sort of wood. Cabbages or vegetable marrows? It seems too large a vessel for market garden

45

produce, though not so very large. Its responsiveness to the tides – I'm nearly sure that there are tides – suggests to me a vessel of medium size, a coaster rather than an ocean-going ship. As for where Minerva, the poet and the child live, that's towards the bows, I think. Minerva may have become suspicious about my efforts with the boy. On the last occasion, she kept him very much under her eye. I had to drink some of the drugged water from sheer thirst. I'm almost intolerably thirsty most of the time. I'm trying to distract myself by remembering things. I still have only the smallest fleeting memories of the attack, but the evening leading up to what happened is becoming clearer, starting with that protest of Harry's: *Going out again. Always going out.* It was in the night nursery. Mrs Martley had given him his bowl of broth and Helena her bread and milk. Helena had been tucked up in her crib and had only opened her eyes for a moment when I bent over to kiss her, but Harry had refused to get into bed, truculent. We'd still been trying to count up to ten when Robert came in, fighting with a collar stud. Between us, we'd managed to persuade Harry into bed, then went to our dressing room. I'd dealt with the collar stud and Robert had helped me fix my dragonfly clip in my hair while we talked about the evening to come.

'I hope you won't find it too tedious, darling. It seems to be a rule of nature that great riches are given to boring people,' he'd said.

'Or that great riches make people boring. I hope we'll never have to risk that. If he comes up with a generous donation for the hospital, it will be worth it.'

Robert's pride and joy – the eye hospital. And yet, what seemed to have turned out to be his role in life had come about almost by chance. A young friend of ours had had his sight restored by an operation at the hospital. Robert's interest in him had turned into a fascination with the work, and for the past three years he'd been training as a doctor and raising funds for the hospital in his spare time. The Maynards – the hosts' name had popped into my head quite suddenly – might donate. Miles and Rosa had bowled up on time to collect us. The leather of their carriage upholstery was the green of holly leaves. They'd had the carriage for two years, at least. Why was I remembering things that didn't matter?

Later. A thump against the side, just now. I'd been half asleep again and it brought me wide awake. My first thought was that some other boat had crashed into us, my second that this was the rescue. Even through my drugged sleep, I'd been more than half expecting it. I was on my feet at once, pulling up my shredded stockings, twisting my blood-clotted hair into a knot, ready to run. Nothing happened. It had been quite a soft thump, no battering ram. Then something jolted down the side of the boat, seeming very close. A rope ladder being let down and a male voice from the deck, saying something I couldn't catch. The hope of rescue faded almost to nothing. This was some visitor, recognized and expected. Still, I stayed on my feet, hoping even now. After an uncertain number of days with so little happening, any change seemed welcome. Then there was a soft, unsteady tap of feet on wooden rungs as somebody climbed the ladder cautiously. Whoever it was must be unaccustomed to boats. More words, then two sets of male footsteps on the deck. So a man who wasn't a sailor had arrived, probably by rowing boat. One lot of steps came back along the deck, and something was thrown down and landed with a thump, presumably in the rowing boat. It must have been the end of a rope, because after that three loads were drawn up, sounding heavy as they bumped down on the deck. Supplies, probably, and there must be some person down in the boat hooking them on. So we were anchored close enough to the shore to be reached by rowing boat. If fresh supplies had been delivered, the intention was for us to remain on the boat for some time. There were more people in the plot than the two-and-a-half that I knew to be on board, but that had been pretty clear from the start. The loads were dragged across the deck. Some minutes after that, voices sounded from the other side of the plank wall, where Minerva, the poet and the boy lived. This was unusual because, as far as I could tell, they mostly went about their business in silence. The new arrival and the poet seemed to be arguing. I heard, '. . . Manage without if we have to . . .' from him and a loud, 'No', from the other man. He must have been standing close to the partition when he said it, then moved away, because the next words were less distinct. I caught, '. . .

There's still time. It's definitely fixed now for Friday the twenty-third, so we know where we are.' Then, '. . . Message to him when he lands . . .' Then the argument probably finished, because I only heard them moving about, nothing else.

Sometime after that, Minerva and the poet came in. I hadn't heard the other man leave, so he must still be in their living quarters on the other side of the partition. Minerva was carrying a candle-stick and an ink stand, with the blotter under her arm. She put them down on the table. The blotter had a blank sheet of writing paper tucked into the corner.

'Come here,' she said.

I stayed where I was on the pallet until the poet made a move towards me, boots squeaking. I didn't want to be dragged, so I got up and moved over, taking my time. Minerva had her veil down, as usual, but I had a sidelong glimpse through it of those eager eyes.

'Write what I tell you, like last time. Whatever you'd call him, then this. *I'm still alive but only because you've done as instructed. Continue to* . . . You're not writing.'

'I'm not going to write.' It was simple stub-bornness because, with my wits coming back, I was sick of being passive. Minerva dipped the pen into the inkwell and tried to force it into my hand. I let it drop on the floor.

'Pick it up.'

I didn't. She hit me a stinging blow across the cheek with her open hand. The force of it made my teeth bite the inside of my mouth. I bunched my fist and hit her a lucky blow right in the stomach, a woman's stomach definitely, yielding a little but not much. She let out a gasp, and the poet who'd been standing behind me grabbed my right arm and twisted it up behind the chair. When I tried to pull away from him, he just twisted more until I was sure if he forced it another inch my arm would snap.

I yelled out: 'I can't write if you break it, can I?'

To my surprise, he let go. I sat there, rubbing my arm, the taste of blood in my mouth, sweat on my forehead, trying to think. Heroism is all very well in opera, but when you're alone, hungry and thirsty with no aria to sing, you realize its limitations. They could, between them, beat me unconscious, though that would defeat their object for the present. Still, I'd have to come to at some point, and then it would begin again, and – sooner or later, more or less damaged – I'd have to write the letter. Or die, I supposed. But then, they needed to keep me alive because I was their hold over Robert, and it was now clear that whatever they wanted him to do was the point of all this. I couldn't imagine what it might be. They must believe that he possessed some influence, some skill or access to somewhere or somebody that mattered to them. But for the past few years, Robert had been leading an even quieter life than I had. True, he had sympathies with Italian patriots fighting to unite their country and had helped some of them, but more recently, his medical studies had taken up most of his time and energy.

'Suppose we discuss a deal,' I said, my voice

sounding thick from thirst and blood. 'I might agree to write under certain conditions.'

'What?' Minerva's voice didn't sound entirely normal either. My punch must have done some damage.

'Stop drugging me. I want a plain cup of water with nothing in it before I think of doing anything.'

Minerva and the poet looked at each other.

'Write first,' she said.

'Water first.'

Their hesitation proved one thing: they did not want to kill me, at least not at present. They exchanged another look, then Minerva went out of the door, leaving me with the poet. He didn't speak or move. It was some minutes before she came back with the cup of water. It looked clear and tasted slightly of mud, nothing else. I made myself drink slowly, savouring every mouthful.

'Now write. *I'm still alive but . . .*'

I wrote down her dictation, my arm throbbing. The complete message was short enough. *I'm still alive but only because you've done as instructed. Continue to obey instructions or you may never see me again.* Then simply my signature, with no love sent. How could I do that when they were forcing him to do something against his will and I was helping them? She blotted and folded the page, then took a step towards the door.

'Do you have to keep me in the dark?' I said. 'I'm doing what you want. At least unblock the window and let me see some daylight.'

I called it window instead of porthole because I didn't want them to know I'd guessed I was on a boat. She didn't answer and they both left, taking the letter and the candle with them.

Soon after that, steps sounded across the deck and down the ladder, and the rowing boat drew away, taking, I was sure, my letter with it. I stayed sitting at the table, blaming myself for writing. After a while, it struck me that line of thought was no use to Robert and I should go on adding together what little I knew. One thing I'd recently learned was that Minerva and the poet were under somebody's orders. They were no more than gaolers, with most of the planning happening elsewhere. The demand that I write a second letter had closely followed the arrival of somebody in the rowing boat. I wished I could have managed to open the porthole to get a look at this new person. I looked up at it, just beyond the reach of my fingertips. If I moved the table underneath it and used the chair to climb up on to the table, I'd reach it, but my mouth, head and arm were aching, my whole body weak from inactivity, my . . . While I was running through all the reasons against it, I found I was on my feet, moving the chair. That went easily enough, so I tried the table, inch by inch, careful not to make a sound. The nearly empty hold would amplify sound like a drum. Some grit must have got on to the floor under the legs, because it made a scraping sound that sounded loud to me but would probably be no more than a rat's scuttling to anyone outside. I tried to take the weight and lift it rather than drag it, and was breathless when I'd got it under the porthole. Then, hurry took over. If I was going to try it at all, it must be before somebody came in with the next meal. I stepped on to the chair, lifted one foot on to the table, took a deep breath and followed with the other. It seemed desperately insecure, with nothing to hold on to, though the table was probably not much over two feet high. It brought my head under the ceiling of tarred planks – too high, in fact, so that I had to bend my head back to look up at the porthole. The view was not encouraging. It was secured by four thick brass bolts, with the nuts on the outside. There was no way of budging it. The cover was over the outside – a metal disc that looked firmly secured, but I couldn't have reached it in any case. I got down, then returned the table and chair as far as I could to their previous positions. The experiment should have left me more cast down, but strangely did the reverse. At least I'd done something for myself. When, sometime later, Minerva and the boy came in with the stew, I ate most of it, leaving only a few chunks of beef for the child that he managed to bolt down when Minerva's back was turned. The water that came with it was like the previous cupful – clear but slightly muddy tasting. It was an expensive bargain I'd made, but at least they were keeping to it.

That night – I think it was night because the small amount of light in the hold turned orange then went – I slept more deeply than I expected and dreamed. I was a child again, with my mother and father still alive. They'd taken my brother and me on some treat. In my dream, the childish rush of excitement came back to me, along with vivid pictures: a man in a leather apron, white-bearded, who seemed very old to us but kindly. His hand had a long iron claw and the claw – a chisel, I could make out now – was biting into a large wooden something clamped in a vice as easily as I could bite into an apple. It was shaping out the mane of a fine horse's head, with wide eyes and flared nostrils. We understood that it was to be our rocking horse. Small curls of wood fell down, white with the faintest tinge of pink like sea shells. I stooped, picked one up from the floor and lifted it to my nose. I was instantly awake, panicking, crying out. It had been the same smell on the sleeve that came across my face from behind just before they hit me – the clean, sweet scent of fresh wood, of a carpenter's workshop. The memory was so vivid that for some time I lay there, shaking. Nobody had come running, so my shout couldn't have been as loud as it sounded to me. It was still dark. After a while, it began to rain – not very heavily, but regular and persistent, drumming on the roof of the hold. The sound of it sent me back to sleep. When I woke, the rain had stopped, daylight was coming in and one side of the blanket felt damp. Part of the pallet was damp too, and at first I was simply annoyed because rain had leaked in. Then the significance of it struck me. I stood up, pulled the chair over to stand on and looked as closely as I could at the ceiling of planks. There it was, two planks in from the side – a darker patch about a foot in circumference, a few drops still clinging, waiting to fall. I heard footsteps outside, and was just in time to get down and put the chair back in its usual place before Minerva and the boy came in with the porridge.

Six

Amos Legge wouldn't have called himself a stubborn man: there were simply things he knew and he stuck to them with the same patience he'd give to training a colt. It was one of the principles of his life that everything that was going anywhere had to go on two feet or four hooves. From the start, in this case, he'd concentrated on hooves. The shoe meant Liberty hadn't gone willingly and, since a woman being carried through the Westminster streets would have been noticed by somebody, that meant a wheeled vehicle. It had seemed at first a comparatively easy task to check what vehicles had been near the Maynards' house when she had disappeared, and he'd carried it out thoroughly, using his vast network of friends and acquaintances in the horse world, from the merest donkey-cart man and cab driver to the coachmen of the great families of Mayfair. Then he went back and checked again until he was certain that he knew the movements of every horse, pony, mule or donkey that had stirred a hoof anywhere near the house that night. Not all of the journeys were entirely innocent, and he found out things that would have rocked the complacency of several noble families if they'd come to the notice of anybody less discreet than Amos, but none of them had any connection with Liberty's disappearance. Then it had come to him quite suddenly, while showing a new lad the proper way of combing out a horse's tail: what about the ones that hadn't stirred a hoof? The comb had checked just for a moment, and he'd gone on with the lad's lesson as if nothing had happened but, as soon as it was finished, he tacked up a cob and rode to the Maynards' house.

Amos had already met the Maynards' coachman, Daniel, in his investigations, and found him pleasant enough but bone idle. He managed to make looking after two carriage horses and a pony for mowing the lawn seem like a full job of work, and in any case, he left most of it to the boy. When Amos arrived, he was sitting in a chair, smoking his pipe and watching the boy wash the carriage, a neat clarence that would carry four people in decent comfort. He accepted a refill of his pipe from Amos, and for a while they smoked in companionable silence. Amos asked if the family went far in the clarence and Daniel shook his head.

'Never more than a few miles from home. Him to work in the mornings, her and the young lady for shopping or visiting two or three days a week, then church on Sundays – their church, that is, not this one. He quarrelled with the vicar here.'

'The evening the lady disappeared, they didn't have the carriage out?'

'Of course not. They were entertaining.'

'That's what I thought.' Amos handed over his pouch for another refill. 'I heard you had a bit of a business with the dogs.'

Daniel nodded. 'She thinks more of those dogs than most human beings. It would have been as

57

much as our lives were worth if some mongrel had got at the bitch.'

'So you were all out trying to get her back in?'

'Yes – bloody nonsense. They should have sacked the girl for letting her get out in the first place.'

'So you were out in the garden in the dark. What about these doors?' He gestured towards the high doors of the carriage house, which were open to the sunshine. 'Were they locked?'

Daniel looked offended. 'We don't bother with that. The wife and I sleep over the stables and we'd hear if anybody tried to take a horse and carriage out at night.'

''Course you would. What I'm thinking is suppose somebody brought something in while you were all occupied with the dogs and left it in the carriage?'

'Why would they do that?' Daniel stared at him.

'I'm just thinking . . . if they'd knocked the young lady senseless and wanted to hide her until they could come and take her away when nobody was about, the clarence wouldn't be the worst hiding place.'

'That's just mad,' Daniel said.

'Is it, though? If they came back hours later when nobody was around, say two or three o'clock in the morning, they might have carried her to a cart or carriage they had waiting on Millbank. Risky, but not as risky as trying to get her away earlier.'

'I'd have heard.'

'A cart or carriage you would, but somebody

on foot? She's not a heavyweight, that lady. Did you notice anything odd about the carriage the next morning?'

'No. It was all right when I took him in to the office as usual.' He took a slow draw on his pipe. 'When I took the ladies out in the afternoon, the young lady did say there was a funny smell inside, but then she's always complaining about something.'

'What sort of funny smell?' Amos tried not to sound too eager.

'As if somebody had been smoking inside it, she said. Stupid. Nobody would have been.'

'All the same, do you mind if we take a look inside?'

It looked as if Daniel did mind, but it would have been uncivil to refuse. He signed to the boy to step back and opened the door for Amos to go in. The inside of the clarence was empty and orderly, but Amos wrinkled his nose. Sulphur.

'There is something. Doesn't smell like pipe tobacco.'

Daniel put his head inside and sniffed. 'I can't smell anything.'

'Very faint, it is.' Amos came out and closed the door. 'Is that a horse rug in the corner there?' Something dark was crumpled in the dark corner behind the clarence.

''Course it's not. If you think we throw horse rugs round anyhow . . .'

Amos walked over and picked it up. 'More like an old bit of blanket. That's what the smell came from.'

He gave it to Daniel to sniff. The coachman,

furious at being caught out in untidiness, turned on the boy. 'If you've been . . .'

'He hasn't done anything. Mind if I take this with me?' He rolled the blanket up and held it under his arm, mounted the cob and rode away.

Amos had to wait two-and-a-half hours to see Sergeant Bevan. He should have been at Tattersalls buying a good calm hunter for a lady, but the lady would have to wait. He'd walked into the police station after taking the cob back to the stables, told the constable who he wanted to see and refused, without rancour, to give any reason. Various constables had tried again, invited information and offered conversation. But he'd simply folded his long legs in their boots and breeches under the bench in the waiting room, so as not to discommode the life of a busy police station going on around him, and waited without impatience. Sergeant Bevan appeared around mid-afternoon in a quiet interval, and the two police constables on duty straightened up and looked busy. He was in uniform, carrying his top hat under his arm. One of the police constables said something to him, and he looked across at Amos.

'Mr Legge.'

Amos took it as no more than his due that people should know him, though he'd last met the sergeant three years ago, in Liberty's company. He stood up and they shook hands. The sergeant was tall, but Amos towered over him by a good six inches, and his gloved hand was swallowed up in Amos's fist. They respected each other but warily, knowing they'd kept things from each other in the past and would do so again if necessary. Bevan was a London man through and through, and Amos – though London had been kind to him – was a country man to the bone. Bevan led the way past the inquiries desk and into a side room, instructing the constables that they should not be interrupted. At Bevan's invitation, Amos sat down in a chair that looked only just strong enough to hold him and Bevan settled behind a plain table, much stained and marked with various initials, and mostly badly carved.

'Well, have you found her?' Bevan said.

'I've come to ask you that, sir.'

The voice was respectful enough but the calm eyes, locked on Bevan's, were challenging. 'I'm afraid we've made no progress.'

'And it's nearly four days. Have you been looking?'

'Mrs Carmichael's description has been issued to all our constables.'

'In case they happen to spot her in the street, like a lost dog? I meant really looking.'

'Mr Legge, have you any idea how many people are reported missing in this city in a single day? Several dozen. Usually they'll turn up in a day or so – fancied a change, annoyed with their wives or husbands, drank too much and lost their way home – any number of reasons. We can't organize searches for all of them.'

'She disappeared into thin air with her husband only a few hundred yards away. You can't say that's ordinary.'

'To be honest with you, Mr Legge, few things about Liberty Lane are ordinary.'

Amos nodded. Bevan, like Amos himself, had known her before she was Mrs Carmichael.

'Any road, I reckon I've got more to tell you than you have to tell me.'

Bevan smiled. 'I thought you might have.'

Amos frowned, not liking the tone. 'I've worked out how they got her away.' He told Bevan about his search. 'So the question in my mind was is there some vehicle I've overlooked? Then it came to me: what about the carriage that wasn't going anywhere?' He unrolled the piece of blanket and spread it on the table.

Bevan sniffed and raised his eyebrows, picked up the piece of blanket and looked at it closely. He raised his head to look at Amos. 'Gunpowder?'

'I reckon so. That's been in an explosion and a fire. See, it's charred there along the edge.'

'And you think that has something to do with her disappearance?'

'I do. They might have gagged her with it or put it over her head. There was no sign of an explosion at the Maynards' place, so whatever happened came sometime before that.'

'The artillery fire guns in the park,' Bevan said. 'And any man of war would have gunpowder on board.'

'Do you think the artillery would use an old rag like that for anything? And I hope you aren't telling me somebody sailed a three-master along the road up Millbank.'

'So what's the significance of this?'

'It might help to look for somewhere where

there's been an explosion of gunpowder in the last few weeks. The police officers on the beat would know, wouldn't they?'

'Not necessarily. Just think how full London is of little factories dealing with substances that would make an artilleryman sweat. Matches, cartridges, fireworks, patent fuels, the sort of firewater that turns people blind. We could probably go down any street in south or east London and collect enough assorted chemicals to blow up half of Whitehall.'

'So you're not going to look?'

'We'll carry out any enquiries we think necessary, Mr Legge. But our resources are limited.' The conversation seemed to have reached its end but neither man was in a hurry to move. After a while, Bevan spoke in a different, less official tone of voice. 'I'll tell you one thing that puzzles me, Mr Legge. Shouldn't it be her husband coming to see me?' He looked at Amos, seeing the blood mount in his suntanned cheeks. Amos could hide things well enough, but as an outright liar he was as blundering as a puppy chasing a butterfly.

'Mr Carmichael is looking for his wife elsewhere.' He was puzzled by Robert's secret journey to the Continent but had no intention of sharing it with Bevan.

'Is he indeed? Do you happen to know where?'

Amos shook his head, looking unhappy. 'But that's not the point, is it? Somebody's taken her and there has to be a reason. I'd have thought it was the police's job to find it.'

'Yes, there has to be a reason.' Bevan had taken

63

the blanket in his hands again and was staring at it. 'You know, Mr Legge, I never thought we'd seen the last of Liberty Lane. As an investigator, I mean.'

'She's not done very much in that line in the last few years,' Amos said. 'There's the children and a house to run.'

'But she has kept her hand in, hasn't she? There's no point telling me she hasn't because we do hear things.' Amos was silent. 'Of course, you'll know better than I do.' Bevan was speaking deliberately, almost teasingly looking up from the blanket at Amos. 'Suppose she was working on a case at the moment and that case required her to disappear for a while. She'd be capable of that, don't you think?'

'She's been taken against her will.' Amos stated it as a fact, beyond stubborn. He knew very well what Bevan's eyes were saying – that she might have chosen not to confide in him. He knew that this wasn't the case, but didn't intend to waste his breath trying to convince Bevan. 'The point is if they'd made their plans so well, knowing about the carriage in the coach house and arranging the dog fight, they're something more than ordinary kidnappers.'

'Or in some cases it happens that there's a falling out,' Bevan said, not looking at Amos now. 'One partner or the other decides to disappear for a while to bring the other to his or her senses. If Mrs Carmichael were to do something like that, she'd do it thoroughly.'

The blood came to Amos's cheeks again, this time from anger. 'It's nothing like that. For God's sake, she's left two young children. She'd never have done that willingly.'

Bevan nodded, but Amos sensed he wasn't entirely convinced. 'I may go round to the house again and talk to the coachman. But the Maynard family have been very much bothered by all this and I don't want to add to the burden if I can help it.'

Amos thought, *That means he won't.* He stood up and thanked Bevan in tones that were the nearest he came to sarcasm. 'Shall I leave the blanket?'

'If you like. You'll let me know if there are any developments?'

Amos nodded and walked out, leaving the blanket on the table. He never lost his temper with a horse and seldom with a human, but he'd come closer to it than he liked. He walked into the sunlight and set out towards the park, turning over in his mind his next move.

Tabby waited just inside the door to the garden until the old gardener stumped towards the back of the house. Toby had seen her as soon as she came in.

'Got the money?'

'Will she talk to me?'

Toby nodded towards the house. A young woman in a black dress and white mob cap was waiting on the kitchen side of the trellis. When he crooked a finger, she came towards them, taking her time. Tabby summed her up mentally in her first few steps – seventeen or eighteen, pretty and knew it too, dark curls escaping from under the cap, a well-rounded figure, lips that had been kissed a few times by men who thought that's what servants were for but she'd probably made them pay for it, so that was all right. Probably not an obedient servant or at her age she'd have been promoted from scullery to parlour. Skirt with some carrot scrapings sticking to it and on the short side, showing glimpses of ankle in cotton stockings too expensive for her station, the sort that might be donated by a thoughtful lady to her maid, but Jane was several rungs below lady's maid, so where had the stockings come from? Altogether, she was a girl who could look after herself, as her first words proved.

'So what've you paid him?'

'That's his business.'

'I expect the same.'

'Depends what you can tell me.'

'He says you're a burglar.'

'I'm looking for a friend, the one who disappeared the night the bitch got out.'

'Friend?' From the tone of Jane's question, she doubted that a guest of the Maynards would have a friend who looked and sounded like Tabby. Tabby let it pass.

'You're the one who feeds the bitch?'

'I look after the dogs, all four of them. Mrs Maynard dotes on those dogs as much as she does her own children – more, probably.'

Toby had disappeared by then. Tabby and Jane were standing by the strawberry bed. As casually as if she owned the garden, Jane stooped down, picked a large ripe berry and popped it between her lips. Her hands were small but rough and red from her work.

'And when the bitch is in season, she's shut up?'

Jane swallowed and nodded. 'Berengaria's her name. There's a big old pantry we don't use any more, just inside the kitchen door. It's all done out nicely for her – blankets and cushions better than we get on our beds, a window with a view of the garden, a ball and an old doll she likes to play with. I look in on her several times every day.' She sounded genuinely fond of the dog.

'When did you last look before she got out?'

'About eight o'clock, just after they'd started dinner. Cook has to do her cuts off the joint, same as the family eat. I take them in to her and watch her eat, then give her a walk in the garden while the other dogs are having their dinner, then lock her in for the night.'

'Lock her in how?'

'There's a big bolt on the outside of the pantry door. If you're going to ask me if I bolted it that night, I know I did.'

'But she got out.'

'I didn't have anything to do with that. I've told Mrs Maynard so. She believes me, even if nobody else does.'

'Could she have got out herself?'

'She's clever for a dog, but not that clever.'

'So somebody else must have unbolted it?'

'Yes.'

'Do you know who?'

'No.'

'Does anybody have anything to do with the dogs apart from you and Mrs Maynard?'

'Most days the stable boy or Toby walk the

males, but they never have anything to do with Berengaria. I've got to go in now – they'll be missing me. So how much?'

Tabby handed over a crown. Jane looked down scornfully. 'You might have made it a half sovereign.'

'I might if you'd told me anything useful.'

'I told you what you asked, didn't I?'

Jane swooped on another strawberry then ran off inside. Tabby stood looking after her, admitting to herself that it was true. Jane could have told her more, only she hadn't known the right questions to ask. It was some time before she realized that she was being watched. Not by Toby, who was bent over, weeding an onion bed. Her eyes went to the greenhouse and cloud shadows sliding over the long leaves of the peach trees inside, and she thought the old gardener might be in there watching. Instead, she saw a sudden shift of bright blue. A woman, or rather a lady in a blue silk dress, was inside among the leaves, looking out. She was tall, with light brown hair caught loosely in a knot at the neck, and her eyes were on Tabby. Tabby expected her to come out and ask what she was doing, but she stayed where she was. Tabby gave her stare for stare and walked over to Toby.

'Who's that in the greenhouse?'

Toby spoke under his breath, without looking up. 'Miss Felicity. Why do you think I'm working all of a sudden?'

'Who's she?'

'The daughter.'

She asked several more questions but he turned

68

his back to her and wouldn't answer, so she let herself out by the side door.

It turned out that Amos Legge knew more.

'Two children, there are. The boy, Mr Oliver, he's at Cambridge, only it's their holidays now so he's up in Yorkshire with friends. Miss Felicity's twenty-one. She broke off an engagement recently. She's pleasant enough most of the time but she's got a temper on her. I've heard her exchange high words with her mother.'

He was grooming Rancie as he talked, Tabby kicking straw into place in the corner of the box. He'd told her about his discovery of the blanket with the explosive smell and his interview with Bevan. She disapproved of having anything to do with the police.

'How come you know all this?'

'From their coachman, Daniel. He's been with the family a while.'

'It was strange, the way she looked at me. Why didn't she just come out and ask who I was, or see me off?'

'Some folks with servants, they hardly know who they've got in the house. She might just have thought you were a new one. So, did you get what you wanted?'

'I got what I expected. Somebody let that bitch out deliberately, knowing it would start a fight. It was a distraction from what was going on at the front, only somebody would have to know the household well to know about the bitch. The girl, Jane, knows a lot more than she's saying.'

'About the kidnapping?'

'They have to be linked. Same people start the dog fight and send in the message for Mrs Carmichael. Then they grab her.'

'And put her in the Maynards' carriage while the coachman and his boy are distracted by the dogs. It's the planning in this that bothers me – every detail worked out. They want something a lot and we don't know what it is.'

'Whatever it is, somebody in this house knows something about it, and I'm going to keep watching until I find out what.'

Tabby walked back to Millbank. When she'd had places to watch for a long time in the past, she'd often called on the more reliable members of the gang of street boys that were the nearest people she had to family. She'd thieved with them, begged with them, fought them for crusts in Covent Garden gutters. Some of them had melted away over the years, several gone to prison, one transported and Drubbin about to go the same way, and one, named Plush, to regular employment as a coal, ashes and empty bottles boy at a Pall Mall club. Still, there were several she could have called on to help watch the Maynards' house, but she was determined to keep this job for herself, not trusting anybody else. In the early evening, with the household occupied with making dinner or dressing for it, she risked an extra half hour away from the watch. She crossed to the far side of Millbank and bought a mug of tea and a pie from the stalls that had sprung up to cater for the parliamentary workmen outside the gates of the building site, then walked upriver as far as Vauxhall Bridge, keeping on the opposite side from Millbank prison and looking up at the great rectangles of brick, pierced with narrow windows. Some of the more desperate members of the old gang were talking about trying to rescue Drubbin. When that was reported to her, she thought it was wild and probably drunk talk late at night, as useless as children plotting to attack an ogre. It would be impossible to force a way in, and everybody knew that the prisoners were tightly penned in solitary cells. Drubbin would be taking his long sea voyage and there was no help for it. She'd seen their first friend go. Some of the gang had found out what day the prisoners were to be taken out to the ship and were in position before the sun came up, watching the gates. Even on a summer day, an impression of damp and cold clung round Millbank prison and, on that February morning, it had felt as if the cold was rooting their boot soles to the stone paving slabs and their gloveless hands were frozen into fists. They waited a long time, but then everything happened quickly. The gates in the brick cliff were opened and two lines of warders carrying stout sticks formed up from the gates to the river. Then a line of men shuffled out in prison uniform, grey-faced and grey-jacketed, their jackets marked with MP in red – the initials of the prison – and blue woollen caps on their heads. They were prodded along the line towards the river, where two long rowing boats had suddenly appeared. The gang member beside Tabby had called loudly, 'Good luck Johnny!' and one of the prisoners had turned and raised a manacled hand in a kind of salute. A warder had caught him with a crack on the arm, not particularly heavy but enough to take the hand down. Talking about it afterwards, they weren't even sure whether the prisoner had been Johnny or some other man grabbing at a last passing kindness from the old country.

Tabby walked back to the Maynards' house. That afternoon, before she left for a consultation with Amos, she'd watched from the pavement across the road as their carriage drew up by the front door. After some time, Mrs Maynard, Miss Felicity, two dogs and a middle-aged maid had come down and climbed inside. Mrs Maynard was plump and cheerful, in a brown dress and bonnet and a yellow shawl. Tabby judged that Miss Felicity was what people would call beautiful, in a dusky pink dress, skin as white as house martin eggs, careful curls of hair escaping from a bonnet of pale straw with pink silk ribbons. She'd looked bored and sulky, her eyes down and mouth set in a tight line. They had set off in the direction of Piccadilly, probably paying calls. As Tabby walked past the coach house now, she looked through a crack in the doors and noticed that the carriage had come back. It looked as if nobody planned to go out for the evening. The side door into the garden was not bolted, so she went in and settled under one of the trees in the miniature orchard, watching the back of the house as usual. The family had no young couples who might want to wander in the garden of an evening, and even if Toby woke up and saw her, he'd assume she was simply going about her burglarious ways. The servants were too busy to come more than a few steps from the back door. As the sun went down, the wall cast a long shadow over the garden. Lamplight gleamed from the rooms on the ground floor. The scrape and clash of servants clearing up the dinner things and a sudden burst of laughter, quickly silenced, came from the kitchen. At dusk, the butler, in full black-and-white uniform, came out on the gentry's part of the terrace and paced solemnly along it twenty times or so, hands linked under his tailcoat, his eyes forward. It didn't look as if he enjoyed it. Meanwhile, a maid with her head done up in a scarf and a long brown apron over her dress came out of the house with a pail of ashes and emptied them into a metal bin. It was an ordinary household with ordinary servants – nothing to indicate that a woman in full possession of her senses, among members of her family, had been spirited away from there as cleanly as a gull takes a fish. Tabby waited in the garden until the last lamps on the ground floor of the house had gone out and there was just one dim light higher up where the last of the servants was probably going to her bed in the attic. The church clock struck one. She was thinking of going to her bed in the church when something happened.

The hinges on the door to the garden had a creak to them, so soft that you hardly heard it by day, but it was as loud as a pistol shot to Tabby's ears in the dark. She was on her feet in a moment, moving closer to the path that ran from the garden door to the terrace. The night had turned dull, with clouds over a half moon.

She could hear the steps of the person who'd come in padding on the grass, but did not see him until he passed only about a dozen yards in front of her. A man, she was quite sure of that from the build, and a smell – not a bad smell but one that was unmistakeable to her nostrils. Women smelled too, but differently. Quite tall and not old, judging by the way he walked. There seemed to be a kind of swagger about him, in spite of his caution, then she realized that it was a slight limp on his right leg, the sort of limp a man would have had for a long time and learned to manage. Other than that, it was too dark to see. She wondered whether he might be a burglar, but burglars usually worked in pairs. Like her, he was a person at home in the night. She stayed where she was but her eyes followed the dark shape as he went up the steps to the kitchen part of the terrace. The trellis screened him then, so she moved enough to see him walking up to the back door. Then, just like that, he was gone. The only way for him to disappear so completely was by somebody opening the kitchen door and letting him inside. There'd been no knock, no light, no words spoken. Whoever opened the door had been there waiting for him, picking up the slight sound of his steps on the terrace. It could still be a burglary, but somehow Tabby didn't think so. She went on watching the house. The servant's candle in the loft went out and no other lights came on. Two o'clock struck. Soon after that, the shape came down the steps to the garden. The cloud was thinner by then, with some moonlight filtering through, so Tabby stepped noiselessly

74

back behind a bush. As he passed, she had a sideways-on glimpse of a pale, beardless face with a prominent nose, certainly no older than thirty. He wore a dark coat and a low-crowned black hat, and wasn't carrying anything. Then the door hinges creaked again and he was gone. Tabby was out of the door before he'd turned the corner into the square.

He walked towards Millbank without looking behind him. She trailed him past the church and into Millbank, keeping about fifty yards behind. It wasn't easy at this time in the morning, with the street empty apart from the two of them, but he seemed to have no suspicion of being followed and Tabby made no more noise than a falling leaf. He turned in the direction of Westminster Abbey but, before he got there, he crossed Millbank towards the Parliament building site. At this hour of the morning, the heavy gates that let in the carts were closed. Tabby had looked in a few times by day and seen great piles of stones and timber, mountains of coal, vats and barrels, sheds and workshops. She lost him for a moment, dark against the dark gates, then saw him to the side of them, opening a small door no wider than a man. He disappeared inside and the door closed. She was about to cross the street and follow him when a couple of policemen appeared from near the abbey, coming in her direction. They were strolling slowly and she heard the murmur of their voices, just chatting by the sound of it, nothing urgent. One of them was smoking a clay pipe, the smoke of it coiling up, which was against regulations, but there was no chance of anybody picking up on it at this deserted hour of the morning. Wary of anything to do with the police, even a pair as peaceful seeming as these, Tabby stepped back into the shelter of a bush. They walked slowly past, not noticing. They were talking about a bet. Tabby waited a few minutes after they'd gone past.

The dark was fading to the grey half-light of pre-dawn, and she knew she'd stand out crossing the road if they happened to glance back. Then she darted across to the door the man had used. It opened on a latch and she was inside. Her feet grated on a clinker path. To her right was a lean-to with some kind of machinery inside it, to the immediate left there were heaps of coal, and ahead was a maze of single-storey buildings. Above them all was the unfinished bulk of the tower, dark against the lightening sky. She stood and listened, and heard nothing but the cheep of sparrows and a distant cart grinding across Westminster Bridge. An army of men could disappear in this place, and she cursed the two policemen for making her lose the trail. She thought her man knew the place well. He hadn't hesitated at the door. All she could do now was work her way round it and hope to find him. At any rate, he wasn't on the clinker path ahead of her, or she'd hear his steps. He might already have heard hers. She turned left on to a path of trodden earth, rutted from heavy vehicles, and walked as far as the scaffolding round the tower. She stopped there and listened for a minute or so. Again, nothing but the sparrows and two pigeons that hoisted themselves clumsily into the air when they saw her. She wondered if he'd heard the sound of their wings but, as far as she knew, he'd no reason to think he was being followed. He could be half a mile away. She walked on slowly towards the river, passing various buildings that looked like workshops and a parking place for wheelbarrows – dozens of them. The river was pewter coloured, the tide going out. Wooden wharves stretched into the water with hoists at the end of them and lines of flat carts waiting on the landward side. A steamboat went down river, sparks flying up from its funnel. She turned back inland, smelt fire and followed the smell. When she saw a man sitting by a brazier outside one of the huts, she felt hopeful for a moment, but he was only a watchman, bearded and elderly, a dog beside him. The dog must have heard her because it gave one sharp bark, but the man stroked it and said something, and it lay down beside the brazier. She looped round the hut, keeping well clear of it, and found herself suddenly in a crowd of figures, more than lifesize. The nearest one was a bearded warrior leaning on his sword. Next to him was a monk with his cowl thrown back, a woman with long braids of hair and a creature that looked like a dragon, all in pale stone. For a moment, she was fascinated then went tense, listening. She'd caught a sound, possibly a footstep, from behind her, towards the river. She went back to it, keeping well clear of the watchman, and saw a man standing on the landward side of the wharves. Immediately she knew he wasn't the one she'd followed – he was too short and square. Her man had disappeared and she had no clue where on the site he might be. Still, he was inside somewhere. If he'd gone back to the clinker path towards the gate, she'd have heard him. It was more light than dark now, and the first workmen would be arriving in an hour or so. She wandered round the site, fascinated by the size and complexity of it. It seemed to be a vast and disorderly village, with barn-like wooden structures pressed up against walls of grey stone and two great towers hundreds of yards apart, one nearly finished but the other still a long way to go, smaller workshops with piles of wood or stone outside them and metal tramway tracks that shone in the morning light. Even at this hour, people were awake. There was the occasional watchman, two workmen strolling together, deep in conversation. But no sign at all of her man. He could have gone inside any of the several-dozen huts or workshops she'd passed. She stopped and listened outside some of them but heard nothing. He must know the site well to disappear so completely, and for a while she wondered if he'd known he was being followed and was deliberately hiding from her. She decided not. The likelihood was that he worked here. Why she was so intent on finding him, she couldn't have explained. It wasn't so great an event that a kitchen maid had a lover from the building site. All she had was a feeling up and down her spine that there was more to it, and she never argued with that feeling.

In the morning, the dogs were walked as usual, and Mr Maynard was driven to his office. Tabby went up to Toby when he was on his own, tying up raspberry canes. He was nervous still and said she should stop coming there. She had to give him another half-crown to calm him down enough to talk. The case was fast wearing down her little stock of money, but she'd never cared much for saving it.

'You didn't tell me Jane has a follower.' It hadn't been a difficult deduction. She'd seen all the servants by then and Jane was the only one likely to have a man coming to the back door at night.

'Not my business. Not yours either.'

'You must have known, sleeping in the green-house like you do.'

'I sleeps deep and I knows when to keep my ears closed.'

'How long's he been coming?'

'Some time.'

'Weeks? Months?'

'Few weeks.'

'How often?'

'Twice a week usually.'

'Always late at night?'

'Yes.'

'Does Jane know you know?'

'I said something to 'er once about 'er young man and she threatened she'd 'ave me dismissed, so I never said nothing else.'

It struck Tabby that a scullery maid would be in no position to threaten even a gardener's boy. Altogether, Jane's confidence puzzled her. The mere rumour of a follower, even too long a conversation with the milkman or coalman, could mean dismissal for a maid. Tabby's work had taken her backstairs in a lot of households, and a scullery maid regularly letting a follower into the house at night was something altogether new in her experience. She was tempted to go and question Jane there and then, but decided against it. Next time, she'd follow the man, find out where he came from and who he was. It was hard to wait, even for somebody with Tabby's patience, but it gave her the first small stirring of satisfaction since Liberty had disappeared to discover some flaw in the Maynards' well-organized household.

Seven

I've got time back now. At least, enough of it back to give me a rhythm of working days. Light crawls in from overhead in the mornings, sometimes golden, sometimes grey, and once with the sound of rain again. It was enough to set the roof dripping, which was awkward. I scrunched up the blanket under it, trying to make it look as if I'd left it like that casually when I got up, and Minerva didn't notice. I believe that she's become accustomed to the routine too, and routines mean that you stop noticing things. Porridge and a glass of water arrive about an hour after daylight, salt beef stew just as the light is going in the evenings. The boy is more alert than Minerva, but that's because these mealtimes are a risk for him. So far, I've managed to distract her long enough for him to gulp down what I leave in the bowl. On the morning after I first noticed the drips from the ceiling, I managed to get hold of the spoon. I'd left quite a lot of porridge for him and he swallowed it as swiftly as before, while I was making a case to her for soap and a bowl of water. As she turned to the chamber pot, the boy was picking up the empty bowl. He had the spoon in his right hand. I looked him in the eye – scared grey eyes – and took the spoon from him, glancing across at Minerva and putting a finger to my lips. His eyes flickered but he said nothing.

81

I held the spoon in a fold of my petticoat and, by the time Minerva straightened up, there was nothing out of the way to see. For hours afterwards, I sat on the chair, clutching that spoon, waiting for an outcry. They probably had little cutlery on board the boat, and the loss of it might be noticed. But the boy must have been clever. Probably they left the washing up to him. Stew arrived that evening with another identical spoon, and the boy didn't meet my eye. By then, I'd spent most of the afternoon sharpening the edge of the spoon. Now, the gritty dust on the floor was precious. I swept it with my hand into small heaps on the firmest floorboard I could find and ground the spoon against it until my hand felt raw and my arm ached. It struck me that the boat might have been used to transport stone, which seemed a great piece of luck. Now I had something to do, my mood swung between fear and an almost insane optimism.

On the second day, I waited for some time after I'd finished the porridge, then moved both table and chair under the site. I felt stronger by then, my head hardly aching at all and my arm not hurting. I climbed up on the table and got my eye as close to the damp patch as I could. It must be a bright day outside because there was enough light to see the darker colour of the damp wood. It was where two planks met, with a damp patch on either side. The table was too high because I'd have had to work with my head bent right back, but the chair was better. I stood on it and raised the sharpened spoon, swaying at first and only just managing to keep my balance. If

I'd fallen, the crash of me and the chair would have brought Minerva and the poet running. When I was steadier, I probed with the spoon and, to my delight, a piece of damp wood about the size of a pencil came away as easily as a slice of cheese under the knife. Another three or four pieces followed and I was looking up through a narrow hole at sunlight on canvas. The canvas had a tear in it, the edges frayed. I couldn't make out how long it was but obviously it was large enough to let the rain through and, judging by the softness of the wood, it had been there for some time. So the hold was roofed with planks and canvas – possibly an old sail, tarred – and nobody had noticed the leak. Of course, if they'd been carrying stone, it wouldn't have mattered much. The easiness of gouging out the first few pieces was deceptive, because after that the wood was still damp but more resistant. My arm and neck were aching, and I had to tell myself that this was long and patient work that would take days, and I must keep to it as industriously as a burrowing bee. I climbed down carefully and found myself shaking from a mixture of exhaustion and excitement. Once I'd moved the chair and table back into position, there was no particular reason for anybody to look up. My efforts hadn't made a large enough hole to let more than a glint of light through, but it was something I'd have to think about for the future. I collected the fragments of wood that had fallen and took them away to a dark corner. They looked pitifully small for so much bother, and my mood dropped right down again, wondering what

Robert was expected to do, where he was, and how unlikely it was that I'd get free in time to do anything about it, if I ever did.

As it happened, it was just as well that I'd left off work, because well before stew time Minerva and the boy reappeared. This time, he was carrying a china bowl full of water, she a rough square of towelling and a piece of soap. Relief at being able to wash at last was more than checked by the fear that she'd look up, but I needn't have worried. Her eyes were fixed on me from behind the veil all the time. I loosened my stays, pulled down my chemise from the shoulders, soaped my face, breasts and armpits. Then I hitched up my petticoats and washed underneath. Goodness knows where the boy was looking. The water was cold, the soap a sliver from a kitchen block. When I took the piece of towel from her, I looked her full in the veil and again caught a glint of eyes behind it. If she thought she was shaming me by watching, I'd let her see I didn't care. When they'd gone I lay down for a while, luxuriating in the feeling of being somewhere nearer clean, and relief that she'd seen nothing in the room to make her suspicious. I was too excited to sleep, so I turned my mind to trying to remember. I'd managed now to piece together most of the earlier parts of the evening – saying goodbye to the children, the coach drive to the Maynards' house, the careless prattle of the dinner conversation. I could even remember what we ate and drank – turbot with a rather sharp hock, lamb with good claret and fresh peas – to the point where Mrs Maynard got up from the table and led Rosa and me through to the sitting room. I remembered Robert catching my eye and smiling as we went because he knew how I detested the convention that separated men and women at the end of a formal dinner. I thought that might have been my last sight of Robert, but I didn't know for sure, because after that everything drifted away into darkness and confusion. All I'd managed to retrieve so far was that smell of freshly carved wood or sawdust, but even that might have been my memory playing tricks. If I tried to press it harder, my head began aching again. So I let it run on the things from further back that I could remember without physical pain, at least. There'd been a morning ride in the park with Amos – quite recently, I thought, but then I didn't know how long I'd been unconscious – that had seemed especially sweet. My mare Rancie had felt as light in the hand as a butterfly, and Amos was riding a big hunter that was a match for her in speed and stamina. We'd raced like two stable boys and drawn up level, laughing from the sheer delight of it. Amos would be looking for me, I knew that, but we might not even be in the same country. Besides, Amos knew about horses but not boats. Rancie would be missing me. As for Tabby – goodness knows what she'd do. If I thought of them, I was too likely to be dragged down into self-pity, so I pictured instead a few recent social events, hoping all the time they'd jog my memory into action. There'd been one in particular that Robert and I had both enjoyed, and it had involved that rapidly rising Member

85

of Parliament, Benjamin Disraeli. He'd been a friend for some time and was occasionally a client, rarely on his own behalf, more often representing somebody of his acquaintance with a problem he thought I might solve. When I say Disraeli was a friend, I mean it, but you never quite knew where you were with him. The whole world was his friend, from the emperor of Russia to beggars on street corners in Damascus. He wanted to know what was going on everywhere, and to be at the centre of it. The rebuilding of Parliament was an example. He'd kept at a distance from the details of it, grumbling about the inconvenience. Now that the House of Lords was almost ready for occupation, Disraeli was as curious as anyone and had arranged to show a party of friends round as if the whole thing had been his idea. Robert and myself were included. The place had been chaos. They were rushing to put the final touches to it before it was opened by the Queen, and the great chamber had been full of stonemasons, gilders, carvers, seamstresses, foremen, wandering peers getting in the way and everybody giving orders nineteen to the dozen, standing arguing with hands on their hips, most things that were said inaudible from the din of banging and the arrival of more delivery carts outside. It had been hot, too. After about half an hour of it, Disraeli had led our retreat. We'd gathered no very clear idea of the new chamber other than that it was very ornate, and that the throne looked fit for Genghis Khan or the Great Cham and altogether too large for little Vicky. I could remember vividly Disraeli's fleeting look of irritation that nobody was noticing him for once, but it was no help at all in going back to what had happened to me in that time between walking out of the Maynards' dining room and being bludgeoned.

The morning after the wash, I was up at the table gouging out wood as soon as the light came in, then down again for the arrival of Minerva and the boy with porridge, then up again all day with intervals for rest. I sharpened the spoon edge regularly in the stone dust on the floor and tore a piece from the blanket so that I could block up the light coming in through the hole. The further I dug from the edge of the planks, the harder the wood got. I looked at the dimensions of the damp stain, wondering if the hole would be big enough for me to squeeze through if I managed to carve all of it out. I thought just, maybe. In any case, there was no point in thinking anything else. What I'd do if I did get out was too far into the future even to consider. Long before the light went, I was simply too exhausted to do more. I pushed the piece of blanket into place, stumbled down off the table and piled the pieces of gouged-out wood in the dark corner. It still made a depressingly small pile. My hand was blistered from the spoon handle, my neck and back aching so much it felt as if they'd snap apart. When the evening stew came in I stayed on the mattress until Minerva and the boy had gone, dreading giving myself away by trying to move. This morning, I tore off another piece of blanket to pad the spoon handle and managed to get up on the chair again, moving like a jointed wooden doll. By evening, the pile of wood chips might just fill a stable bucket, and the hole between the planks is big enough to get my arm through. Perhaps, with luck, another two or three days will do it. I'm too tired to even try any more remembering.

Eight

He arrived early in the afternoon, thirsty and unshaven, with the sun spreading layer upon layer of heat over the city from a cloudless sky. He'd hired a private carriage from Aosta because nobody seemed to know when the public conveyance would be going, or perhaps by then he was too tired to care. Urgency had driven him on until the point where time itself hardly seemed to exist any more, just a succession of light and dark on his long journey southwards. Calais to Paris, over the hills to Dijon, more hills then down to Geneva. He hadn't slept at an inn or hotel at any stage of the journey, flinging himself straight into the next vehicle or waiting at the tables of public houses while servants cleared plates and glasses around him, or hunched in his greatcoat on benches in stable yards, listening for the trumpet of the vehicle that would carry him onwards. The long climb from Geneva over the Alps, once the highlight of his journeys south, was now just another obstacle. He'd wake from a half-doze to feel the wheels spinning, hear the driver shouting and cracking his whip, and urge the coach on with every fibre of his body. Now, with the journey over, all the tiredness from it caught up with him at once. The river, the buildings, the people hurrying by all seemed unreal, and himself no more substantial than the rest of them.

He walked slowly up the Via Po, past the Café Fiorio. Some years ago, he'd spent a lot of time there, talking politics. The ideal of a united Italy and the various heroes, scholars and downright bandits who were fighting for it had fascinated him. They still would, if the brain in his head had been as it was before that letter arrived, but since then there was only one thing in the world. If he'd gone into the café he'd almost certainly have met an old friend or acquaintance, but this time there were only a very few people he wanted to meet. In between the politics, he'd taken an interest in science and known that some interesting work was going on at Turin University. Now and then, by letter, he'd kept in touch, and still knew some names. The one that concerned him was known to him, though he'd never met the man. He went on up to the Piazza Castello, not far from the university, and turned into an alleyway off the square. A letter waiting for him in the inn at Aosta had given him directions. He couldn't remember the alleyway from previous visits, which wasn't surprising because it did not look very inviting – buildings leaning in from both sides and a mangy dog scratching itself in the gutter. Halfway down it, as described, a tarnished copper cooking pot hung out on a bracket, indicating a café. He went in, stooping at the doorway. A plump, middle-aged woman was sewing something long and grey behind the counter.

'Is Marco in?'

His Italian was good, but the accent marked him as a foreigner. The woman raised an eyebrow and went on sewing.

'He's out. Don't know when he'll be back.'

He said he'd wait and asked for water and a coffee. She took her time but both were good. He felt some life coming back into him as he drank, ordered another cup of coffee and accepted her offer of cheese. As he sorted out coins to pay her, she glanced at his bag.

'You need a room?'

He shook his head, instinctively wary of the place. It was an hour or more before a figure appeared in the doorway. The woman nodded her head towards him.

'Marco.'

He looked to be in his early thirties, shorter than average and very thin. His face was pale, skin tightly stretched over a high forehead and a chin that projected like Mr Punch's. He sat down across the table without being invited. His expression flickered from what seemed to be a habitual resentful look to a welcoming grin, then back to resentment. The woman put two cups of coffee on the table and Marco emptied his cup in a few gulps, as if afraid it would be taken away from him.

'You said in your note it was urgent.'

'You still work for the professor, Ascanio Sobrero?' Robert asked.

Marco nodded. 'Still his laboratory assistant. I could be a professor myself. I know as much as any of them, but . . .' A twist of the wrist and a hand turned flat indicated his lack of money, a familiar theme with Marco.

'I could put you in the way of earning money. I need your help.'

Marco's eyebrows rose in a question and stayed

arched as Robert leaned across the table and talked quickly in Italian, in low tones. At the end of it, Marco whistled.

'Some risk.'

'Could you do it?'

'How much?'

Robert told him and Marco considered, turning his coffee cup round and back, round and back. After six or seven revolutions, he nodded without looking at Robert.

'Probably. I'd need half upfront now.'

'A quarter now. Another quarter when you tell me you can definitely do it.'

Robert passed over a folded pile of notes. Marco counted them, turning his back to the woman who was trying to see how much, then put them in his pocket.

'When will you let me know?' Robert said.

'Here, same time tomorrow. Have the money ready.' Another turn of the coffee cup, then, 'It's hard to handle.'

Robert finished his coffee, walked out into the sunshine and took a room in a boarding house near the university. He was brutally tired and slept insensibly for a few hours on the narrow bed, but after that the dreams came and he saw her reaching out to him, being pulled away over some edge into darkness, shouting words he couldn't hear. After that, he lay awake, knowing that nothing on the journey had been as bad as this waiting.

In Paris, Miles Brinkburn sat wearily down in the writing room of his hotel and wrote to his brother.

Dear Stephen,

I'm sorry to tell you that the trail, if there ever was a trail, has gone cold. As I told you in my note from Calais, I had some hope. We know from Amos Legge that he crossed the Channel and I had a report of a tall, dark-haired gentleman with no more than a travelling bag taking the coach for Paris. But if the man was Robert – and I'm beginning to doubt even that – I've lost him. I've been here for five days now, asking round the hotels, and it's hopeless. The place seems to be plagued with tall, dark-haired English gentlemen, and I've had some embarrassing times encountering several dozen of them, with no luck. If he registered at any of the hotels, it wasn't under his own name. I even wasted a day at the medical school in case he had some associates there, but nobody seemed to know anything about him apart from a professor who had some memory of the name from years ago, but nothing now. Of course, I've inquired at some of the main coaching stations that take passengers on from Paris, but on to where? He might have travelled south, east or west, and there are so many coach companies. He might still be here in Paris – assuming that he ever reached here – but in that case, surely I'd have had some trace of him in five days. In the circumstances, I think

93

it best that I travel home in the hope
that you may have better news.
Your distracted brother, Miles.

Miles sent one of the hotel servants to the post with the letter and enquired dispiritedly about coaches back to Calais. After the shock of Robert's disappearance, he'd travelled out with high hopes of catching up with him and finding out about his new information. Both he and Stephen had agreed that whatever it was, they could surely work on it together. But following a person's trail was more difficult than he'd expected. Several times, it had occurred to him that his sister-in-law's strange occupation had more skills to it than he'd realized. In a city full of foreigners, with French that was no more than politely adequate, Miles felt totally out of his depth. He clung to the hope that he'd return to find Liberty restored and Robert's behaviour explained, but had seldom in his life felt more completely at a loss.

Nine

Amos knew some of the men in the Fire Engine Establishment because he'd sold horses to them – good, solid animals that didn't panic at flames or clanging bells, even if they weren't elegant enough for his aristocratic clients. The Fire Engine Establishment was funded by the insurance companies, so would only tackle fires at premises that had paid their premiums, which wouldn't apply to the kind of backstreet places Bevan had mentioned. Still, fires were their business, and they'd probably know more about them than the constabulary. They covered the capital from thirteen stations, and over three days he spoke to twelve of them, asking if they'd heard of any explosions over the past few months. It took time because he had to fit it in between his normal duties and his daily visits to the Carmichaels' house for anxious talks with the children's nurse, Mrs Martley. There were no results from any of the stations. On the third day, he got to the last one that covered the area north of the river around Vauxhall Bridge, just up from Westminster. It was a quiet day and the leading fireman was happy enough to talk to him, but at first couldn't think of anything to the point. Then, at Amos's gentle prompting, a memory came to him.

'It was a month ago or more. We were just on

95

our way back from a fire in a baker's shop – it was easy enough, nobody hurt and most of the building saved – when we heard this explosion. It wasn't that big either, but a bit out of common. It sounded as if it came from the area near the prison. We still had a drop of water in the tank, so we thought we'd go for a look. You know there was this area they mostly cleared, on the Vauxhall Bridge side when they were building the prison? There's still a ruckle of buildings left there, and that's where it was – a house pretty well destroyed, two of the walls and half the roof gone and the other two not very steady – a bit of a fire burning in what was left of the timbers and two people, a man and a woman, standing by it all singed and smoky looking as if they were lucky to be alive. We could tell at a glance that it hadn't been in the insurance-paying class and we'd have been in our rights to leave it be, but since we were there I went over to ask the man if we could help. He bad-worded me as if we meant to do him harm, so we went away and left them to it and didn't bother to report it.'

'Was it gunpowder?' Amos asked.

'From the smell of it, yes. I don't know whether it was a case of thieves who had fallen out and somebody had hidden a keg of gunpowder and a slow fuse in the house, or whether they were mucking about with it themselves and just got out in time. Either way, it wasn't our business.'

Amos told Tabby about it when she came to see him after evening stables, taking time out from her watch on the Maynards' house. They had visitors in that evening, which meant more

96

work for the servants, and the scullery maid's lover probably wouldn't be calling.

'We should go there,' she said.

'Won't be much to see after a month or more.'

But he agreed with her, so they went together across Hyde Park and Green Park to Vauxhall Bridge. With Tabby comparatively demure in her grey dress, they could have been brother and little sister, except they walked faster than people out for a family stroll. They stopped on the north side of the iron arches of Vauxhall Bridge. From there, the bulk of Millbank prison seemed even more oppressive than on the Westminster side. The low sun gave its walls a thin wash of brass colour but didn't take away any of the grimness. Tabby stared at it for a while then looked away.

'What are those?' Two new workshop buildings stood close to the bridge.

'For the woodworkers from the Houses of Parliament,' Amos said.

They walked away from the bridge, towards the prison. The fireman had been right about the ruckle of houses. A rough triangle with a few ramshackle buildings and paths of trodden earth in between them made it seem as if the city planners and everybody else had forgotten about it. One side was bounded by the great brick wall of the prison, another by the approach road to the bridge, with an endless stream of traffic going across. Perhaps it had been a works yard when the prison was built. Certainly, the houses there looked as if they'd been cobbled together with materials meant for something else, mostly red brick but beams and planks too, and the occasional square of stone sticking out at an odd angle. There were a dozen or so houses altogether and, standing a little apart from the rest, a heap of singed rubble. They walked across to it, picking their way over solidified mud and bits of bricks. No adults were visible but a couple of ragged children, five or six years old, were playing in the rubble. One of them glanced up and said something through teeth that looked like an ancient ruin.

'She says this is the place that got blown up,' Tabby told Amos.

Various smells hung in the air, sewage, brick dust and horse dung. Under it all, a faint, sulphrous whiff of the end of a firework display. Saltpetre.

'Who blew it up?' Tabby had no squeamishness about questioning a child so young.

The girl shrugged. 'A man.'

The children stood watching as they walked round the rubble. Most of the bricks were smashed and blackened and bits of them had been blown twenty yards or more away.

'My fireman got it right, then,' Amos said. 'I reckon that bit of blanket came from here.' In his heart, he knew he couldn't prove it, but he was desperate for something to make sense. Tabby nodded but said nothing. He went on, 'So the people who took her had gunpowder and it nearly killed them. And they took her because they want Mr Carmichael to do something and he's gone abroad. What are they doing?' Tabby was looking away from him, staring at the wall of the prison. The bronze light had faded; it was

98

now just a great cliff of brick with narrow slit windows. She didn't answer. 'We should talk to the people in the other houses,' he said.

'Won't be any use.'

Two of the houses were empty, almost ruinous inside, and hadn't been inhabited for some time. Three, standing in a truncated terrace and looking as if they were holding each other up, were occupied by one sprawling Italian family with a donkey housed in the backyard. The inhabitants of four of the others told them to go away in terms that left no doubt they meant it. Tabby had a look round the backs of the houses while Amos was being bad-worded at the front, and reported nothing out of the ordinary – unless you counted several years' worth of bottles. An elderly woman, bent almost double and profoundly deaf, occupied a sliver of a place next door and might or might not have been willing to answer questions if she could have heard them. That left one house slightly more substantial than the rest, its ground-floor windows boarded up. They hammered on the door and, when nobody answered, Amos hoisted Tabby in through an upper window at the back and caught her effortlessly when she came out.

'Anything?'

'Nah. Looks like some people slept there not long ago. There are a few blankets and a mouldy bit of bread the rats have been at. Not a sniff of gunpowder.'

Amos walked with her along Millbank, past the prison to the turning for Smith Square. She said very little on the way, but that didn't bother him because he had his own thoughts. So had Tabby, and they weren't cheerful. She had nothing against lying and was good at it when needed, but there were a few people she didn't like telling lies to and Amos was one of them. She'd said there'd been nothing in the boarded-up house except blankets and gnawed bread, and that was true in terms of things that could have been carried away. But something else in it was worrying her, and it wasn't anything she could talk about to Amos. She muttered a good night to him when they parted, but that was all.

Back at the Maynards' house, it seemed to Tabby that they'd resumed their social life at indecent speed considering they'd had a guest snatched from under their noses just nine days before. Two carriages were waiting outside the front door. The front windows on the ground floor were brightly lit, the curtains not yet drawn. The night was still warm, so the sash windows were open at the top, allowing gusts of men's laughter to drift into the square. Through a window, Tabby glimpsed the bare shoulders and flower-trimmed hair of one of the female guests. The meal had ended but the gentlemen had not yet rejoined the ladies in the drawing room. The evening might go on for an hour or more. The coachmen evidently thought so because they were standing together on the pavement, smoking pipes. Knowing that all the indoor servants would have their hands full, Tabby felt even safer from being spotted than usual as she slipped through the side door into the garden. She risked a look into the greenhouse and saw a long bundle rolled up in

100

sacking under one of the benches. It was Toby and, from the snores audible even through the glass, he was fast asleep. She left him to it and took up her usual position in the orchard, sitting on the grass with her back against an apple tree. The little Jersey cow strolled over to have a look at her, breathed a few grass-scented breaths into her face, then wandered away. It was probable that Jane's follower had been warned not to come that night because of the dinner party, but she'd lose nothing by waiting, and the Maynards' garden was more comfortable than the alleys and doorways where she usually watched her subjects. She stayed in the same position, unmoving, trying to decide what she should do about what she'd seen in the boarded-up house. Ten o'clock struck. The butler had failed to do his walk along the terrace; he was clearly too busy. Soon after ten, Jane let the bitch out on to the lawn at the bottom of the terrace then called her in again after a few minutes. She was wearing a fresh white cap and apron over her black dress, possibly promoted for the evening to carrying empty dishes from the dining room to the scullery. By then she was not much more than a silhouette against the light from the house, but Tabby was struck again by the confidence of the way she walked and the authority in her voice when she called to the dogs. Once Jane had gone in, Tabby settled herself for a long wait, but only a few minutes afterwards, a man and a woman appeared on the gentry's part of the terrace. Enough light was coming through the windows for Tabby to recognize the woman as the Maynards' daughter,

Felicity. She wore a gold-coloured dress with many ruffles at the neck and elbows, and matching ribbons in her elaborately piled hair. The young man was yellow-haired, full-faced and nothing remarkable. He said something to the daughter and touched her elbow, very lightly. She drew it away and walked down the steps to the lawn, the young man following her. When they came to a rustic seat on the edge of the lawn, he spoke again and she sat down, which was a relief to Tabby, who'd been afraid they might stroll further into the garden. He took the other end of the seat, and Tabby could see from the way his head and shoulders moved that he was talking urgently. Felicity kept her head down. She had her back turned away from Tabby, so there was no chance to read her expression, but the whole line of her body, stiff and unmoving, showed she wasn't impressed by what the young man was saying. When he stopped, she raised her head and spoke a decisive few words. The young man's head slumped. Felicity stood up and walked on her own back up the steps and into the house. The young man sat on the bench for some time, head down, until an older man came out to the terrace and called to him, then went back inside, walking heavily as if through knee-high water. So Felicity had turned down a proposal of marriage, and not very graciously by the look of it. For Tabby, the whole business of marriage was slightly less interesting than horse fairs. She simply registered that with an engagement broken off and at least one other marriage proposal rejected, Felicity was not easy to please.

After that, she waited for a long time, her acute hearing catching goodbyes from the front door steps and the sound of two carriages leaving. With a dinner party to clear up, the servants worked later than usual. Tabby hoped they at least had a chance to eat the leavings – the fat tail end of a salmon perhaps, a half dish of peas. She felt hungry herself, picturing it. It was well past one o'clock before the lamps went out in the kitchen. By then, various windows on the upper floor had been lit with lamps for a while then turned dark again – presumably the family had gone to bed. By two o'clock, the last of the candles in the servants' attics had been blown out, leaving the back of the house in complete darkness. By now, the warmth of the day was long gone, the moon down. Tabby stood up and stretched, sure that Jane's follower was not coming that night. She'd taken a few steps when she heard the soft creak of the garden door hinges. She froze, then darted behind the nearest tree. The gate closed, very softly. Somebody had come into the garden. At first, he was no more than a dark shape, and she thought he was the same man as last time but, after he'd taken a few steps, she knew that this was somebody different. He was slighter in build and moved more hesitantly, with no limp but less confidence. He strayed from the path on to the strawberry bed, stumbled and almost fell. As he came nearer, blundering through vegetables, she saw that he wore a long travelling cloak and a dark hat tipped down over a pale, young face. He found his way on to the lawn and sat down on the rustic seat, then twisted round so that he was looking towards the house with his back to her. He stayed like that for a long time, no more than a hunched shape in the dark. Tabby settled back down by the tree and considered. She was no romantic, but she had observed the likes of him on several occasions in her work and knew the conventions. A young man in love, too shy to declare it, creeping in by night to stare at the window of the one he loved. Another victim for Felicity. When, after an hour or so, he stood up and came back along the path to the garden door, she decided against following him. Lovesick young gentlemen were no more than a distraction. The question of Jane's mysterious visitor was more promising, and she decided suddenly to make another early morning visit to the parliamentary site in the faint hope of tracking him down. It was too close to daylight for sleeping, and in any case, she'd probably lie awake from the thing that was nagging at the back of her mind. She let herself out of the garden and walked back across Millbank to the gate into the site.

Ten

The rowing boat came back in the afternoon, when I was standing on the chair and daring to think that another day's work with the spoon might produce a hole just large enough for me to squeeze through. Up until then, I hadn't thought seriously about the problem of getting through the hole, or what I'd do when I got outside, because the sheer labour of making it was more than enough. Now there was so much light coming through that it sometimes threw my shadow on the wall of the hold as I scraped away. I'd already had to tear off a larger piece of blanket to plug the hole when I wasn't working on it. I was afraid Minerva would notice, but so far the rhythm of meals and chamber pot had gone on as usual. I think the boy may have noticed, but he ate the food I left and kept his eyes on the floor. The first I heard of the rowing boat was the creaking and splash of oars, much closer than any other vessels came. Then, before I could even scramble off the chair, I felt the small thump of the boat against our side. I managed to get down, pick up the piece of blanket, scramble up again and plug the hole. Footsteps came across the deck – the poet coming to let down the ladder for whoever was in the boat. I was afraid he might see the hole in the hold cover through the torn canvas, but his attention must have been on the new arrival. Just one man again, though there may have been another left in the rowing boat. Two sets of male steps crossed the deck only a few yards away from where I was standing and went below. I carried the chair back where it should be, collected the fragments of wood from the floor and stowed them in the corner, then used my hands to brush woodchips from my hair, stays and petticoats. Was it to be another letter? Would it help if I tried to hold out against all they could do to me and refuse to write? It was the same male voice as last time. I went close to the partition and crouched down with my ear up against it. I think he must have been standing close, because I heard quite clearly.

'. . . Can't trust him. He's drinking, and when he drinks, he talks. He may have said too much already.'

Then Minerva's voice, less distinct but sounding both angry and apprehensive, asking how long they'd have to wait. The man spoke again, but I missed part of it because he must have turned his head.

'. . . Tomorrow afternoon, just after the tide turns. Somebody will be coming on board an hour before to help you.'

'So who, if it's not Jonah?' The question came from Minerva.

'You'll recognize him.'

'Do you want her to write another letter first?'

'No. The last one she wrote hasn't been delivered yet. We've had what we want from her.'

I started sweating. The finality of the voice rather than the words themselves told the story.

Tomorrow afternoon, the boat would sail and I shouldn't be going with it. Not alive, at any rate. The poet was saying something. He was further away and I couldn't hear him because my heart was beating so hard. In any case, the other man didn't stay long after that. The two sets of steps came back across the deck, and one pair went on down the ladder. The rowing boat banged against the side then drew away, oars creaking in the rowlocks, then there was silence, apart from the lapping of the water. I heard the sounds from where I was kneeling on the floor. I thought, as far as I was capable of thinking anything, that this would be the last thing I'd feel – the grit on the hard floor. I'd never see the light again, only this near darkness, then total darkness. I couldn't even think of Robert or of Helena and Harry, because it would be more pain than I could deal with, worse than anything they'd do to me. Every slap of water against the side of the boat sounded to me like their footsteps coming for me. But they didn't come. What there was of light round the sides of the porthole changed to the orangey glow of evening. Two hours of daylight were perhaps left. Would they do it by candlelight? When they didn't come, I decided that they were waiting for the other man. Until tomorrow, then, near the turn of the tide. One more day and the hole might have been big enough. Slowly, it came to me that I might have something like that single day.

They didn't bring in the beef stew that evening. I didn't expect them to. Why feed somebody you're going to kill? I got the chair back in position and worked until the light went, splinters in my wrist and blood running down my arm, but no matter. At first light, I was up and working at it again. Every sound from outside, every boat going past, made my heart beat harder, thinking it was the man arriving. I heard movement from the other side of the partition but nobody came. The light coming through the hole I'd made turned from pale to bright, the sun coming up. It was enough, possibly. It would have to be. I climbed down and considered. Getting through the hole was likely to be a more difficult business than I'd imagined while I was making it. I'd have to stand on the table, grab the edges of the hole, take all my weight on my arms and somehow hoist myself up. I'd have only one chance because, if I fell back on the table, the clatter would bring Minerva and the poet running. At least my body was a good deal lighter from my days in captivity, but my arms were already as stiff as billets of wood. And then, suppose I did manage to scramble through it on to the hatch cover? The only place to go was the water – the sea or the river. My father had been greatly influenced by the teaching theories of Rousseau and had brought up my brother and me according to his principles as what he called 'educated savages' – at home in pools, fields and woods, but with a very unsavage insistence on Latin, French and trigonometry. I could swim, but what water would I be swimming in? I still had it in mind that we might be near Edinburgh in the Firth of Forth, or possibly Dublin Bay. No use worrying about that. If I were to do it at all, it must be kept

108

simple – climb through the hole, dive into the sea or river and swim for the shore. What I'd do there, in chemise and petticoats with no money, was a question so complicated I daren't even think about it. The only plan was to get away, but my body didn't want to do it. It wanted to curl up on the floor, sleep and give up trying to save itself. It seemed the sweetest thing in the world to stay where I was for just a few minutes longer, but I knew that if I didn't force myself to get up, I'd never do it.

Clothes were the first thing. I took off my stockings – they were full of holes by now and smelt foul – and left them with my garters on the floor. Then my stays had to go because they'd be too stiff for getting through the hole. I felt oddly vulnerable without them in just my chemise and petticoats, bare feet grating on the stone dust on the floor. Then, after some consideration, I unhooked my upper petticoat. I was in two minds about that because I'd once heard a story of a lady who fell in a river and was buoyed up and saved by the air under her petticoats, but its bulk might have stuck in the hole. In nothing but my chemise and under petticoat, I was shivering, which couldn't be tolerated, so I got the table in position and climbed on it, the wood harsh and knotty underfoot. I tore away the blanket and the early morning sun streamed in, so bright that for a while I stood there, blinded and blinking. Then I curled my fingers over the opposite edges of the hole, reached up on tiptoe for a firmer grip and swung myself up with one foot on either side of it. At least, that was what I'd intended to do, but I must have swung unevenly. My right foot braced itself alongside my hand, but my left foot was treading thin air then falling, threatening to drag me down. I still don't know how it was possible but I heaved up my foot and pushed my head and shoulders through the hole. I was stuck like a cork in a bottle. It was only just big enough, and my upper arms were pinioned against the sides of the hole, hands still underneath. I dragged them up, first right then left, feeling whole areas of skin being scraped off, and planted them on top of the canvas of the hatch cover. By now, my whole body was trembling, and I knew there were no more than a few seconds of usefulness in it, if that. I braced my hands flat and pushed, brought my right knee through, catching my toe in the under petticoat, then scraped my foot and ankle out to join the hands. After that, the left leg followed as easily as a chick coming out of an eggshell. A chick, though, that was not far off being dead. I just had the strength to crawl clear of the hole but then lay there curled up on the hatch cover, shivering, crying and only half-conscious. If Minerva and the poet had come for me then I couldn't have done anything about it. In fact, I more than half expected them to come, sure that I'd made enough noise to bring them running. When I felt someone looking at me, I was sure that it was Minerva, and uncurled enough to put out an arm in a useless attempt to protect myself. Nothing happened. I opened my eyes and there was the boy. He was just standing there on the deck beside the hatch cover, staring at me. I pushed myself to my knees and stared back. There was no hostility in his eyes, not even curiosity. This was just one of the things that happened in a world beyond anything he could understand. I put a finger to my lips. He just went on staring. I was sure that, however confused, he'd shout out at any moment and raise the alarm, so I pushed myself to my feet. There was blood on my chemise and my under petticoat, and it felt as if it could be coming from anywhere in my body. I half walked and half fell off the hatch cover on to the narrow strip of deck beside it, only a few feet from the boy. I was so intently focused on him that at first I didn't look anywhere else. Only when I was leaning against the rail on the outside of the deck – a low and tarnished rail – I looked up to catch a lungful of air more than anything and gasped at what I was seeing. It was a river wide and crowded, the tide going out, the water brown and surging along. I'd never seen anywhere with so much shipping – steamships, barges, rowing boats and long vessels with copper-coloured sails rushing out with the tide. Almost opposite was a grim, modern fortress of brick, oddly shaped. There was an area just down-river that seemed to be a magnet for the barges and sailing ships, with dozens of them clustered round. High forests of scaffolding stood up out of the river. Further along, a great tower shone in the rays of the morning sun. It wasn't completely finished – a jagged crown of more scaffolding sat around the top. Looking just beyond it, a fine stone bridge of many arches spanned the river. It was a great, busy city, and one I knew almost as well as I did my own hands.

The fortress was Millbank prison, and the ants' nest building site was the Palace of Westminster. I'd stood, several times, on that great grey stone bridge with Wordsworth's lines in my head: *Earth hath not anything to show more fair . . .* Whether it was fair or not at that time didn't bother me. What took my breath away, so that I had to struggle to make my lungs work, was the shock of familiarity. Not Dublin. Not Edinburgh. London. What was more shocking, it was a London I knew well and only a hop, skip and a jump from my last memories before I was kidnapped. We were moored on the north side of the Thames off Millbank, practically within sight of the house where we'd gone to dinner. Downriver, I could even see the towers of St John's Church. Before I could take in the shock of this, my attention was pulled back to the boy. He was still watching me but he was listening to something and his eyes were scared. I listened too, and heard the shuffle of feet somewhere below decks. Minerva's, I thought, making for the hold. The boy's mouth opened. He didn't say anything, or perhaps he couldn't, but his eyes went to the low rail round the deck. It wasn't a case of thinking any more because there was only one thing to do. I went over to the rail, grabbed the middle bar of it in my cold hands and swung myself under and out. I spent a moment in the bright air, then the water closed over me. The shock of the cold meant that for a few moments I didn't even think of swimming, then instinct took over and I struck out, away from the boat, then turning – I hoped – towards the north bank, feeling the pull of the tide. At that point, I had no plan at all, only the wish to get away and the fear of hearing Minerva's voice shouting after me.

Eleven

I whirled round and round, water in my eyes and too much light after the darkness, my head dragged back by a weight of hair. I turned on to my stomach and saw, some distance away, the iron arch of a bridge. Vauxhall Bridge, that must be, and the tide was going out, carrying me away from it and down towards Westminster Bridge. I was some way out from the bank so I started swimming, aiming for Millbank on the left. It was a forest of great square wooden pillars, jetties jutting out where the sloops carrying stone for the Houses of Parliament unloaded their cargoes. I'd seen it from the landward side and knew there were cranes up there, only I couldn't see them from the water, or see anything of the building site, just a few sloops moored among the wooden pillars and what looked like a steam tug. If I could only get among the timbers and jetties, there'd surely be steps or a ladder where I could climb out, or perhaps there'd be somebody on one of the boats to help. But the current was carrying me along so fast I'd be past the building site and under Westminster Bridge before I could get to the bank. A thumping sound came from behind me and to the right, getting nearer and nearer. I screwed my head round to look and saw another tug, steam rising out of it, seemingly coming straight for me. I shouted something, uselessly of course, because nobody would hear me above the engine, and pulled desperately to the left. It missed me, I think, by quite a wide margin, but it didn't feel like that. I'm sure nobody on board noticed me. I experienced a moment of calm and relief as it went away, then I was caught by the wash of it – waves that flung me around like a piece of rag. I lost all sense of direction and just concentrated on trying to keep my head above water most of the time. When the waves subsided and I could see again, I found that the steamboat had done me a favour. The wash had pushed me much closer to the forest of wooden pillars than I'd have managed on my own. I was near the end of the wharves, coming close to the great coffer dam that closed in the main building site on the river side. A half-dozen strokes with what felt like the last of my strength brought me alongside one of the wooden pillars. It had a piece of slimy rope looped round it and for some time I clung to the rope, though it felt old and frail enough to break at any moment, my chest heaving and my whole body shuddering. When I recovered enough to look around me, I saw that an unloading jetty came out to within a few dozen yards of my wooden pillar. I couldn't make out any steps up to it, but it had huge wooden supports that might be possible to climb.

Reluctantly, I let go of my rope and swam towards it, my body more than half wanting to give up and sink down into the brown water. About halfway along it, I came to a vertical post with two diagonals leading up, and clung there. If I could climb one of the diagonals, then get my fingers over the edge of the jetty, I might just be able to pull myself up. Exhausted as I was, it looked to me to be nearly hopeless, but it was all I could think of. I managed to get a hold on the diagonal, dragged one foot out of the water and jammed it into the angle between the vertical and the diagonal. Then it was a matter of lifting myself up enough to get the other foot there, but my body just wouldn't do it. I leaned out too far and fell back into the water with a splash that sounded like an Atlantic wave, and a yell of fear and frustration that seemed to echo all around the empty wharves. Then, as I thrashed to get back my hold on the post, I heard a man's voice shouting, first from some distance, then nearer.

'Who's there? What is it?' Then steps, running along the jetty, and the voice right above me. 'What have you gone and done?'

I looked up and saw a craggy brown face and a trim beard the colour of pewter. When he saw me, his mouth dropped open. I thought maybe he was surprised to see it was a woman, though I didn't know why he should be. Then, in a quieter voice, 'Wait there.'

I didn't see how he thought I had a choice. Perhaps I'd expected him to plunge into the water straight away, but not everybody's a swimmer or a hero. Then the steps came back at a run and the end of a long pole splashed into the water beside me. It was about the size of a young birch tree. I grabbed it, understanding that he intended to tow me to where there were steps, and let it drag me through the water. Then something went wrong. I thought I must have shifted my

116

grip or my weight, because suddenly the pole was pulling me down. I opened my mouth to yell to him but my mouth filled with water. To loosen my grip on the pole might mean losing my last chance, so I clung to it, going down and down. Dimly, I heard more shouting and another voice. Then I was going up again, my head breaking the surface, being towed along – this time faster. A stone wall came up on my left, then a series of projecting stones that made steep steps. A different, younger man was halfway down the steps, holding out his hand, telling me to let go of the pole and take it. The voice was Welsh. I plunged towards him and he caught my wrist in a grip that nearly broke it, hauled me out of the water and somehow got me up to the bank where the older man was standing, looking shaken.

'A close thing,' he said. 'It seems I wasn't as strong as I thought I was. A very good job that Evans came along.'

He was perhaps in his late forties, and there was something calming about him – his grey eyes looked as if they'd seen a lot of things. The Welshman said he was going for a blanket and it struck me that I was practically naked in my chemise and under petticoat, both soaked and clinging to my body. I stayed crouched on the stones and we waited until the Welshman came back with an armful of blankets. Between them, they got me upright, draped blankets round me and supported me to a workman's hut with a bench to sit on. For some time, I was too weak to say anything, shivering under the blankets. A stove stood in a corner of the workshop, and they

117

lit it and produced tea from somewhere. My teeth juddered against the cup and the Welshman helped me to hold it. While they'd been getting the stove going, I'd heard them talking to each other in low voices, and gathered that they thought I was a failed suicide. It was mainly the Welshman's idea. He seemed a kindly man but religious, and while I was drinking he said things were never as bad as that, not ever, and the Lord would always provide. I couldn't explain, and a small part of my mind was waking up and wondering how much I should explain in any case. The older man stood at a little distance, looking down at me. The Welshman called him Mr James and spoke to him with respect in his voice.

'Where is it you live?' the Welshman asked.

I gave my address. It was a respectable one, and I could see they thought I was a servant there.

'I'll take her back,' Mr James said.

The Welshman suggested they might get a message to the family, who'd surely send for me when they heard. I'd decided to remain the disgraced servant woman until my mind caught up with what was happening. He added that there were few cabs to be found this early, and in any case it would be hardly proper. I imagined myself in wet underthings and blankets, crushed against the dignified Mr James on a cab seat, and could see what he meant. But Mr James was determined and the Welshman gave way. As a final kindness, he found a pair of wooden workmen's clogs for my bare feet. They were too big but, with the support of the two men, I managed to stand up and shuffle to the door. We went slowly through what seemed to be a village of large huts with wide avenues between, laced with iron tram tracks. There were quite a few workmen around even this early, and we got some curious looks. The partly built tower of the great building loomed over us. As we went, some of my strength came back and I was able to shuffle unsupported. We came to a tall wooden gate, which stood open with dozens of workmen coming in now.

'It's all right, Evans, I can manage from here,' Mr James said.

The Welshman seemed relieved not to be seen on a public highway with me and left with murmured advice that I should always pray. Mr James gave me his arm and we walked out into Millbank, the workmen moving politely aside to make room for us. The shock of vehicles trotting past and scores of people on the pavement in the fine summer morning hit me, as if I'd expected the world to stop what it was doing while I was imprisoned. Mr James was looking up and down the road for a cab. We had to wait some minutes before one appeared in the distance, and he signalled to it urgently. It was about a hundred yards away, coming at a slow walk, when I was aware of somebody running up on my other side.

'Well, where in the world did you get to?'

We both turned at the question. Mr James, I suppose, saw a young woman in a grey dress, no hat and her hair all over the place. I saw a vision.

'Tabby.'

Mr James jolted with surprise and looked questioningly at me.

'You know her?'

'We work together.' I still wanted to be the servant he'd assumed me to be because explaining anything else was too complicated. I knew Tabby was quick-witted enough to back me up.

'What's happened to you?' she said.

'We pulled her out of the Thames,' Mr James told her. Not surprisingly, he seemed disconcerted.

'We've been looking for you everywhere,' Tabby said. 'You're coming home with me.'

By now, the cab had stopped beside us and the driver was looking down from the box. Smartly, Tabby pulled the front cover open, waited while I got in and settled herself beside me. Since there's only room for two in a cab, that left Mr James standing, looking disconcerted at the speed of events. I didn't blame him. Tabby had mumbled the address to the cab driver as she got in, and he shook the reins to impel the horse back to its slow walk. As we drew away, I called to Mr James that I was very grateful to him and I'd bring back the blankets. I owed him a proper thank you, and I told myself I must come back and find him, but for now my mind was too full of the miracle of being back with Tabby.

'How in the world did you come to be there?'

'Business. I'll tell you later.' She was frowning, worried. 'But where the bloody hell have you been?'

On our slow journey to Mayfair, I told her. She listened, making no comment. 'It's because somebody is trying to force Robert to do something, only I don't know what,' I said. 'Now, at least, I can ask him.' In the amazement of travelling home alongside Tabby, I didn't doubt that I'd find Robert waiting there. At least now we could deal with it together, whatever it was. But Tabby's frown grew darker.

'No, you can't, because he's not here. He went abroad two days after you disappeared and we've none of us got any idea of where he is.'

It was the worst blow of all. After the first shock of it, I asked questions and found out about Amos tracking him to the Channel and Miles failing to find him in Paris.

'How long have I been away?'

'Ten days.'

I sat, slumped and shivering, almost beyond curiosity, until the cab slowed to an even slower walk, jolting on cobbles, then stopped outside a gateway.

'It's Abel Yard,' I said, expecting to have been taken to our house.

'That's where I told him.'

She helped me out of the cab, reached up to pay the driver, then gave me her arm through the gateway and across our yard. The staircase to the parlour seemed steeper than I remembered and I stumbled in the clogs on my wrapping of blankets, Tabby coming behind to catch me if I fell. Sun was coming through the parlour window, gilding the motes of dust that whirled up as I opened the door. It was probably a warm day but my teeth were chattering. For the first and only time in our partnership, Tabby actually acted as a maid. She sat me in a chair, went downstairs for coal and kindling and got the fire started, then found a towel from somewhere. She slid off the clogs and started drying my feet.

'I'll have to take those back, too,' I said.

'Your feet are all cut.'

'Probably from the post, trying to get out. If Mr James hadn't happened to be there . . .'

'Later. You stay there. I'm going upstairs to get you some clothes.'

I always kept some clothes at Abel Yard, and it was an odd assortment of them that she brought down – winter petticoats, an old chemise, thick stockings and a wool dress. With no sign of embarrassment, she helped me out of the blankets and thin underwear and got me dressed. She made tea, even stronger than I'd usually make it, and took a jug down to Mr Colley's cowshed at the end of the yard for milk. After two cups, I could feel my blood circulating again and my mind coming back into some kind of order.

'I can walk,' I said. 'We'll go round to the house together.' The urgency was to find Robert. I was sure that there must be something the others had missed. Now I was back, it was unthinkable he shouldn't be here too. Helena and Harry would be at the house with Mrs Martley. I'd have to find a way of explaining things to them, but for now all I wanted was to have both of them in my arms, holding them close until they wriggled and giggled to be let go. I moved towards the door and looked at Tabby, expecting her to come with me. She stayed where she was.

'You think that's the best idea?'

'Of course. Don't you?'

'Nah. I was thinking it might be a good thing if you stayed out of the way.'

'But we have to find Robert. Whatever's going on, it's something they want him to do. Now they haven't got me, they have no hold over him.'

She gave me a long look. 'It's eight days he's been gone, so I reckon whatever it is, he'll have done it or be doing it by now. I don't know what's going on, but it's something big.'

'I still don't know what happened that night.'

'Mr Legge and I have been making enquiries. He'll tell you.'

I put my head in my hands and winced when my fingers touched the place where I'd been hit. The water seemed to have opened it up again.

'What were you doing at the Parliament site?'

'Looking for somebody, but I didn't find him. I'll tell you about it, only you should be in bed. I'll fetch Mr Legge.'

'Following who?'

'I don't know the name. There's a fellow who's been visiting the scullery maid there, secretly at night. I reckon he works on the site.'

'What scullery maid, where?' My head felt as if it weren't attached to my body; it was still floating.

'The Maynards' place. It all started there. Somebody knows what was going on and I'm trying to find out who. I reckon she was the one who let the bitch out.'

I tried to follow what she was saying. 'There'd be quite a gap between them.' A scullery maid would be some steps below a skilled workman.

'That's what I thought,' Tabby said. 'Why's

he going to all that trouble? And she behaves quite high and mighty for a scullery maid. I reckon somebody in that house was helping whoever took you. She's probably the one who let the bitch out in the back garden to distract the servants.'

'Bitch?' Dogs again. I couldn't keep up.

'I told you it'd be too much for you to take in. Are you going to get up those stairs to bed or do I have to carry you?'

She'd have done so, too. I started laughing, then it combined with the shivering and wouldn't stop. I let her help me upstairs and on to the bed, still fully clothed, and rolled myself into a cocoon of sheets and eiderdown. She drew the curtains, asked if I'd be all right then went, presumably to fetch Amos.

I tried to think about it all as the bright light of a summer day came in through the gap in the curtains, along with the occasional moo of a cow and the continuous crooning of chickens coming up from the yard. Then I slept, only I kept seeing Robert in my dreams and couldn't understand what he was saying to me. I didn't know what it was, only that it was urgent. Around mid-afternoon, I woke up suddenly, my mind as clear as it was likely to get. Tabby was sitting on the floor, playing with the cat that had got in somehow. She dropped the stocking she was using to amuse the cat carelessly into its claws. It had been waiting for Mrs Martley to darn it but was a lost cause now.

'I went for Mr Legge but he'd gone out some-where to see a horse and they didn't know when he'd be back. I said to tell him it was urgent and he should come here as soon as he gets in. I went to your house on the way back here but didn't say anything to Mrs Martley about you being found. She even talks to me now, she's so concerned. She says the children are as sound as pippins and not worried.'

A fleeting thought that they should be crossed my mind, but still, pippins were a good thing, and in my head I could hear her saying it. Again, with Tabby's help, I stood up and went downstairs to the parlour.

'What about his brothers?' I said.

'We shouldn't tell them. Mr Miles talks. Can't help it, he just does.'

She was right. Now my mind was clearer, I could see the point of keeping away from everyone until we knew what Robert was doing. While we tried to find a way out of this thicket, the brothers would have to do without news. I'd no fears that anybody in Abel Yard would talk. The cowman and carriage builder we shared it with stuck to their own affairs and let the rest of the world go its way.

'So all we have to decide now is what we do next,' I said.

'What I've been thinking . . .'

I never found out because somebody was hammering at the door downstairs. Tabby went to the window.

'Mr Amos.'

She went down to let him in. He came pounding upstairs the moment the door was opened, practically running, hat in hand, his face red. He said,

'Thank heavens . . .' Then stopped, speechless. I'd known Amos in several tight places and a number of moods, but never incoherent before. His yellow hair was all over the place, streaked with sweat. His hat looked as if it had rolled in the dust. He just stared at me. I told him, as coherently as I could, what had happened, and gradually his face returned to its normal colour, though he was still as agitated as I'd ever seen him. Tabby, still in her unfamiliar ministering role, brewed tea and persuaded him to sit down, then took up from when she'd been interrupted, speaking to Amos.

'What I've been thinking is she shouldn't go back to her house. The people that took her will be mad she got away from them, and they'll come looking for her.'

'Why should they?' I said. 'They've got what they wanted. The whole point of taking me was to make Robert do whatever it is they want, and he's probably doing it.' I was sick at heart, thinking of those letters, wondering what Robert was involved in.

'Because you know about them and what they're trying to do,' Tabby said.

'But I don't. I've only seen two of them – one of those was under a veil – and I'm sure they're not the main ones. All I know is that whatever it is, it's supposed to happen on July the twenty-third. And I've no idea what it is, except that it must be big for them to go to all this trouble.'

Tabby looked away from me. 'But they don't know you don't know.'

Amos broke the silence. 'Anyway, we'll have to tell Sergeant Bevan you're back.'

'No.' Tabby practically shouted it at him. 'If you do that, she'll have to tell him about whatever Mr Carmichael's doing, and it must be something bad, so they'll arrest him and put him in prison, and what's the point of that?'

I started saying that none of us had any idea what Robert was doing. Tabby's certainty that it was something very serious was scaring me even more. Her view of wrongdoing was usually a pretty tolerant one. I had the idea she knew something she wasn't telling us. But Amos interrupted me for once, speaking across me to Tabby.

'We can't not tell him. He's been looking for her.'

'Not looking very hard, from what you tell me. He already thinks she might have just been pretending to disappear.'

'Why should he think . . .?' I said.

'He'll know she wasn't when we tell him about it,' Amos argued.

'No, he won't. He's just a raw lobster like the rest of them. Even if you tell them the truth, they don't believe you.'

'Will you both please stop talking as if I weren't here.' It came out as a wail, which I hadn't intended, but at least it stopped them arguing. Reluctantly, because like Amos, my instincts were to trust the police, I was on Tabby's side. I'd got Robert into this, against my will, and it was my job to get him out of it. The problem was we'd no idea where to start. Amos accepted, reluctantly and temporarily, that he wouldn't tell

Sergeant Bevan, and we discussed what to do instead. He was in favour of going down to the Thames and looking for the boat, but Tabby and I said there was no point. Minerva and the poet had been intending to sail with the tide, and in any case, one sloop looked much like another to our landsmen's eyes. The only possible trail was Tabby's conviction that somebody in the Maynards' household, probably the scullery maid, was involved in whatever it was. Neither Amos nor I was convinced, but we had nothing better to suggest. Tabby would continue her observation of the house and I was to stay at Abel Yard, out of sight. Amos returned to his stables for the evening round but insisted he'd come back and keep watch in the yard all night. With difficulty, I convinced him that he'd be better off in a chair in the parlour. His notions of propriety were surprisingly strict sometimes. While he was away, Tabby didn't let me out of her sight but, as soon as he reappeared, she went. I didn't discuss with Amos my feeling that Tabby knew more than she was saying, partly because I didn't want to start another round of discussion. I went upstairs, pole-axed by tiredness, but kept waking with the bedclothes twisted round me, thinking I was back in the river.

Twelve

When I came downstairs in the morning, Amos had gone and Tabby was sitting on the hearthrug, staring into the fire's ashes.

'What time is it?'

'After eight. I just got back.' She spoke without turning round.

So if Amos had stayed until she arrived, he'd have been late for morning stables, an event so rare that it scared me to think how everything was disrupted. I made tea, discovering in the process that there was nothing to eat in the place. Tabby accepted a cup, gave a long sigh and hoisted herself on to a chair.

'I stayed to see him come out.'

'See who come out of where?'

Another sigh, but she stirred herself into making a proper report. 'The fellow who's seeing the scullery maid. I went back to watching the rear of the house last night. Sometime after one o'clock, there he was, coming across the garden to the kitchen door as usual, only this time she wouldn't let him in.'

'I thought you stayed to see him come out.'

'I didn't mean from there. He went up to the back door like he did before, but it didn't open to him. He waited for a bit, then he knocked on it with his fist, but not loud. I heard the door open and she must have said something from inside, only I didn't hear it, then the door closed again pretty sharply. He stood there for a while, then went. I followed him again. He went pretty fast, in spite of the limp. I thought he'd go in the building site like the last time, and I could find out what bit of it he works in. Only he didn't. He kept going all the way to Saint Giles and went into a house just off there.'

There was something about the way Tabby said *house* that showed she didn't mean residence. From infancy, she'd known the dark ways and places of the city, but she could be almost puritanical sometimes in talking to me about them. She meant brothel. Considered squarely, that was hardly surprising. His scullery maid had closed the door on him, so he'd paid for consolation elsewhere. I still couldn't see what this kitchen-door affair had to do with my abduction but didn't want to tell Tabby so.

'And he stayed there all the rest of the night?' I said.

'Yes, which means he's got a bit of money, whoever he is. I watched him leave sometime between seven and eight, but then I thought I'd better get back to you, so I don't know where he went.'

'You got a good sight of him?'

'Better than in the garden. Tall, dark hair quite long, early thirties probably. Needed a shave, but then he wouldn't have got one in there, at least not that kind. Pretty well dressed if he's a workman – good black coat and hat but no gloves. Walks like a man in a hurry.'

The day passed slowly. I found some coins in

a drawer and wanted Tabby to go out and buy bread, cheese and anything else she could get, but she wouldn't leave me so long. The most she'd concede was a five-minute absence to give the money and instructions to a maid the carriage repairer's wife had taken on. We lunched on the provisions she brought back. Most of the time, I thought about Robert. He'd been away for nine days now, which should be enough to go to Paris, for instance, and come back. The trouble was we had no idea where he'd gone, except that it was on the far side of the Channel. I found a calendar and managed to establish, with some help from Tabby, who was pretty vague about days of the week, that the day's date was Thursday the fifteenth of July, just eight days away from whatever was due to happen on the twenty-third. Since the smell of explosive on the blanket was one of the few clues we had, I suggested that we should all go back together and have another look at the site by Vauxhall Bridge. Tabby was against it – nothing to see there, she said. I didn't insist. The problem was that my recollection of being kidnapped was still patchy, and I was prepared to try anything that might fill in the blanks.

We expected Amos back in the early afternoon because things were quieter at the stables then, but he didn't arrive until after four. By the time we heard his knock on the outside door, we were both nervy and tired of each other's company. I called to him to come up and he arrived looking almost as perturbed as the day before. My thoughts flew to the children.

'Amos, has something happened to Helena and Harry?'

'No, they're safe enough. It's . . . it was something that bothered me, that's all. Only it's all right. That is to say, it isn't all right, but it's not what I thought it was.'

We sat him down in an armchair. It was normal with Amos to make me wait for his stories, but this time he wasn't teasing. He rubbed a hand over his eyes as if trying to wipe away something, and told his story.

'I was in the stables and a constable came in with a message from Sergeant Bevan. He wanted to see me urgently at the Westminster police station. My first thought was that he'd found out you'd escaped and wanted to know if I knew, so I went in a bit cautiously. He asked me to sit down, quite politely, then got straight to the point. A young woman's body had been taken out of the Thames at Westminster Bridge, and he wanted me to look at it and see if I could identify it.'

'To see if it was me?'

'That was the size of it. My first thought was that it couldn't be you, but then I thought I didn't know what might have happened after I'd left, and perhaps . . .'

Tabby was on her feet, and I thought at first she was going to hit him because of the anger blazing off her. 'You knew I was looking after her. You should have known it couldn't be her. It was a trick, and I suppose you fell for it.'

'I didn't fall for anything.' He turned away from her, back to me. 'He hadn't seen the body himself because it had just been taken out of the river that morning, but it was a brown-haired young lady, well dressed. Yes, it was in my mind that it might be a trick of some kind, but more that it might not be. So we went together in a cab to the mortuary. Right up until they took the cover off her face, I thought it might be . . . only it wasn't.'

The lurch my heart gave was odd, as if it had somehow been me and the river had swept me along, as it might have done if it hadn't been for the steamer.

'When did it happen?'

'They think she must have gone in last night or very early this morning. She didn't look like the sort who drowns herself – a nicely dressed, a handsome young woman.'

Was there a sort? 'Was she injured?'

'Her . . . her head was battered. They think it might have been when her body struck against the bridge. It was a boatman who saw her and pulled her out.'

'So they don't know who she was?'

'They didn't when we saw her, but they do now. When we came out of the room in the mortuary, there was an elderly gentleman with another police officer waiting to go in. Sergeant Bevan said we should wait. They were out in a minute, with the gentleman leaning on the policeman. It turned out she was his daughter.' He paused, but it was clear that there was part of his story still not told.

'So who was she?' Tabby asked the question sharply, but Amos replied to me.

'The daughter from the house where all this started. The Maynards' girl.'

'Felicity.' Tabby said the name flatly. 'She's not the kind to drown herself. If she's dead, it's because somebody killed her.'

Amos, still looking shaken, took a long breath. 'So what do we do now? Tell the police about the man and the scullery maid?'

'It might not have anything to do with it,' I said. 'Why would he want to kill Felicity?'

'It's got everything to do with it,' Tabby said. 'The two of them must have had some kind of hold over Felicity. I knew from the start that Jane was too uppish for what she was. But if you think I'm going to tell the police anything, you can put that idea where the monkey put the nuts.' The unusual vulgarity of that showed just how strung-up Tabby had become.

'So they were blackmailing her?' I said. 'In that case, why kill her?'

'Perhaps she'd found out they had something to do with you being kidnapped.'

'The bitch again?'

'Yes, the bitch. Somebody let her out and it was most probably Jane. Somebody knew about the coach house and made sure it was unlocked so they could hide you in the carriage. It all comes back to Jane and this man she's been seeing.'

'So when he came to the back door last night and you think he was turned away, it might have been just to tell Jane he'd killed Felicity?' In spite of my doubts, she was carrying me along with her.

'It might have been, I suppose, only it wasn't.'

'Oh?'

'Because when I left to follow him, sometime after one o'clock, Felicity was still inside the house. I know she was in there because earlier she'd come out on the terrace and gone back inside. She didn't come out of the back door because I was watching all the time. If she'd walked out of the front door, somebody would have heard her.'

With anybody else I might have doubted it, but Tabby's observation skills were infallible.

'So are you thinking that Jane bludgeoned her to death inside the house?' I said. 'It would be a noisy, messy business, and surely Felicity would have fought back. Besides, how did she get in the river? I don't suppose Jane carried her all the way across Millbank.'

'She looks like a strong girl to me.' Tabby sounded discouraged, but only for a moment. 'If Felicity was still alive, she could have come out of the back door any time after I left and gone to meet whoever it was killed her.'

'Who, from your account, couldn't be the man Jane was seeing. Unless he got out of that house in St Giles.'

She shook her head. 'He didn't. It backs on to another house, so the main entrance and the tradesman's entrance are both at the front. He didn't come out of either until sometime after seven o'clock in the morning.'

Amos had been listening intently to all this. 'So do I tell Bevan about this man and the maid? I don't have to say I got it from Tabby.'

'He'd probably guess,' I said. 'We should tell him and let him decide whether it's got anything to do with Felicity's murder. We need to keep in touch with Bevan to know what he's doing, even if we're not telling him I'm free.' It was in my mind that he might have news of Robert before we did.

'What about Tabby's idea that it's got something to do with you being kidnapped? Do I tell him that too?'

'I don't think we'll need to. He must suspect already that it's more than a coincidence – the same house involved.'

Tabby wasn't looking pleased at the thought of giving any information to Bevan, but would stand for it as long as her name wasn't mentioned. 'Let me go back to the house before you say anything to anyone,' she said. 'I can talk to the servants.'

'Including Jane?'

'Especially Jane. The garden boy, too. Somebody must know whether Felicity walked out or was carried out.'

So we settled that Amos should go and see Bevan again, but not until after Tabby had reported back. He had to go back for evening stables but would then return for another night on guard, freeing Tabby to go back to the Maynards' house. I wanted to go with her but knew she'd be more effective on her own. Amos came while there was still some light in the sky and Tabby slid out without even saying hello to him, still angry. I tried to will myself not to dream, but it didn't work.

136

Thirteen

Tabby came back quite early in the morning, so Amos left in plenty of time for the stables. I made tea for us.

'What's happening at the Maynards'?' I said.

'You sure you're strong enough to talk?'

I must sound worse than I realized. She'd never been so solicitous before.

'Yes. Do I still look that bad?'

'Like a hen's carcass a dog dug up. They're all at sixes and sevens at the house, lights on all night. The police have been round, talking to the servants.'

'Did they include the scullery maid?'

'Nah, they wouldn't expect her to know anything. Only the upper servants like the house-keeper, the butler and Mrs Maynard's maid. They knew she didn't go out by the front door because the butler locked it at midnight and put the key in his pocket, and she was seen after that by Mrs Maynard's maid.'

'Are they treating it as murder or suicide?'

'Dunno. The only one I could get to talk to was the gardening boy, Toby, and the police didn't bother to speak to him either. They think he only comes in by the day and don't know he sleeps in the greenhouse. If they did, they'd have saved themselves asking about the front door. Toby saw her go out through the garden.'

'When?'

'He doesn't know the time but says it was just before it got light, so that would be around four o'clock. He says he usually sleeps sound but he heard a noise. He thinks it was her stumbling on the gravel path. He woke up and looked out because he thought it might be me. He's got it in his head that I'm a burglar.'

'Why would he . . .?'

'Don't worry about it. Anyway, there was this woman in a cloak with the hood up. He says he didn't know at the time it was Miss Felicity, but she was moving like a young woman and he thought somehow she was quality. Then, later, round about their breakfast time, the place was in an uproar because Miss Felicity was missing, so he knew it must have been her that he saw.'

'Didn't he tell anybody?'

'Wasn't his place and nobody asked him. One thing, if she went out the back way, Jane should have known. She sleeps in the kitchen.'

'So Felicity went out just before first light. To throw herself into the Thames?' Up till then, I'd accepted Tabby's belief Felicity would not commit suicide. I didn't know the girl – she'd been absent from the dinner party at the Maynards' – but it had to be a possibility.

'Nah. I reckon she was going to meet somebody, or was looking for somebody.'

'Who?'

'I told you – Jane and the man she'd been seeing had some sort of hold over Felicity. Suppose they were blackmailing her and she'd gone to talk to him or hand over money?'

'At the building site?'

'That's what I reckon. She knew he came from there and she'd gone to find him.'

'And he hit her on the head and threw her in the river? Very neat. The only problem with that is that he couldn't have. Before Felicity came out of the house, you'd followed him to St Giles and he stayed there.'

'So we come back to Jane. I said she'd have known if Felicity went out the back. But suppose she wasn't asleep in the kitchen? Suppose she'd told Felicity to meet her somewhere outside the house and was waiting for her?'

'And killed her? But would Felicity have gone out to meet her?'

'If she had no choice. We don't know what they had over her.'

'How big was Felicity?'

'Tall, quite slim.'

'And Jane?'

'Not so tall, and broader across the hips and shoulders. Looks strong.' I still found it hard to accept that a woman could bludgeon another over the head, but suspected Tabby would know of examples, so said nothing. 'Anyway, I'll need to go back there and make her speak to me.'

'Will she, do you think?'

'She'll have to, if I threaten to tell the house-keeper about her having a lover calling on her.' I doubted that Tabby would do that, her sympathies usually being with scullery maids, but she'd make it an effective threat.

'I'll come with you.'

She looked me up and down. 'For one thing,

you're not up to it yet. For another, we don't want anyone knowing you've come back.'

'They won't. I'm sure Jane never saw me at the Maynards'.' A scullery maid wouldn't wait at the table. 'You can just say I'm a friend of yours.'

In the end, she gave in, on condition that we went to Westminster by cab. We put together an outfit for me from the clothes upstairs, a plain blue wool dress and a bonnet that came well forward over the face. The dress was too hot for the day but I welcomed the warmth with my bones still cold from the river. We got out of the cab on the north side of Westminster Bridge and stood for a while looking down at the water. The tide was going out again, brown water sucking against the stone pillars. I imagined a body being bludgeoned head first against the stones, not sure whether I was thinking of Felicity's or my own. When I looked back upriver there were the familiar landmarks – the partly finished towers, the abbey, the prison. We walked past the building site along Millbank, the road clogged with a mixture of smart carriages and wagons loaded with building materials, then crossed into the open area surrounding St John's Church. Two carriages were parked outside the Maynards' house. Friends or family condoling, I supposed. The blinds were down in mourning over all the windows, so there was no fear of Mr or Mrs Maynard looking out. In any case, after ten days in the near dark and a ducking in the Thames, I knew I was looking very different from the light-hearted woman who'd arrived for the dinner party. We went into the garden by the side door. The gardening boy, picking French beans, glanced up at us then warningly towards the greenhouse and mouthed two words. Inside it, a gardener with his back to us was doing something to espaliered fruit trees. I looked questioningly at Tabby.

'Dismal Jim. He'll go inside soon. We'll get you in the cowshed and I'll go and talk to Jane.'

The cowshed was occupied by the little Jersey sheltering from the sun, but she was obliging enough to share it with me while Tabby walked up to the kitchen door as if she belonged in the place and disappeared inside. She was gone for about ten minutes and came back looking grim.

'She's scared, but I made her see she's got to talk to us. She'll come out to the greenhouse when Dismal Jim goes inside for his beer.'

We watched as the gardener shuffled towards the house. Soon afterwards, a young woman in a black dress, white cap and apron came out of the kitchen door, glanced round her and started walking towards the greenhouse. We met her at the door and I opened it for us to go inside. The air was hot and heavy. Perfect downy peaches hung from trees espaliered along the wall and melons were ripening, each one netted in its miniature hammock, filling the air with tropical scent. I led the way to the far end, our feet echoing on the metal grating, and stopped by a big lead water tank. Jane's eyes were red-rimmed and terrified, her breathing heavy. In happier circumstances, she'd have been pretty enough – curly hair, big brown eyes, a pleasant roundness of

141

figure. Now she leaned back against the tank, trying to put as much space as possible between herself and us, and the sharp whiff of her sweat mingled with the fruit smells.

'We're not going to hurt you,' I said.

'Wh-who are you?'

'Friends of the family. We're just trying to find out what happened.'

'She's dead.'

'We know that. We're wondering why she left the house. You keep a watch on the back door, don't you?'

'I sleep there. It's handy in case the dogs bark in the night and I have to go to them. I've got a bed to myself that folds up in the day, and it's warm from all the cooking.'

'So you saw her go out?'

A nod.

'Did she say anything to you?'

'Not then, no. Earlier, she'd been angry with me.'

'Why?'

'Because of something I'd done.'

'What had you done?'

Silence.

'Had she found out that you were seeing a man from the building site?' I said.

It's odd when you're questioning somebody and suddenly find out that you've made a mistake. I saw it in her eyes. She was still terrified, and yet somehow I'd just said something that made her feel a little more secure. When she replied at last, her voice had an edge of defiance.

'She couldn't have, because I wasn't.'

Tabby had been silent up to then, but she broke in. 'No point in saying you weren't. I saw him being let in, and you're the one in the kitchen.'

'I didn't know he was from the building site. I never knew where he was from.'

'But you let him in,' Tabby said. She looked ready to shake the truth out of Jane. I put out a hand to stop her.

'Only because I was told to.'

Tabby and I looked at each other. 'Who told you to?' I said.

'She did. Miss Felicity.'

Her eyes, staring into mine from a few feet away, were now more hostile than terrified.

'Miss Felicity told you to let him in? Why?'

Just the glimpse of a grin from her at my supposed naivety. 'Why do you think?'

'She's dead. You won't gain anything from bad-wording her.'

'I'm not bad-wording anybody. It's God's truth. She gave me things – money and stockings and underthings. It was her secret and I had to keep it. I liked her. Better than I liked the rest of them, anyway.'

'And after you'd let him in?'

'She'd take him into the parlour. I didn't spy on them. It was nothing to do with me. Then I'd let him out.'

'How long has this been going on?'

'Since May. Twice a week, most weeks.'

'And the night before last, he came as usual?'

'She hadn't told me he was coming. She'd always told me before. He just arrived at the back door, no warning. I knew she was up in her room with a headache, so I told him she was indisposed and he went away.'

'Had she known he was coming?'

'Can't have, or she'd have told me. She'd had another argument with her mother that evening. We all knew about it from Mary – her mother's maid. Miss Felicity and her mother were always arguing. This time it was over a man that proposed to her but she wouldn't have him. So she'd gone to her room and didn't want to be disturbed. Then, later I thought maybe she should know he'd called, so I went up and tapped on her door and told her. She was mad with me for turning him away, but I don't see what I could have done.'

'What time was this?'

'Late . . . after midnight. I went back down to the kitchen and went to sleep, and the next thing I knew, a few hours later, there she was, walking out.'

'And you didn't tell anybody?'

''Course not. Then, at breakfast time, there was all the fuss because she wasn't there, and of course I didn't tell anybody because it would all have come out about the man. Later on, the police were round here asking questions, but I kept clear of them. You won't tell them, will you?' She glanced at Tabby. 'She said you wouldn't tell them if I talked to you.'

I'd have hesitated to give that assurance, but Tabby would never willingly talk to the police. I'd have to decide later whether I was bound by what she'd said.

'Why didn't you want to talk to them?'

'Because if it came out about me letting him in, I'd lose my job and get no reference – then what would I do?'

It seemed such a small matter in the circumstances. I had to remind myself that for her it would be a disaster far above Miss Felicity's death. She turned and looked out to the garden. 'Dismal Jim'll be back any time. I have to go.'

'Just one more thing. Do you think Miss Felicity was going out to meet the man?'

'I don't know. She couldn't have expected to meet him that night or she'd have told me to let him in.'

We stood aside to let her walk past us to the greenhouse door. She turned after she'd taken a few steps.

'You won't tell the police, will you? It had nothing to do with me, her being dead.' The door closed behind her and we watched as she hurried across the garden.

We let ourselves out of the garden and started walking back towards the abbey.

'Do we believe her?' Tabby said.

'Yes. She was too scared to lie. Still, it's almost incredible the risk Felicity was taking. The police should know about it.'

'Why? We know he can't have killed her.'

'We need to speak to him. That means we must go back into that site.' We looked across at it. A team of six horses was pulling a wagon of timbers through the gate. 'I wonder if the police have been talking to the workmen there. It's one of the places where she might have been put into the river.'

'You could do that anywhere. Still, if we could walk round I might see him.'

'I still have the blankets that Mr James wrapped round me, and the workman's clogs. It would surely be only civil to return them.'

We walked on in silence for a while, looking for a cab.

'I've been thinking about that bitch,' Tabby said. I almost groaned. She seemed obsessed by the dog. 'Suppose it wasn't Jane that let her out. Suppose it was Felicity.'

'Why would she do that?'

'Because the man who was seeing her told her to.'

'So, by your theory, she's not only let a lover into the house, she's involved with whatever plot is going on?'

'Is there anything else that makes sense of this?'

We waited on the corner by Westminster Bridge. Several full cabs trotted past. 'You've seen Felicity,' I said. 'Did she strike you as remarkable?'

Tabby shrugged. 'Only a couple of times, from a distance. Why should she?'

It was a fair enough question, but it was in my mind that Felicity must have been quite remarkably daring. For a girl from her sheltered background to take a lover was surprising enough, even more so that he seemed to be from the working class. How in the world had she met him? Then to bribe a servant to let him into the house secretly was something altogether out of the common. A girl capable of that would surely be capable of anything.

An empty cab appeared. Tabby signalled to it

146

to stop and we folded ourselves into it. On the slow journey back, I worked out in my head the details of our return to the building site. What we'd do if she came face-to-face with Felicity's lover was something we'd have to deal with when it happened. An odd recklessness had come to me after my time in captivity. I'd escaped from that and didn't see what could be worse. If Tabby's suspicion turned out to be right – and I was still by no means convinced of that – then this was a trail that at some distant point led to Robert. With nothing else to point the way, all we could do was follow it.

Fourteen

At Dijon, Robert was negotiating with a fish-monger. It was heavy going, partly because they were down in the man's cellars, where it was almost totally dark and the air practically swam into your nostrils with the smells of fins, scales and guts, and partly because his French was less fluent than his Italian. The fishmonger, a small, dark man, was holding his shielded lamp over a pit in the corner of the cellar to illustrate how little of the commodity he had for his own use. He was explaining, Robert thought, how far it had to be brought to him and at what expense.

'But I'll pay you well. You can send for more.'

The man shook his head doubtfully and looked at the hessian sack Robert had brought with him. 'Not so much. Not half so much, without robbing myself. It's the worst time, July.'

That was one thing that had been easier when he crossed the Alps. At every coach halt there'd been some boy who could be paid to run up with the sack and an axe to the glacier fringe, but now he was well west of the glaciers and with less than half an hour before the coach left for Paris.

'Half full, then, and name your price. Only, please hurry.'

The man named his price – a high one – took the sack and clambered slowly with the lamp down some steps into the pit. Robert stood, trying not to fidget with impatience, while he hacked at a block that gleamed golden in the lamplight, and loaded shards of it into the sack. One of the worst things about this nightmare was the urgency that was drilled into him, combined with the times when there was nothing he could do but wait. Back in Turin, he'd learned every knot in the woodwork of that awful café, waiting for news from Marco. Then, on the second night, Marco had arrived, sweating from the weight of a wooden box about eighteen inches high and two feet long. He'd put it down on the floor with what seemed like exaggerated care and almost jumped out of the door when Robert lifted the lid.

'Be careful. A knock's enough to set it off.'

Marco had kept his distance while Robert looked inside. There were two bottles like squat wine bottles but with thicker glass, packed in straw, each containing about a pint of pale yellow, oily liquid. Robert had been surprised, both at the fact that the stuff was a liquid and not a powder and at the small quantity of it. Marco had flashed a humourless grin.

'Just one bottle's enough to destroy this place and probably half the street besides. The professor says it's the deadliest thing ever made. He didn't want to make it at all, only it came out by accident from something else he was doing. He's been trying to keep it secret but people talk.'

'What does he call it?'

'Pyroglycerine.'

He'd impressed on Robert that the dangerous instability of the stuff was lessened if he could

149

keep ice packed round the bottles. The box was tin-lined to stop melting water seeping out, and a friend of his could supply a bag of ice, for a consideration. Robert would have to do the best he could to renew it on the journey. Robert had slept that night with the box under his bed and taken the first coach out from Turin in the morning. Every jolt of the journey over the Alps thundered inside his skull, and he remembered what Marco had said. He hoped Marco had been exaggerating. He supposed it should have concerned him that he was risking the lives of the other passengers, but the whole thing was happening in such a fog of unreality that only the box, its need of ice and the letter from Liberty in his pocket really existed for him. Now, striding up the street in Dijon, his thoughts were on the journey to the Channel and the hessian sack already sweating moisture in the hot sun.

Fifteen

By the time we got back to Abel Yard, we were both hungry, so Tabby went out for a couple of meat pies. Amos wasn't due back until the evening, so we had time to get to Westminster and back without discussing it with him. I suspected he wouldn't approve, but by now Tabby was fired up by the chase and had stopped treating me like something that would come apart. While she went out to find another cab, I searched the bookcases in the parlour, most of them full of Robert's books. It took me some time to find the object I remembered but I came on it at last, snuggled between Aesop's Fables and Catullus. It was a tobacco pouch embroidered with pink rosebuds, forget-me-nots and ribbon garlands – exactly the sort of gift an effusive lady might make for the man who'd saved her life. Robert and I had found it years ago when we were unpacking his books. He'd laughed and explained that once upon a time, when he was trying to smoke a pipe, it had been made for him by a young lady of his acquaintance. Both the pipe and the young lady were long since left behind, but somehow the pouch had remained. He'd said to throw it away, but I'd felt sorry for it and the unknown girl, so had stowed it on the bookshelf. Now, when I needed an excuse to visit the site, it had found its hour. The blankets and clogs might have been left with anybody but a gift for my preserver would have to be presented personally. In fact, Mr Evans had been more effective in the rescue, but I'd had the impression that Mr James was a man in some authority and I intended to use the acquaintance for what it was worth. I'd never made anything like it myself, and it struck me that it would probably have taken many more hours than had been available to me, but if I were uncertain about that, it was likely that Mr James would be even more so.

This time we asked the cab driver to let us down by the big gates to the building site. I hesitated there for a moment because the place on a normal working day was so busy. Loads of materials were trundling in all the time, with men who looked like clerks standing at the gates to tick them off in notebooks and direct them. The noise from inside sounded like dozens of stonemasons' yards, blacksmiths' shops and regiments of navvies all competing. I walked up to one of the clerks and asked where I might find Mr James. I had to repeat the question twice because of carts trundling in and, even when he heard it, he didn't seem to find much sense in it. He said I should ask at the office and directed us with a wave of his hand towards the smaller of the two partly built towers. Once we were inside the gates I saw his difficulty, because the place was the size of a market town and a lot louder. There were hundreds of men – workmen in shirtsleeves and corduroy trousers, more clerkly types, supervisors in city suits and top hats, all of them seeming intent on what they were doing. I even saw a few women, though our presence was unusual enough to bring second glances as we picked our way towards a solid-looking wooden hut that luckily turned out to be the office. Inside was almost as busy as outside, with plans pinned to the walls and men on tall stools writing in what looked like account books. When I found somebody to ask, it turned out that there were at least three Mr Jameses on the site – a blacksmith, a scaffolder and a foreman in the woodcarving department. I opted for the foreman and a clerk was told to guide us. As we followed him deeper into the site, my hopes began to rise slightly because at least it looked as if I'd chosen the right one. We were heading towards the river and the wharves, and I thought I recognized some of the huts I'd passed on my way out. The clerk stopped by an enclosure with an open-fronted shed on one side of it. Pieces of carved timber were piled inside the shed and several men were standing round a large piece outside that looked like part of a door surround. My Mr James was hunkered down, peering closely at a piece of carved foliage.

'Lighten it here and remember to balance it up on the other side. But whatever you do, don't take it back any further than this.'

He stroked his long-fingered hand over it as a person might stroke an animal. When the clerk called out that he had visitors, he straightened up, turned round and saw me, and for a moment looked almost alarmed. I was prepared for that. Two days ago they'd taken me for a suicidal servant. Today, even in my far-from-best clothes,

I looked more respectable. He walked over to me.

'I've come to thank you and Mr Evans,' I said. 'And to return these. This is a small token of my thanks.' I presented him with the tobacco pouch. He stared at it as if unsure what it was, glanced up at my face and away again. Some of his men were openly sniggering. Unsurprisingly, they suspected that the slightly crazy woman their foreman had fished out of the river was setting her cap at him.

He glanced at Tabby. She dumped the blankets and clogs on a convenient bench.

'You've recovered very quickly, Miss . . .'

'Miss Black,' I said. I wore no wedding ring. It must have been taken on the sloop, along with my clothes. Thank you, Minerva. I didn't like lying to him, but there seemed to be no alternative. 'How it happened . . . I'd gone for a walk by the river further up Millbank and I fell in. I was carried along so terribly fast and I believe I must have hit my head.' I didn't add that I'd lost most of my clothes in the water but hoped he'd assume it. The look he gave me was reassuringly steady and those grey eyes just mildly amused. His pewter-coloured beard was as neat as one of the carvings. He knew I wasn't telling the truth, or at least not all of it, but he was prepared to let me keep my secrets.

'Your family must be relieved to have you safe.'

I thought the voice might be Midlands originally. He was obviously an educated man. Again, there was just the hint of amusement. He was right that somebody from my family should have come with

154

me. Right, too, that I seemed to have recovered quickly. A family would surely have kept me at home in bed.

'Very relieved.' I smiled at him. 'I truly am most grateful. I shouldn't have managed to get out of the river without you and Mr Evans.' No need to remind him that he'd almost fatally bungled the rescue attempt. His intentions had been good.

'I'm very glad that we were there to be of service, Miss Black.'

It should have been the signal to go, but I chattered on like the featherbrain he probably took me for. 'What an amazing place this is, so many people. I should love to see round it.' There were a few more sniggers at this blatant invitation.

'I'm sure that could be arranged if you write to the site office.' He smiled, but his politeness was now close to frosty.

'I once met a gentleman who worked here, only I can't remember his name,' I said. 'I think he was a craftsman of some kind.' From Tabby's description, her man had been respectably dressed and had enough money to stay all night in a brothel.

'Eight hundred people work here,' Mr James said. 'Many of them are craftsmen.'

That confirmed my feeling that this was a hopeless errand because of the size of the site, but I blundered on. 'He was in his thirties – early thirties, I'd say. Rather long dark hair, and he walked with a limp on the right leg.'

'I'm sorry I can't help you. Thank you for the pouch. Now, if you'll excuse me, I'll ask one of the men to show you out. It's hardly safe to walk here unaccompanied.' He nodded across to the men and one of them came over to us, young and square in build, with a broad grin showing two missing front teeth. 'Bitten here will escort you.'

We began to walk. Tabby fell in behind us. Once out of sight of Mr James, Bitten appeared in no hurry. It was possible he enjoyed escorting two women past the various gangs of workmen, because he led us on an informal tour of the place. That over there was the House of Lords, finished now and ready for occupation. This would be the House of Commons, and those wooden sheds were for the railway committees, supposed to be temporary but would probably be there for years more. That would be the clock tower when they finished building it, but they kept chopping and changing the plans so goodness knows when that would be. While we were standing watching work on the clock tower, Bitten became more personal.

'You'll have to excuse the guvnor for being a bit short.' He was clearly trying to console me for my failed romantic mission. 'He didn't like the police coming round – thought it reflected badly.'

'Police? When?'

'Yesterday – a sergeant and two constables looking round the stone wharves. Still, they have to do their job, don't they?'

'Why were they here?'

'A woman got pulled out of the river same as you did, only that one wasn't so lucky. From a good family, too.'

'Why did the police come here?'

'I asked one of the constables that. He said he had no idea, reckoned she could have gone in anywhere upriver. He said the sergeant had a bee in his bonnet about her head being bashed before she went in and thought it might have happened on the site here, only they didn't find anything. Still, the guvnor thought it was unsettling the men. Bit of a mother hen, he can be.' A wooden platform piled with stone blocks was being slowly winched up the tower, with men waiting for it on the scaffolding thirty feet up as easily as if they were standing on the kerb edge. 'That man you were asking about – I reckon I know who he is.'

'What?' I'd been half hypnotized by the progress of the stone blocks, resigned to the failure of our attempt.

'Sounded like Whalebait to me. He's a wood-carver like I am, usually up at the main workshops by Vauxhall Bridge. That's where most of the woodwork gets done, then it's moved down here for fitting. I'm mostly on the site here so I don't see him that often, but we've had a drink together now and then. He walks with a limp and usually wears his hair longer than most. Fancies himself a bit. Educated man, though, I'll give him that. Knows languages.'

'What languages?'

'Don't know. But there's always parties of foreigners coming round looking at us working – prince of this, lord high something or other of that, regular tower of Babel. We just bow and get on with it. But it struck me that Whalebait knew quite often what they were saying in French or German or whatever it was. Once we had a group from Russia with their ladies round the workshops and he was laughing to himself quietly – said something under his breath in what sounded like their language. I asked him what and he said never mind, he'd just been talking gibberish, only I don't think he was.' He paused. 'A bit of a man for the ladies, Whalebait is.' He gave me a side-long look. I think it was in his mind that I might have been one of the man's conquests.

'And his name's Whalebait?' It seemed unlikely.

'It's what we call him. He's Cave – Jonah Cave. Jonah and the whale, see?'

'Do you know where he is now?'

From the glance he gave me, I'd confirmed his suspicions. 'Haven't seen him for a week or two. I suppose he'll be at the workshops, unless he's moved on.'

He possibly thought he'd been indiscreet, because he said no more and started to lead us back towards the gates. We were almost there when another visitor came towards us. A gentleman in his early twenties was being escorted by an obviously official man in a top hat with a sombre expression. The young gentleman's face was pale, his eyes red-rimmed. He was staring straight ahead, not noticing anything round him. As they passed us, the official said something to him in a soft and respectful voice, and I just heard the words *Mr Maynard.*

When we were outside the gates, Tabby said, 'I've seen him before. He was out in the garden on Wednesday night, looking up at the house.'

'The man called him Mr Maynard. He must be Felicity's brother.'

'So what was he doing outside the house? He should have been inside.'

'He was supposed to be with friends up in Yorkshire. If the police think she went into the river here, I suppose he wanted to see for himself.'

'Do you think he knew she was seeing a man?' Tabby said.

'Is it something you'd tell a younger brother? I very much doubt it. At least we know the man's name now and where he works. Jonah Cave.'

'If the police have been asking questions round the site, that means they think she was murdered.'

'Or suspect it, at least.' I wondered if the sergeant had been Bevan.

We crossed into St James's Park and took the path alongside the lake. Normally it would have been an easy walk, but I was weaker than I'd realized and wished we'd taken another cab. I wanted more than anything to walk through the door at home, see Robert and hear Helena and Harry running to me, but they seemed as far away – or even further – than when I was in darkness on the sloop, and I couldn't see how to get back to them. Tabby was silent for most of the walk and disappeared into the yard when we got back. I saw her through the window, scuffling the dust, deep in thought. She came back up to the parlour when Amos arrived soon after seven o'clock, and we all had our supper of tea, bread and cheese together while I told Amos about the events of the day. He was sure that we should tell the police about the identity of Felicity's night visitor. Tabby, as usual, was against it.

'We know he couldn't have killed her, so what's the point?'

'He's probably the reason why she went out of the house,' I said.

She argued less than I expected, and we agreed that Amos should tell Sergeant Bevan about him the next day, though not saying where the information came from. He'd probably suspect it was Tabby but would know it would be a waste of time trying to question her. It seemed important to me that Amos should keep up communications with Bevan, though hiding from him the fact that I was free. Somehow, I still didn't feel it. There was no reason for Tabby to watch the Maynards that night, so we agreed that she'd stay with me and Amos would go back to the stables for the night. I lit the fire now that the heat of the day was going and brewed another pot of tea, going over things in my mind.

'Why would Jonah Cave have wanted to kidnap me?' I said, speaking mostly to myself. 'What would he want Robert to do?'

'I know.' Tabby said it so quietly, almost under her breath, that at first I hardly knew she'd spoken. We both stared at her. She was kneeling on the hearthrug, not looking at us.

'What?'

'They're trying to break somebody out of Millbank prison. I reckon they want Mr Carmichael to get him settled with his money somewhere abroad.'

Silence reigned for a few heartbeats while I tried to take it in. 'Who?'

'Baron Kidson's people.'

This time it was Amos asking, '*Who?*'

'He's the leader of a big criminal gang,' I told him. 'He's not really a baron – that's just what they call him.'

I'd never met him, but once an associate of his had figured on the fringes of a case I was investigating. His name had only been mentioned obliquely and very quietly. Kidson was dangerous. Sergeant Bevan had once confided to me that it was one of the great ambitions of his career to arrest him.

'It's not just a gang,' Tabby said, still not looking at us. 'He's got his fingers in most things. He talks like he's a lord and he's rich enough to buy up half London if he wanted, but he just lives in different rooms, all over the place – never sleeps in the same house longer than three nights on the go. Most of the working women in London pay him for their beats, not directly but through whoever's in charge of them. Same with people taking bets and gambling clubs. Likes going to the races and owns a lot of horses, and they say he's never lost money on a race in his life, one way or another. Any bet that goes on in London, fist fighting, cocks, cards, he'll have a share of the profits. He's never once been arrested, because he keeps three or four removes away from where the money changes hands. If any of his people do get taken, they know to keep their mouths shut, then he'll see they're all right when they come out. If they blabbed, they'd probably never live to get out of prison. Anybody who crosses him ends up dead, probably in the river.'

'And never once arrested?'

'Well, not till two months ago. He's got enemies, naturally, but they'd never dare take him on direct. There's been a new gang coming up in Seven Dials, though – younger men, and they want what he's got. They've got in with one of his women, somebody he trusted as far as he trusted anybody, and managed to set him up as being behind a jewel robbery from Hatton Garden. The police burst into one of his houses and there he is, his hands in piles of emeralds and diamonds and whatever, guilty as hell. The thing is he wasn't, not that time. For one thing, the jewels weren't as valuable as they looked, and for another, he hadn't had anything to do with the robbery. He didn't do jewel robberies – too risky. Everybody knew that, except the police, of course.'

I said I supposed the Seven Dials gang had organized witnesses.

'You bet they did, and pretty thoroughly. Some of the best liars in the business, well paid and with a promise from the Seven Dials lot that they'd be protected from the baron's people, which they have been mostly. Only three have died so far, and two of those were after they'd given their evidence in court, so it didn't matter.'

I had about enough sense not to comment on the ethics of London gangs. 'So he was convicted?'

'Just for receiving stolen goods. Of course, the police, the judge and everybody else knew it should have been for several dozen murders and fraud and blackmail and everything in the book since he was old enough to hold a knife. So he was sentenced for about the only thing he'd never done. Seven years' transportation.'

'It seems fairly little in the circumstances.'

'He didn't think so. He stood in the dock and told the judge to his face that he was innocent and he'd never serve the sentence. And now he's in Millbank, listed to go out on the next boat to Van Diemen's Land.'

'And his gang want to rescue him? But how do you know about this?' The fear that Kidson's web might have spread wide enough to include Tabby was in my mind.

'Because there's one of ours in Millbank too, and some of them had this plan to rescue him, only Kidson's lot found out about it and we'd have got in their way, so they made us drop it. They came up to this friend of mine, right out in the open, slit his nose, cut off the top of his ear and told him there'd be worse if we went ahead with it. We'd just be getting in the way of them rescuing the baron, and they wouldn't have that.' She looked me in the face at last, defiant.

'You were planning to get somebody out of Millbank?'

'I wasn't in it properly. I knew some of them were thinking of doing something, but not how far it had gone. I only knew that when Mr Legge and I went to that place near where there'd been an explosion.'

'That boarded-up house,' Amos said. 'I thought there was something.'

She nodded. 'I told you there wasn't anything inside and it was true – not anything you could

163

carry away anyhow. But there were some scribblings on the plaster of a wall with a sharp bit of slate, a game one of my friends plays when he's got nothing better to do. It's one he invented himself so I knew he'd been there. I went and asked him about it, and he told me because by then it didn't matter and they'd given up. He and some others had been using that house as a lookout because it's so near the prison. The plan was that they'd get our friend away when he was being taken out of the prison to be put on the transportation boat. I don't suppose they'd have managed it anyhow, but now Kidson's lot have put the fear of God in them.'

'Was that explosion your friends?' Amos asked.

She shook her head. 'Nah. That must have been Kidson's lot.'

'It would take a great deal of explosives to blow a hole in that prison,' Amos said. I was relieved his mind was turning on the practicalities rather than being angry with Tabby. 'If I were doing something like it, I reckon I'd just use the explosion as a diversion. You say your gang were going to rescue your friend outside the prison on his way to the boat?'

She nodded.

'That would be it, then. Cause an explosion near the prison to draw as many of the guards away as you can, then snatch him away.' Amos was essentially law-abiding, but he liked to know how things worked.

Tabby nodded again. 'Could be. Then they'll have a boat waiting to get him hidden away somewhere and he'll be across the Channel before the dust has settled.'

'You think the baron's people can do it?' I said.

'Why not? He's still got hundreds of people working for him, and most of them respect him. Not just ordinary people, either. There's high-ups he's met racing and gambling who have to do what he says.'

'So blackmail? But what can he do from inside Millbank?'

'Anything. He sends his instructions out and gets reports in as easily as a general in a battle. Some prisoners get visitors and most warders'll take money.'

'What are they planning to do with Kidson if they get him away?'

'He'll settle abroad somewhere.'

It seemed all too likely. I was very much afraid that she was right and this was where Robert came into it. They'd need to spirit Kidson away to the Continent along with as much of his money as possible. A respectable gentleman speaking several languages who knew his way round the banking system would be essential. There were surely hundreds of those, and I wondered why they should have gone to so much trouble to recruit Robert. Was it possible that somewhere in my career as an investigator I'd crossed Kidson's interests worse than I knew, and this was delayed revenge? I asked Tabby if she'd found out when the next batch of prisoners was to be transported.

'The twenty-fourth of July. Saturday. It's been changed. It was supposed to have been the day before, but something else is happening that day and they didn't want the transportation ship there.'

I remembered the conversation I'd overheard on the sloop. They'd been talking about something fixed for the twenty-third of July – surely the transportation, now put off for one day. Eight days from now. 'We should tell somebody,' I said. 'We can't just let Kidson's people go ahead.' It was in my mind that if Kidson's escape attempt failed, nobody need ever know that Robert had been coerced into helping to prepare a foreign bolthole for him.

'Who? Sergeant Bevan?' Amos said.

'No. He's suspicious of us already. It will have to be somebody who can do something and not give me away.'

'Are you thinking of the one I'm thinking of?' Amos's head moved by a few degrees so that he was looking towards Park Lane.

I nodded.

'You reckon you could trust him?'

How to answer? In general, with Mr Disraeli, the answer was probably not. His love of plots and stratagems and a fondness for releasing cats among pigeons meant that he wasn't the most discreet of men. And yet he could keep secrets when necessary. I'd usually found him – in his way – honourable. Above all, he was an important man in Parliament (though nothing like as important as he should be in his opinion), and if he told the police about the Millbank plot, they'd listen and not press him too heavily for his sources.

'To this extent, yes.' I suspected that he'd have

166

heard by now about my disappearance. I'd have to judge carefully how I made contact with him.

Before we parted, Amos told me he'd been to see Mrs Martley at our house. He made a point of calling in there every other day but we'd decided, reluctantly, that she couldn't be trusted not to let out the news of my reappearance.

'I saw the children,' Amos said. 'Lively as elvers, the two of them.' Then, more quietly, 'Harry wanted to know when his mother and father would be back. Soon, I said. Just be good and wait.'

How long? I couldn't even let myself think about it. I found a pen and paper and wrote a note to Mr Disraeli.

Sixteen

It turned out that the Disraelis had already left for a weekend in the country, expected back either late on Sunday evening or Monday morning. Tabby found that out when she went round the corner into Park Lane to deliver my note. Saturday was a restless something or nothing day with Tabby and I cooped up together, she even quieter than usual. Amos arrived in the afternoon with his account of the meeting with Sergeant Bevan.

'He was interested, right enough. They had the inquest on Miss Maynard yesterday. The jury brought in accidental death, probably to spare the feelings of the family, though Bevan thinks the coroner was trying to guide them to suicide. He's keeping an open mind between suicide and murder, but reckons if she was seeing this fellow, Cave, it makes suicide more likely.'

Tabby made a derisive noise.

'Makes sense from his point of view,' Amos said to her. 'Overcome with shame and does away with herself.'

'But none of us believes that,' I said. 'Did you tell him about Cave being in the brothel when she was killed?'

'No, because that would have made him sure that Tabby was trailing Cave. He might guess that we know about him because of her, but there's no sense handing everything to him on a plate.'

168

'We need to speak to Cave before the police do,' I said. It was in my mind that he might know something about Robert. 'We know he's at the Vauxhall Bridge workshops.'

'He won't be there on a Sunday,' Tabby said. 'I could watch on Monday and follow him home or wherever he goes.'

That seemed to be one clear thing we could do in the maze we were in, so it was agreed that Amos should take over the watch at Abel Yard from around midday on Monday, freeing Tabby to hunt for Cave.

By now, I was becoming tired of being guarded. It was three days since I'd escaped from the sloop and nothing had happened, which suggested that the gang did not consider me dangerous. They'd got what they wanted from me already. Amos and Tabby, though, were both adamant that I shouldn't be left alone, and I had to accept it. But as Sunday wore on, the combination of tension and boredom became nearly insupportable. I tried to read in my study but by evening, as the sun moved low down the sky after another fine and hot day, I felt I had to do something. It was just possible that the Disraelis might be home. Tabby had gone down to the end of the yard with our jug to get more milk and was probably chatting with the cowman. There was no reason why I shouldn't have waited for her to come back but a foolish spirit of rebellion had come over me. I put on my cape – too heavy for the weather – and my face-concealing bonnet and slipped out of the yard, along the mews and into Park Lane. Their butler answered the door. He was an old ally of mine and butlers do not chatter, so I saw no reason to conceal my identity. He regretted that I'd had a wasted journey. The Disraelis were not expected back until Monday morning. He'd make sure that Mr Disraeli saw my note as soon as he arrived. I walked slowly back, turning over in my mind what I'd say to him and how much I should take him into my confidence. The gates from the mews into Abel Yard were partly closed – one side pulled right across, the other slightly open. This was unusual because they were normally left open, but I supposed somebody had come in with an urgent job for the carriage repairer. They were stiff on their hinges, and I had to put my shoulder against the slightly open gate to push it wide enough to walk through. It was just starting to yield when the world exploded. I heard a shout, feet running, then something cannoning into me, sending me flying on to the cobbles. Above my head, there was a heavy thud against the door, more shouting, and the clang of something heavy hitting the cobbles just a few feet away from me, striking sparks. Then more feet running – two pairs, at least. I pushed myself to my knees and looked up. Three or four of the ragged lads who live in the mews were staring down at me. One of them bent down to help me to my feet but, before I was properly upright, Tabby arrived like a tornado. She seemed to be blaming the lads, and they were defending themselves.

'. . . Two of them. Must have been . . .'
'. . . Iron bar, look. If that had . . .'
'. . . Seen them waiting, but didn't know . . .'

The smallest of the lads was holding an iron bar about three feet long. Gradually, the story became clear. One of the lads had noticed that I was pushing the door and had come running up to help, naturally expecting a penny for his trouble. At the same time, two men who'd been spotted hanging around the mews earlier had moved in with an iron bar. The lad, showing great presence of mind, had pulled me out of the way of it, and the others had run up to help him. Two of them had tried to trip up the men as they ran away, but unsuccessfully. I asked if they'd had a good look at them and got a description of two men in their twenties – one black-haired and one brown – that might have applied to half the young men in London. All this time, Tabby was standing there, fuming. I thanked the boys and went into the yard with her.

'They deserve something. I'll go upstairs and get some silver and—'

At various times in our partnership, Tabby had been critical, but that was nothing compared to the tongue-lashing I had from her now. The theme of it was that if I was determined to get myself killed, in spite of her and Amos, I should tell her now and be done with it. I apologized as best I could.

'Why should they wait three days, though?'

'They might have been here all the time, just waiting for you to do something stupid, like you did.'

'We'd have known if they'd been here for long.'

When we got upstairs, I persuaded her to go down with some coins for the lads, but only on

171

the condition that I shouldn't stir from the chair by the fireplace. I lit the spirit stove to boil a kettle and steam out the dents in my bonnet, and considered. Clearly Kidson's gang – if this was Kidson's gang – still thought I was a threat. They were right, too, because I knew about the rescue attempt and was going to expose it, but how could they have known that? Could they have been following Tabby? I put the idea to her when she came back upstairs but she was scornful: if anybody had been trailing her, she'd have known about it.

On Monday morning, she insisted on coming with me to Disraeli's house and took up position by the front door when I went inside. The butler sent up my name and, almost at once, I was shown upstairs to Mr Disraeli's study. He came over and took my hand.

'Mrs Carmichael, this is an unexpected pleasure.'

He sounded as if he meant it. He used my married name, but I guessed he still thought of me as Liberty Lane. We'd known each other from the time of my first case, when he was an ambitious and youngish MP. Now, in his early forties, he was an important man in his own party and acknowledged as one of the best speakers in Parliament. I noticed that with success his style of dress had become quieter; he wore fewer rings, had only one gold chain with a signet ring on it, and his waistcoat was a comparatively subdued brocade in dark green. A half-dozen copies of his latest novel were piled on his desk. He offered coffee and I accepted. I could see he was amused at my unfashionable costume, but he didn't ask any serious questions until the coffee had arrived and the servant withdrawn.

'So what brings you here, Mrs Carmichael? I'd heard that you were absent from your usual haunts.'

That meant he knew about the kidnapping, which wasn't surprising. The smile he gave when he said it meant that he was at least as sceptical as Sergeant Bevan and thought I'd arranged it for my own purposes. Well, let him think so. He might suspect that, but if he took my story to the police, or more probably to the Home Secretary himself, he'd find it amusing to keep my supposed secret. So I gave him a smile over the rim of my coffee cup and murmured that yes, I'd been away. Then I got down to business. Without saying how I came to know it, I told him about Kidson's sentence of transportation and the plot to free him as he was transferred from Millbank Prison to the ship. I told him about the accidental gunpowder explosion by Vauxhall Bridge and my suspicion that at least one worker from the Parliament site was involved. What I didn't tell him was anything about Robert's part in it, or the possible connection with the death of Felicity Maynard. I needed to know more before I said anything about those. As he listened, his expression grew more and more serious.

'And you say it's the twenty-fourth when the convicts are being transferred? That's this Saturday.'

'Yes. Probably the explosion may be just a diversion. My guess is that the rescue attempt will happen as they're being put into boats to go out to the ship.'

'Have you told anybody else about this?'

'No, not about the rescue plan.' He knew about Amos and Tabby. When it came to keeping secrets, the three of us counted as one.

It was part of Disraeli's vanity that he didn't ask why I hadn't told the police about the escape plan. In a matter of importance, naturally I'd come to him.

'I shall speak to the Home Secretary this afternoon. I suppose I can't tell him the source of my information?'

'I'm afraid not.' But it was all I'd hoped. With the government alerted at the highest level, they'd have the army out at Millbank if necessary. They could do what we couldn't and search the Parliament building site and workshops for explosives. It was just a matter of me finding Robert now before the police got to him. I thanked Disraeli, and he asked if he could get word to me at the usual place. I said I wasn't supposed to be there, but any communication to Mr Legge at the livery stables by the Bayswater Road would reach me.

Amos arrived as arranged and Tabby left to take up an observation post by the Vauxhall Bridge workshops. I asked her to call in at the Maynards' house on the way and see if the staff knew when and where Felicity's funeral would be. I wasn't sorry to see her go. Amos was concerned about the attack on me but less judgemental. It was after seven o'clock when Tabby got back, her mood a lot better than when she'd

174

left. Which was surprising at first, because she had a failure to report.

'If he works there, he wasn't in today. I was there by the gates when they all came out and I wouldn't have missed him. Saw no sign of him.' She took a gulp of tea. 'Somebody else was there, though, waiting at the gates. He stood out a mile. You could see the men wondering who he was. If our man had been there he'd probably have missed him. He was fidgeting around, eyes everywhere and nowhere, like a cow in a swarm of bees.'

'So who was this man? One of Kidson's?'

'Nah. You saw him yourself, three days ago at the Parliament site. Her brother.'

'Felicity Maynard's brother, watching the woodwork shops?'

'That's right.'

'So does he know about Jonah Cave?'

'Seems so. Perhaps she told him about Jonah after all.'

It seemed the most likely explanation but I still found it hard to believe. I asked if Tabby had found time to go to the Maynards' house.

'Funeral's tomorrow. We going?'

'Yes.' At least peace seemed to be breaking out between Tabby and me. We went upstairs together to find black clothes.

The search was not very satisfactory, producing only a cotton dress I'd forgotten I'd ever had made in a blackberry colour which would just about do under my long black cloak and the usual bonnet, provided nobody looked too closely. I had no intention of being observed closely. The funeral was not held in St John's but in a church where, presumably, the family usually worshipped, not far from Abel Yard but in the fashionable part of Mayfair. Tabby and I walked there on Tuesday morning, Tabby in her usual respectable grey. The Maynards and their many friends seemed to have decided that the violent nature of Felicity's death should be masked by the grandeur of the funeral. They'd wasted no time in organizing it, probably while that merciful inquest verdict of accidental death was still in people's minds. The hearse was drawn by four black horses with funereal plumes of feathers swaying on their heads, followed by a parade of at least a dozen coaches, mostly with people inside and not just sent for show – many gentlemen in tall black hats, and more carriages packed with wreaths. Inside the church, every space in the pews was taken. Tabby and I wedged ourselves in at the back. The vicar preached about the sadness of a young life cut off in its prime and God taking to himself those he loved most, and I guessed that I was not the only one picturing a body taken from the Thames or even thinking about those arguments she'd had with her mother. There'd been nothing in the newspapers – probably the Maynards had friends influential enough to prevent it – but I guessed everybody present was speculating about the cause of her death. Nobody was openly calling it suicide, or she couldn't have had a church funeral. As for murder, the family had not acknowledged the possibility, but the question of why a fashionable young woman like Felicity should have been wandering by the Thames in the early hours must have been in other minds, besides mine. I was sitting on the end of a pew at the back with Tabby next to me, my face hidden by the black bonnet pulled forward and my cloak fastened. It was stiflingly hot and the whole church seemed like a suffocating mass of black. I was sure that Mr and Mrs Maynard wouldn't recognize me even if they looked my way, which was unlikely. The scullery maid, Jane, was more of a risk. She was sitting a few pews forward from me on the opposite side of the aisle with what were clearly the rest of the servants, all in black clothes that looked new. There'd have been a great deal of sewing in the past few days. At least the garden boy, Toby, was not among them. Jane seemed genuinely grieved. I noticed a couple of times that she had her head in her hands and, once, the woman next to her put a comforting arm round her. I was tempted to try to get more information from her afterwards, but supposed she'd be hustled away with the other servants.

The Maynards, of course, were in the front pew. The tall, young man next to Mrs Maynard was presumably Felicity's brother, but I could only see his back. Either side of them were various people, mostly elderly and presumably relations. It was a shock to see Sergeant Bevan, in plain clothes, sitting at the end of a pew a few rows in front of me. I wondered if he'd come from simple respect or the almost equally simple theory that a murderer couldn't resist attending the funeral. Either way, it was essential that he shouldn't see me. We knelt for final prayers, then stood as the funeral mutes carried out the coffin. It was piled high with white roses and delphiniums, tokens of purity for a young woman who'd died unmarried. Mr and Mrs Maynard followed behind it, the wife leaning on her husband's arm, and yes, the young man was her brother. I glanced at his face as they went past. He was all in black and much tidier than when I'd last seen him, but still looked pale and desperately unhappy. Would she have confided in a younger brother? I guessed not, and that if she'd had any confidante at all it would be a woman friend, but how to pick her out from all the rest? Sergeant Bevan went past me without a glance, and when I got outside there was no sign of him. I followed the procession to the graveside, keeping well back. Words were said, the coffin lowered into the ground and the family led the way back to the waiting coaches. Most of the others fell into line behind them in small and silent groups, with no chance that I could see of finding anybody to question.

But there was one person there beside myself, standing close to the grave and watching the diggers as they piled earth on to the coffin in large spadefuls – businesslike after the restrained dust-to-dust pattering of the service. It was a woman I hadn't noticed in the church, and she'd have stood out because she wasn't wearing mourning dress. After the mass of black, her simple grey dress and jaunty bonnet looked positively springlike. Her posture was quite the reverse, though – shoulders drooping, white gloved hands pressed tightly together. A leather bag, larger than a normal reticule, hung from her elbow. I walked over and stood beside her. A tremor in her body showed she was aware of somebody else there, but she kept her eyes down, and we watched together as the last gleam of the coffin disappeared under the earth. Then she looked up at me.

'It shouldn't be so final, should it? Alive, and then just not.'

The voice was flat but educated. She was in her early twenties, some inches shorter than me, and probably near enough to beautiful when in normal spirits. Her chestnut hair came down in two orderly curves under the bonnet, her eyes were large and brown but with deep purple shadows under them, and her skin was as pale as skimmed milk. I knew what she meant and should probably have replied with some comforting piece of convention from the service, but I agreed with her.

'So final, yes. You knew her?'

'I shouldn't be here.' Her eyes were on me, but I wasn't sure she was seeing me. 'My mother thinks I'm with friends so I wasn't even properly dressed to go inside.'

'I don't suppose it would have mattered.'

'My mother didn't care for her anyway. She thought she was worldly. Then, when she . . . when she got . . .'

'Murdered?'

She flinched as if I'd slapped her, then nodded. 'She said somebody must have pushed her in the river and that respectable women didn't get murdered. She said I should forget I'd ever known her and not mention her. But I knew they were burying her today, so I couldn't . . . couldn't not be here.'

The gravediggers were looking at us, wanting us to move so they could work from our side of the grave. I looked at a bench by the churchyard wall and suggested we go and sit there. She moved as if she didn't care where we went. Tabby loitered by the wall, not missing a move.

'Had you known her long?' I said.

'Over a year, but it seemed longer, as if she'd always been there. I'd always wanted a sister, you see, but there were only brothers – five of them.' We were close together on the bench, and she had to turn her head to look at me. She seemed quite incurious about who I was.

'And she was like a sister to you?'

'A real sister, she'd have been. At any rate, my sister-in-law, and that's almost as good.'

It took a moment to sink in. 'Felicity was engaged to your brother?'

'To my second oldest one, Christopher. Both sets of parents wanted it and Felicity seemed not to mind. I think she was quite looking forward at first to being married and getting away from home. Once they were engaged, I was their chaperone for quite a lot of the time because of Mama being ill. We had such a grand time last summer – balls, theatre, picnics on the river. I didn't want it to end. Then, of course, Christopher had to go and spoil it. I know everybody said Felicity broke it off, but that's just because it has to be the girl who breaks engagements, never the man. He's so dull, Christopher. Felicity and I used to laugh about it.'

'How did he spoil it?'

'He always had work to do. I know he's reading for the bar, but everybody does that and a lot of other things as well. There'd be things Felicity wanted him to go to with her that he wouldn't, and Felicity isn't . . . I mean, she wasn't a girl who liked being said no to and she said she couldn't see the point of being married if her husband wouldn't do what she wanted, so . . .' She gave a little despairing lift of the palms. The leather bag was by her foot now.

'And your parents were angry?'

'Furious. They blamed Felicity, and I was totally forbidden to see her again.'

'But you did?'

'There were always chances to see each other – friends' tea parties, sketching classes, shops. I couldn't have avoided seeing her sometimes even if I didn't want to, and of course I did want to. Then she needed somebody she could really trust to confide in. I was the only one.'

The brown eyes were still fixed trustingly on mine. She needed to talk, and if I hadn't been there she'd probably have told the story to the dog that was scratching the earth by one of the gravestones.

'Confide in you about her love affair?'

I detected a faint jolt of surprise, then a relieved smile at a shared secret. 'Yes, it was such a romance. Her parents didn't know anything about it, of course. They'd have forbidden it.'

'Because he was just a workman?'

Her eyes opened wider. 'Only he wasn't, that was the point. He was several rungs above the

Maynards, Felicity said, the heir to an earldom, but his father had disinherited him because he wanted to be a sculptor instead of going in the army. That's why he was working at the Parliament buildings. They met when Felicity and her family were being shown round. She fell behind to look at something he was carving, and that was when it started. They arranged to meet again, and that was when he told her.'

'What was his name?'

'Jonah Cave. I think that might be the name he went under when he was working. I'm sure she knew his real name but I didn't like to ask.'

She must have made the perfect confidante: open-mouthed at her friend's daring and too naive to ask awkward questions. I asked if he worked as a woodcarver and she nodded.

'Did she tell you he went to her house?' I said.

'They'd meet in the garden at night. She'd go down to him. She said he was such a gentleman she knew she could trust him. But, of course, they had to be careful.'

I decided not to tell her he'd been inside the house regularly. What good would it do to pull apart the fairytale she'd made of the affair? 'Careful to keep it from her parents?'

'Yes, but more than that – there were his parents.'

'But you said he'd been disinherited.'

'Yes, but his father thought he'd come crawling back and was angry when he found that he'd disgraced the family by taking on a workman's job. Jonah told Felicity that his father was paying

182

men to keep a watch on him. He thought they might try to kill him.'

'Jonah told Felicity that?'

She nodded. 'That's how it must have happened. Somehow Felicity must have found out that Jonah was in danger that night and gone across to the site to warn him. Perhaps she found him, then they killed her, or killed her before she could get to him. Or perhaps they were both killed and his body hasn't been found. That's one of the reasons I wanted to be at the funeral. I thought if he's alive, he'd want to be there.'

'Would you have recognized him?'

'No, I've never seen him. But if he'd been there, wouldn't he have said something, let them know that she died trying to save him?'

I almost smiled, thinking of the conventional funeral being disrupted by an aristocratic wood-carver. It would have been something from a novel, and I was sure this girl would be a keen consumer of them. Her gloved fingers settled on my wrist.

'You were inside the church? Was there anything at all?'

'Nothing.'

'Oh.'

'I don't suppose you've told the police anything of this.'

Her mouth dropped open and she drew away from me. 'Of course not. Her parents would find out about him and my parents would know I'd been seeing her and . . . No, I couldn't. You won't tell them, will you? Say you won't.'

'I won't tell anybody in authority that I've seen

183

you. I don't know your name and, if you like, we can keep it that way.'

She nodded, still scared, realizing for the first time how much she'd given away to a stranger. In any case, Sergeant Bevan wouldn't have thanked me for bringing him such a farrago. She lifted the leather bag on to her lap. It looked surprisingly heavy. She saw my eyes on it, considered for a moment, then opened it.

'He did this.' She opened the bag and took out something swathed in pink silk. A feeling of unease, almost of panic, came over me. Under the silk was a carving of a pair of lion's hind feet. They were beautifully made in unvarnished oak wood. The lion they belonged to must have been sitting upright on his haunches, because an inch or two of upper leg curved out above them and a tail wrapped round. It was a clever piece of work, and at first I couldn't account for the feeling it was giving me, as if I wanted to run away. Then it came to me that it was caused by the smell. I made myself take in my hands, my heart thumping. Curls of freshly chiselled wood were in my mind and the frothing mane of a rocking horse. The smell from my childhood. The smell of the jacket arm that had been round my face when I was captured. The girl's eyes were on my face, anxious.

'Is something wrong?'

'No.' I made myself look at it closely. The inside of the carving was hollowed out, making a space that might take a small bird's nest, and a groove ran round the upper edge, suggesting that it might be a drawer. If the rest of the lion were to scale it would be a moderately large piece, too big for a mantelpiece or a dressing table but too small to stand on the floor. I handed it back. 'It's beautifully carved. Where did you get it?'

'Felicity gave it to me for safekeeping. It was his present to her.'

'Just the hind feet, not the whole lion?'

'I think it was from something he'd been working on. She knew if she hid it in her room her mother's maid would find it. That was when she told me about him. I thought that if he'd been here at the graveside today I'd have found some way of giving it back to him.'

'And now?'

'I think I'll leave it here, on her grave. It should have been with her in the coffin, but I couldn't see how to do it.'

We looked across to the grave. The sextons had finished their shovelling and were placing the wreaths over the raw earth, handling them surprisingly carefully. We waited until they'd finished and walked away, then went over to the grave. The girl stood for some time, her head bent and her fingers clasped over the carved wood in its silk covering. Then she slid it out of the silk, knelt and tucked it quickly in between two wreaths of roses, just a corner of the wood showing.

'If he comes to her grave, he'll see it there,' she said.

No sense in telling her that Jonah Cave was unlikely to come anywhere near it. We stood there in silence for a while until the clock struck.

'Oh, no. I'm supposed to be meeting Mama in

Bond Street. You won't tell the police about me, will you? Promise?'

I promised. She picked up the leather bag and hurried away out of the churchyard gate.

I waited for a few minutes, resisting the temptation to follow her and see where she lived, and when Tabby and I started walking towards the gate, another figure came in. We stood back against the church and watched as he went over to the graveside. At first, unreasonably, I imagined that the young woman's gesture had really conjured up a grieving Jonah Cave, but this was nothing of the kind.

Tabby breathed, 'Him again. Felicity's brother.'

His black clothes were new and stiff. A black gloved hand clutched a top hat with its mourning bands trailing down among the flowers. I'd have stood there and waited for him to go, but suddenly he looked up and saw us. Puzzlement was on his face as well as sadness. He was probably trying to place us among the relatives and friends who'd attended the service. I made a sudden decision and walked over to stand opposite him. He watched me all the way.

'We almost met before,' I said. 'At the Parliament building site.' The edge of the carving was just visible among the roses, but he'd given no sign of noticing it.

He blinked, swollen pink lids coming down over moist grey eyes. A shallow cut on his chin showed his hand had not been steady when he'd shaved that morning. 'I . . . I don't . . .'

'My name's Liberty Lane. I'm a friend of your parents.' He might have heard the name Carmichael among their friends, but my maiden name would have meant nothing to him.

'Oliver Maynard. How d'you . . .' But his voice trailed away before he could finish the conventional greeting. I decided that the intense stare he was giving me wasn't personal – he was simply trying hard to find his bearings. It was cruel perhaps to unsettle him even more, but something had been in the back of my mind since I saw him.

'I think you were trying to find out what had happened to your sister.'

A nod.

'You got there very quickly,' I said.

'What . . . what do you mean?'

'I gather you were visiting friends in Yorkshire when she died?'

Another nod.

'Your family didn't know she was dead until Friday. The news of it can't possibly have got to Yorkshire before Saturday morning. The fastest coach in the world couldn't have got you to London by the time I saw you, could it?'

'Why . . . why are you asking this?'

'Because I'm trying to find out what happened to your sister, too.'

Silence. He looked away from me at last and down at the grave.

'You were very close to her,' I said.

'Close, yes.'

But I wondered if he'd felt closer to Felicity than she to him. 'Did you know she was seeing a man in secret?'

His whole body gave a jerk, as if I'd hit him. 'How did you know?'

I said nothing.

'She . . . She wrote to me.' His voice was hardly audible.

'Telling you she was seeing a man?'

'Yes.'

'And you didn't approve?'

'I . . . I needed to discuss it with her. I left Yorkshire on Wednesday and got to London late on Thursday. I went to the house on Friday hoping to see her before I spoke to our parents and found . . .'

'That she was dead?'

'Yes.'

'Did she tell you the man's name?'

'No.'

It came too promptly. I suspected he was lying.

'Do you think the man she was seeing killed her?'

'I don't know.'

I wondered whether to tell him that I knew the man's name and that he couldn't have killed Felicity because he was in a brothel at the time, but it was too complicated and I was becoming sure that young Mr Maynard was lying about some things at least.

'I have to go,' he said. 'My parents will be wondering . . .'

He turned without so much as a good morning and walked quickly towards the churchyard door. When it closed behind him, Tabby came over to me. Her hearing is the sharpest I know, but she'd been standing too far away to hear our conversation. I gave her the details of it.

She whistled. 'So she's seeing a man in secret

and she puts it in writing to her brother. You believe that?'

'There's something wrong somewhere, but I don't know what it is.'

'Something's wrong everywhere, if you want to know what I think. For one thing, he says he got here on Thursday, but I saw him in the garden on Wednesday night. He's up north with friends, right? Somebody writes to him to say his sister is letting down the family so he comes straight back here, gets a message to her telling her to come out and meet him, hits her over the head and throws her in the river. Family honour.'

I couldn't argue, beyond saying that young Mr Maynard did not strike me as the type to do anything so decisive and violent, and we both knew from experience that this was hardly an argument at all. I told Tabby about the smell of carved wood and my memory, though I left out the rocking horse.

'So it was Jonah Cave that grabbed you?'

'Among others, yes, I think so.'

She said she'd keep a proper watch on the Vauxhall Bridge workshops as soon as we'd worked out the timings with Amos. She wasn't risking letting me out of her sight.

Seventeen

Amos arrived that evening with a message from Mr Disraeli: would I please go and see him at my earliest convenience. I gave Amos a quick summary of what had happened after the funeral and he went back to the stables to look after a sick horse. As before, Tabby escorted me to the doorstep of the house in Park Lane. The Disraelis had guests. Talk and laughter were coming from the drawing room, but he must have made some excuse to the company and met me upstairs in his study. He offered port and I accepted. He was in good humour.

'I know you won't tell me your sources, but they were accurate up to a point. There has been a very elaborate plot to free Kidson. We've taken measures. This afternoon, Kidson was transferred from Millbank to Pentonville. I'm told he was very indignant about it. He'll be given his own private transfer to the ship, closely guarded, with no time for his friends to bribe anybody. He'll have seven years in a warm climate to think of all the money and effort he's wasted. Not for the first time, I should tell you that you've served your country well, and certain people in the Home Office are properly grateful.'

The tone of the last sentence was ironic. He knew there was precious little gratitude in government. I sipped my port and tried to look

190

moderately complimented while thinking that Kidson would not now need whatever arrangements had been set up for him on the Continent, and what mattered was to keep Robert clear of the wreckage of the escape attempt. I might even have started to hint something along these lines to Disraeli – who was unshockable – but as usual he went on speaking.

'As it happened, there were other sources. Word had reached the Metropolitan Police that something was going on. Certain people in Kidson's organization have been under observation ever since he was sentenced. The upper reaches of the police have been in communication with the governor of Millbank, and he was able to pick up the men who'd been bribed without much difficulty. Some of them were surprisingly senior men on the prison staff, but then the bribes were enormous. Kidson's men must have spent tens of thousands of pounds.'

'Bribes?' This was a new factor in the case.

Disraeli nodded. 'It was the old business of substitution, but very thoroughly done. A warder would change clothes with Kidson on Friday night. There'd be checks, of course, before the men were put on the boats, but everybody likely to be involved had been well paid. The warder would be hustled on board the transportation ship with the rest. He'd been given assurances that the plot would be discovered before he reached Gravesend. He'd plead that Kidson had overpowered him by force and be taken off. He'd lose his job, of course, but he'd been paid several times his year's wages. Of course, the beauty of this was that the warder wouldn't be taken off at all. The longer the substitution remained undiscovered, the longer Kidson would have to get well away. The warder would be carried all the way to Australia, protesting that he was a wronged and innocent man. Naturally, the guards would have heard that one before. Quite elegant in its way.'

'So no explosion?' I said. The feeling that something was going badly wrong was beginning to stir.

'No. Nothing so crude. In fact, the more routinely the transportation went ahead, the better for Kidson. I'm afraid your sources were wrong on that one.'

'I suppose Kidson intended to escape to the Continent?' I was still trying to feel my way to talking about Robert.

Disraeli laughed. 'He was quite clever in that respect as well. Naturally, that's what he thought the authorities would expect. If the substitution had been discovered early, which wasn't likely in view of the precautions they'd taken, there'd have been police at all the Channel ports. Kidson, meanwhile, would have been going in the opposite direction towards Scotland. From Edinburgh, he planned to take a boat for Copenhagen. I'm told he'd already had a quite comfortable nest built for himself there. It seems his father was Danish and he'd kept up a network. A large amount of money has already been transferred there from his various activities. We may try to get it back but I doubt if we'll be successful.'

I hoped my face didn't show the confusion in

192

my mind. The one thing we knew about Robert was that when last seen he'd been heading south, crossing the Channel. He had no interests or friends in Denmark. And explosions, so it seemed, had nothing to do with it. There was no reason at all in this story why I should have been kidnapped and Robert gone abroad. None of it fitted.

'So an eminently satisfactory conclusion,' Disraeli said.

He wanted to get back to his guests. I may have managed to echo the 'satisfactory', although from my point of view it was anything but. I let the footman show me out and discussed it with Tabby on the way back. Her first reaction wasn't entirely what I expected.

'What a waste.'

'You mean Kidson?'

'I suppose that's a waste as well. I mean our man. If it hadn't been for Kidson's lot we might have got him away, but now they'll all be on the alert, so there'll be no chance of trying it, even though it probably wouldn't have worked anyway.'

I tried to bring her back to our concerns. 'Why did we think this was all about an escape from Millbank? We were as wrong as we could be and we've wasted all this time. Can you remember what you told me about it?'

I was ready to blame anybody and she must have sensed that, but she answered more patiently than I deserved. 'I told you Kidson's people wanted to get him out when they were transporting the next lot, this coming Saturday, the twenty-fourth. I didn't know how they were going to do it.'

I'd done the connecting – the explosion, the convenient closeness of the parliamentary site and that date I'd heard them discussing on the sloop, the twenty-third. 'You said they'd changed the date?'

'That's right. They were supposed to have been transferred the day before, the Friday, only there was something else going on then so it got changed.'

'So where are we? I was kidnapped to force Robert into doing something, and he's doing it. A woodcarver who might have been Jonah Cave was one of the people who kidnapped me. Jonah Cave was deceiving Felicity Maynard, but he can't have been the one who killed her. Where does that leave us?'

We found no answer to that. I went upstairs to bed early, with Tabby down in the parlour, and woke up early. I was feeling almost restored to normal health, so we walked all the way to Vauxhall Bridge, getting to the workshops before most of the men arrived. Traffic was already building up with carts and carriages crossing the bridge in both directions, and Tabby said keeping a watch unobserved in such a busy place was as easy as falling off a log. We bought ourselves cups of tea from a woman who'd set up a stall opposite the gates and took a good look round. The workshops covered perhaps half an acre of ground – two long sheds surrounded by a wooden fence about five feet high. The fence had two gates – one large double one for wagons to bring in wood or carry away the finished carvings, now shut, and one smaller one nearer us for people, also shut. Even from across the road, the smell of freshly cut wood was so strong that I had to stop myself being carried back again to that evening and the arm across my face. As we drank, men began to arrive, and most of them came over to the tea stall. We stood back, and I tried to copy Tabby's ability to merge into the background. These were skilled workmen, not labourers, neat in their dress and mostly moderate in their conversation. They wore flat caps and corduroy trousers, and some of them carried working jackets rolled up under their arms. One of them was coming in for some teasing, having become the father of a new baby – his third, it seemed. He looked barely old enough to be out of apprenticeship. Nobody was talking about Felicity's death, but then, that had been nearly a week ago, and probably never more than of passing interest. We kept our eyes open for Jonah Cave but knew it would be expecting too much to find him so soon. Towards eight o'clock, the men began drifting over to the smaller gate, and a steady stream of them went through. Tabby and I took up position on a stone horse trough opposite, sitting on the edge of it. It was still too early in the morning for horses to be thirsty. There was plenty to watch. Although most of the workmen were in by eight, a lot of visitors went in at the little gate. Some of them were obviously clerks with lists in their hands – one a distracted-looking gentleman in a top hat carrying a portfolio, others unremarkable but all in a hurry. At half past ten a carriage with what looked like a group of important visitors went in at the wider entrance. All the world except Jonah Cave.

'Do you think we missed him?' I said to Tabby. She shook her head.

Another man walked up to the smaller gate, middle-aged and upright, walking fast, wearing a low, crowned black hat. He had a neat beard the colour of pewter.

'Mr James,' I said, caught by surprise. But on second thoughts, I shouldn't have been surprised to see him there, because his work would involve liaison between the woodcarvers at the workshops and the building site. It would have been awkward if he'd seen us, but he didn't glance across the road.

'Do you think he's looking for Jonah Cave too?' Tabby said.

It seemed possible. Amos had given the police the name of Felicity's visitor, and if they wanted to talk to him they'd naturally have gone back to the Parliament site. Mr James struck me as a conscientious man and, even if he hadn't known Cave personally, he'd have made it his business to find out about him. It looked likely that Cave was absent from his work and Mr James would want to know why. He came out again about half an hour later and crossed the road, coming quite close to us, and turned towards the building site. I thought he looked troubled.

'If he was, he hasn't found him,' Tabby said.

Half an hour or so passed with nothing much happening, then a gentleman walked up to the smaller gate. So far, everybody going in and out had looked busy and purposeful but, even from the other side of the road, you could see this one's indecision. He stood as several other people came and went, took a step towards the gate and stopped. He was tall and fair-haired, early twenties, his face white.

'Young Mr Maynard,' I said.

Then, in a rush, he was through the gate and it closed behind him. I moved towards the kerb.

'We following him?' Tabby asked.

'Why not?'

We dodged a cart as we crossed the road. The door opened to us and a man standing inside it looked questioningly at us.

'We're with the gentleman who's just come in,' I said.

The doorkeeper just nodded to the left. He'd seen too many people come and go to be curious. The workshop seemed enormous – another world. Outside was a bright summer day, but the inside flared with gas lamps, and it took a while for my eyes to adjust. The air was full of the grinding of machinery and, under that, the sound of chisels, softer than the clink they made on stone. A kind of succulent bite, as if great caterpillars were eating and eating. We went left as directed and saw a long aisle in front of us, full of men working, but no sign of young Mr Maynard. We'd been standing for some time before a man in a moleskin waistcoat came up and asked politely if we had an appointment.

'I've come to see Jonah Cave,' I said.

There seemed to be no point in going a longer way round. The man looked uncertain.

'I believe he might have left. He was in Mr Casey's division. You can ask him.'

He called an apprentice who led us past machines and what looked like a complete set of choir stalls. As we went, I glanced between machines to a parallel aisle and caught the back view of a gentleman walking in the other direction. Oliver Maynard. I was tempted to follow him, and decided that since we were on the same trail we could easily catch up with him. The apprentice introduced us to Mr Casey, a genial man with a completely bald head under a working cap settled on top like the lid on a teapot.

'Mr Cave seems to be very popular suddenly. As I told the gentleman, I regret I can't help you because he left us ten days ago.'

'Left for where?'

'He didn't say. I assumed that he'd found other work. He hadn't been with us long so maybe he's of a restless nature. Some craftsmen are.'

'A gentleman's been asking for him?'

'Hardly five minutes ago. He must have only just left.'

I nodded to Tabby and she melted away. 'Do you know where he lives?'

'I don't, but I believe our record clerk does. I sent the gentleman to him.'

Another apprentice led me to a cubicle at the far end of the workshop where a clerk had the book already open from the gentleman's inquiry. An address in Chapter Street, off Vauxhall Bridge Road. Outstanding wages had been paid up to Friday, 9 July. A line was neatly ruled underneath this. I went out and found Tabby waiting at the gates.

'On foot. He asked directions from the woman at the tea stall,' Tabby said, 'then went straight up the road a couple of minutes ago, walking fast.'

We walked fast too, and he must have slowed down because we soon had him in sight on the other side of the road. He was walking like a man unsure of his ground. Once he stopped to ask a boy the way and was pointed on up the road. By the time he turned the corner into Chapter Street, we were about two hundred yards behind him. He stopped somewhere in the middle of the street, knocked on a door and waited, knocked again and looked up to the window on the upper floor.

'Try round the back,' Tabby said under her breath, but he wasn't the sort of man who went to the back door of houses. He didn't look, either, like the sort of man who walked into people's houses uninvited, but after more knocking and a few more minutes of waiting, he did exactly that – opened the door and went in. We moved closer and stood opposite, on the other side of the street, not trying to hide ourselves. I had to admit that I was more impressed than I'd expected by young Mr Maynard's nerve. He believed Jonah Cave had killed his sister and had gone to confront him. But then, wasn't that odd in itself? A young man of his background would surely be more likely to let the police deal with it. I suppose if there'd been shouting or signs of a struggle from inside the house, Tabby and I would have had to do something about it, but there was nothing but the sound of traffic going up and down Vauxhall Bridge Road. Then, suddenly, he was blundering out of the front door, hunched over. He looked dreadful, his face grey, lips compressed, and I thought at first that there had been a fight and he'd come off worst. He stared at us, hardly focusing, then lurched to the edge of the pavement and was sick into the gutter. We crossed the street to him.

'Good morning, Mr Maynard,' I said.

He stared at me, wiping the vomit from his face with the sleeve of his jacket. He obviously didn't remember me. 'He's dead,' he said.

'Who? Jonah Cave?'

He didn't answer. I glanced at Tabby and we went through the front door that he'd left open into the house. Another door stood open into a room off the narrow hallway. The light was dim, the curtains drawn across the windows. It was empty except for a table. A kitchen on the other side was empty too, the range cold. I went upstairs, Tabby following, and we found him in the bedroom. He'd probably been asleep when his attacker came into the house. He was still in bed, wearing nothing but a flannel shirt, his body thrown back against the bolster, a thin blanket over his lower half. His right arm was drawn back as if trying to fend off something and his mouth open in what might have been a protest but it was probably simply that his jaw had dropped. Just one shot to the head. Most of the blood had soaked into his shirt and the bedding, but a pool of it on the bare floorboards was congealed, dry at the edges.

'Is this the man you saw visiting Felicity?' I heard my own voice asking Tabby, sounding fairly calm.

'Yes. Did Maynard shoot him?'

'This was done hours ago.' I made myself touch the bare flesh of the drawn-back arm. 'Cold. It might have been done last night.'

'Maynard might have come back. They sometimes do. Or he could have paid somebody else to do it and come to make sure.'

That sounded more likely to me, but what would an undergraduate from a good family know about hiring a killer? 'We'll talk to him.'

He was leaning against the wall of the house, his eyes closed. A few children had begun to gather, as they do when strangers appear on their territory, and were watching him from across the road.

'Did you pay somebody to shoot him?' I said.

He moved his head marginally from side to side. 'Was . . . was he shot?'

I reminded myself that he'd probably never seen a dead body before. 'We should go. The police will be arriving.'

In fact, there was no good reason why they would. The cold kitchen and the empty downstairs room in the house suggested that Cave had lodged there alone. He'd left his workplace and there might be nobody who'd miss him. The body might lie there until the smell or swarms of flies forced neighbours to do something. Of course, it was our duty as the people who'd found the body to report it to the police, but duty had changed its shape in the past two weeks. Still, the prospect of the police was enough to make Maynard's eyes open.

'We should talk, only not here,' I said.

Tabby and I managed to get him to walk to Vauxhall Bridge Road and we stood on the corner, waiting for a cab. He didn't say a word and still looked like somebody who'd run headfirst into a brick wall. When a cab stopped at last, I gave it the address of Abel Yard. Since there's no room for a third person in a cab, Tabby set off on foot. Given the weight of traffic and the slowness of the cab horse, she'd probably be home as soon as we were. On the journey, Maynard leaned back into the corner of the cab and closed his eyes. I decided to save the questions until Tabby could hear the answers. By the time I'd got him out of the cab, through the yard and upstairs to the parlour, she'd arrived. We sat him down and offered him water, which he accepted, and I opened the window to disperse the smell of vomit.

'Did you have anything to do with killing Cave?' I said.

'No. You say he was shot. I don't even have a gun. Until this morning, I didn't know where he lived.' Some life was coming back to him, but he still looked very young and very scared.

'So what were you going to do?'

'I don't know. I wanted to talk to him . . . find out if . . .' He glanced down at his hands – slim hands that had been elegantly gloved, but now the gloves were balled up together in his left fist.

'If he'd killed your sister?' I still wasn't ready to tell him that Cave couldn't have killed her. 'Why not leave it to the police?'

202

'They're doing nothing. They won't even admit for certain that she was murdered. It's a nightmare, the whole thing, just a nightmare.' He gazed at me as if I could get him out of it.

'Why did you suspect he'd killed her?'

'Because they'd quarrelled. Then I thought he couldn't have, because . . . but then perhaps . . .'

'Why couldn't he have?'

'He's my brother.' He practically yelled it. We both stared at him. He started talking very quickly. 'Or, rather, my half-brother. Our mother married a second time. She had him when she was very young, so he's a lot older than we are. Jonah quarrelled with our father – a bad quarrel. I don't know the details of it because it happened while I was away at school, but he went away. We didn't talk about him. Or, rather, Felicity and I talked about him sometimes but not with our parents.'

'How did you know he'd come back?'

'Filly – that was my name for Felicity – wrote to me. She'd met him quite by chance. She was taken on a tour of the new Parliament buildings with the parents, and there he was, among the workmen. He kept clear of Mother and Father but slipped her a note.'

'And she met him in the house at night.'

'Yes. Filly was taking a terrible risk with her reputation, but she was always headstrong. And she had this romantic idea about Jonah – wrongfully treated by his family, driven into exile and so on, the lost heir, like something from one of the novels she read. To be honest, it annoyed me, but there was no arguing with her. She wrote and told me soon after I got to Yorkshire. I wrote back and said she should tell the parents, but of course she didn't take any notice. Then I had this second letter, about two weeks later.' He took a sheet of paper from his pocket and handed it to me. The outside had a penny stamp franked with a date twelve days ago. I unfolded it and saw bold, slanting handwriting with no address at the top.

Dear Oliver,

In confidence, I am becoming worried about Jonah. I positively forbid you to gloat over me and say that you warned me, but I am anxious about what he might do. In his last visit, he was talking quite wildly. I think it possible he may have been drinking. He also asked me to do something, which I did, and now regret. But if I tell father, I shall have to reveal that I have been seeing Jonah, and the consequences are unthinkable. I do not know what to do. From your affectionate and anxious sister, Filly.

'You left Yorkshire when you received this?'
'As soon as I could. It was what I did, you see, from the time we were in the nursery: get Filly out of situations. I'm the younger one but she was . . . not wild exactly. I suppose I'm steadier. Or thought I was.'
The last four words were followed with a sigh that quivered through his body. I supposed that up to now the most risky thing he'd done was

probably climbing into college. 'Was your sister alive when you got to London?'

'Yes. I arrived on the Monday afternoon. I couldn't go home, of course, or the parents would have known something was up. I got a message to her and arranged to meet her when she was supposed to be going shopping. It was worse than I thought. He was short of money and I'm afraid she . . . stole a pair of our mother's diamond earrings and gave them to him. They were quite valuable. Mother doesn't know yet. She only wears them once in a blue moon. Filly said Jonah had started talking about doing something that would amaze her when she heard about it. He told her he'd be one of the most important men in the history of the world. She thought he might be . . . might be mad.'

'So what did you advise her to do?'

'Nothing. I said she shouldn't see him again and should have him sent away if he came to the house. I'd deal with him.'

I looked at his boyish complexion and the fluff around his jaw. 'How did you propose to do that?'

'I intended to meet him and tell him to go away. He'd disappeared once and he could do it again. One night, I waited in the garden in case he came, but he didn't.'

'So how did you propose to get in touch with him?'

'I wrote him a note, saying who I was and asking him to meet me. He'd been working on the Parliament site, so I left it at their administrative office for him. But when I enquired after

205

Felicity was dead, he'd never collected it. He'd left his work.'

'How did you discover your sister was dead?'

'I wanted to know whether he'd tried to see Filly again, so I took the risk of going to our house, by the back door, and it was in chaos. She was missing.'

'And, of course, you connected that with Jonah?'

'I couldn't believe he'd kill her. She was his sister – she'd been kind to him. I thought she'd been impatient because I didn't seem to be doing anything, that she'd gone out to try to find him and perhaps had an accident and fallen in the river, or been killed by chance by some maniac on the streets. Still, I wanted to find Jonah.'

'And hear him say that he hadn't killed her?'

He nodded and hung his head.

'He didn't,' I said. 'Tell him what you saw, Tabby.'

She told him about Cave going to the back door of the house and being sent away, then following him to the brothel. He nodded, without looking up.

'You said Cave boasted to your sister that he'd do something that would amaze her,' I said. 'I don't know what it is, but Cave was involved in something important, some crime. Can you think of anything else she told you about him – anything at all?'

'At first, just after they met, he wanted her to go away with him. He said he'd had enough of England and he'd go abroad when he'd finished some work he had to do. He told her it would be finished soon and he'd have plenty of money. I don't think she would have gone. She wouldn't have done that to our parents.'

'What sort of work?'

'She thought he meant woodcarving on the Parliament site, but it can't have been that.' He'd been staring into the ashes of the fire; now he raised his head and looked at me. 'Do we tell the police about finding him?'

'I don't think so, do you?'

He shook his head. 'I think it would kill Mother. I hope she never finds out. He disappeared once, and she might never have to know he appeared again.' Families being what they are, I thought the chances of that were small, but didn't say so. He pulled at the kidskin gloves, trying to straighten them, and tore a finger. 'Do you know who killed him?'

'No.'

'Or Filly?'

'No.'

He looked at me. I think he was wondering for the first time how I came to be involved in all this. 'I think I may have heard Mother and Father speaking about you. You were once an . . . an inquiry agent?' He said it as if it were something indecent.

'Yes.'

That seemed enough to explain my role in this to him, for the while at least.

'If you find out, will you let me know?'

I said I would but didn't add that it seemed a remote possibility at present. I asked what he intended to do next and he said he'd go home, he supposed. Tabby and I went with him to the corner of Park Lane and saw him into a cab. On the way back, Tabby said, 'That letter, making her do the thing she regretted. I reckon that means she was the one that let the bitch out.' I had to admit that I agreed with her.

Eighteen

Robert took the first coach of the morning out of Dover, which dropped him at Dartford in the early afternoon. It was the final stop before London, and the coach was running twenty minutes late, so the guard was impatient about unloading the box and annoyed because water was dripping from it. Robert told him sharply not to jolt it and took it from him. When he opened the box in a quiet corner of the court-yard, he saw there was very little ice left. He'd managed to buy a few scoops of ice in Dover but the day was hot and he'd felt the sun drilling down on the coach as he tried not to wince at every jolt in the road. Inside the inn, he arranged with the landlord to keep the box in an outhouse and stowed it away himself, to wait until called for. He ordered cutlets and a pint of beer for lunch. He couldn't remember when he'd last eaten or what and he wasn't hungry now, but he was about to start on the last stage of the journey and the headlong rush that had brought him all the way across Europe now had to give place to something slower and more intricate. As he sat down and ate a few mouthfuls of meat, his body and most of his mind were still full of the need to rush on, waste no time, get back to England at all costs. He made himself think calmly, going over the plans he'd made on the journey again. He was expected to deliver the contents of the box to an address in Chelsea. When it was received, Liberty would be released. That was what he'd been told in an anonymous letter, but of course it was a lie. When he delivered the box, they'd kill him. That was obvious. What point would there be in letting him live? Equally clearly, they'd kill Liberty too, if they hadn't done so already. When he let himself think of that, any attempt at calm became a grey waste where nothing mattered, where he might as well deliver the box and let events take their course. Even the thought that other people would die as well didn't seem very important in comparison. The idea came to him that if he knew for sure that she was dead, he could at least do something to save those theoretical others. In handing over the box, he could actually cause the thing that he'd been trying to avoid on the journey and let the contents of it do what they were meant to do. It was, he supposed, what she might have wanted. But for the present, he must assume that she was still alive and use the only card he held in trying to free her. The other decision to make was whether to try to let anybody know where he was going. He'd been told in no uncertain terms not to, but when it came to it he couldn't give up the hope that something might happen to save him from the final decision. The image of steady, trustworthy Amos came to him. He found a piece of grubby paper and a stub of a pencil in his pockets, scribbled a few words and addressed them to the livery stables. If the chance came to send it, all well and good. If not, it would probably make no difference anyway.

He left a handful of coins on the table and stood up to go into the yard. At the doorway, one of the inn servants came up to him.

'You Mr Carmichael?'

He nodded and the servant pushed a piece of folded paper into his hand. His heart somersaulted as he opened it and saw the writing. *I'm still alive, but only because you've done as instructed. Continue to obey instructions or you may never see me again.* He found he'd grabbed the servant's sleeve and was holding on to it.

'Who gave you this?'

'Gentleman left it this morning. Didn't see him myself.'

He released the sleeve and the servant went away. He reread it. The paper was criss-crossed with several folds, splattered with tiny drops of ink, as if from a bad pen. The first reaction, that she was alive at least, drained away when he saw it wasn't dated. For all he knew, it could have been written at the same time as the earlier message. He took the next coach into London, only able to afford a place on the outside. He'd taken a sizeable amount of money out of England with him – half his savings – and now it was almost gone. No matter. The coach was held up in the middle of London Bridge by the weight of traffic and he looked up the river at the dozens of ships coming in with the tide, the dome of St Paul's, the brick-and-stone fronts of warehouses, offices, homes and everywhere tides of people,

211

hurrying, loitering, strolling or just standing and watching, all presumably with lives that made sense to them. He was aware of the heat of the sun and the usual awful smell from the river, but distantly, as if they were all in a different world with a great pane of glass between him and everything else. He assumed it was probably tiredness, but that didn't matter as long as he could keep his head clear. The coach journey ended at Holborn and he decided to walk from there, doubtful if he had enough money for a cab all the way out to Chelsea. He gave the note to the first reasonably sober-looking crossing sweeper he saw, along with his last half sovereign to deliver it. He kept mostly close to the river, not wanting to go anywhere near Mayfair and home. Wherever she was, she wouldn't be there. Along Millbank, he crossed the road to avoid the building site, and went on past the prison and Vauxhall Bridge on the long stretch to Chelsea, with fewer people and vehicles now, and more trees. He was sweating in the heat. He couldn't remember when he'd last washed, and the beard that he'd grown to save time shaving was prickling and itching. At Chelsea Hospital, a trim pensioner in his red tunic looked disapproving when he stopped to ask for directions, probably expecting him to beg for a copper or two. The address was simply the name of a public house, the Compass. It stood in a street of newish brick houses not far from the river, and looked as ordinary as a hundred other London public houses, neither especially old nor especially new, not quite rundown but not so well-kept either. Its outside was red brick, like the houses, with stone facings at the corners that might have been white once but were now grey from soot. A round board marked like a compass, paint slightly faded, hung above the closed front door. Robert opened it and stepped into an empty parlour, smelling of stale beer. Curtains were drawn halfway across the windows, and it seemed almost dark after the sun outside. A few heavy wooden tables with chairs drawn up round them were the only furniture, apart from a counter with barrels behind it facing a fireplace, its grate filled with large stone pebbles. A narrow staircase went up from an opening beside the fireplace. He stood in the middle of the room and called.

'Is there anybody here?'

Silence, then a movement above his head, the floor creaking, then footsteps coming slowly downstairs. A woman stepped into the room – tall, broad-shouldered and unsmiling. Her dress was black and her thin hair was scraped back from her prominent forehead.

'We're not open.'

'I was told to ask for John Smith.'

Her expression changed, though he couldn't have said quite how. She still looked grim, but the obviously false name meant something to her. Without another word, she turned and went back upstairs. Almost immediately, different steps sounded on the stairs. A youngish man in a black jacket and open-necked flannel shirt, without a hat, passed through the room without glancing at Robert and went out of the front door. The woman followed him down.

'He's being sent for. You can wait.' Then she went back upstairs.

He sat in a chair at one of the tables and waited for nearly two hours. Flies buzzed in the window. A cart went juddering past on the potholed road outside. Children's voices sounded from a long way off. The sun was low enough to throw an orange rectangle through a gap in the curtains on to the wall before the door opened and two men came in. One was the messenger, the other a middle-aged man of medium height, pot-bellied, clean-shaven and round-faced, wearing a long grey jacket, black trousers and a low-crowned hat. His eyes were dark, protruding a little and also round. The rotundities of belly, face and eyes might have given him a soft look but there was nothing soft in the stare he was giving Robert. It wasn't hostile exactly, but seemed to be sucking in every detail of his face and travel-stained clothes. He sat down opposite Robert at the table.

'You've taken your time.'

His voice was a Londoner's, quite educated, the comment sounding no more than a mild criticism. The round eyes were taking things in but letting nothing out. Robert stared into them but it was like looking at wet slate. He was tempted to defend himself and say truthfully that not a minute he could help had been wasted, but resisted. Let the other man talk.

'Where is it?'

'Where is she?'

The two questions hung in the air for what seemed like a long time. The messenger, standing by the door, shifted his weight from one foot to the other. The pot-bellied man broke the silence.

'She's safe.'

'Can I see her?'

'When you deliver it to us. Have you got it here?'

Robert shook his head. 'That would mean trusting you. I want to see her released first.'

'And that would mean trusting you.'

Another silence. Robert kept his eyes fixed on the other man, hoping they'd give as little away as the man's, and stated his terms. 'I want to see her released first. I don't even need to talk to her and she doesn't have to know I'm watching. Once it happens, I'll tell you where it is.'

The man moved his head slowly from side to side, still expressionless.

'It's the only way you'll get it,' Robert said.

At last, an expression. The man's lips curved into a smile that was worse than the blankness. It faded quickly. He looked towards the messenger and gave him a nod. The man went out of the front door and returned almost immediately. Just behind him was another man, entirely unremarkable, from the grey cap over his mid-brown hair to his worn black boots, his face round and pale, his eyes nondescript. Nothing would have picked him out in the crowd or even in the bustle of a Dartford coaching yard, where most of Robert's attention had been concentrated on unloading the box. And yet, as soon as Robert set eyes on him, he jerked upright in his seat, knowing that was where he'd last seen the man only a few hours ago. Before that, too, in the coaching yard in

215

Dover, he'd seen a man who'd looked very like him, but why notice that particular man in the hurry to get on the London coach? There were half a dozen like him anywhere people gathered. Of course, they'd have had a man at Dover, waiting for him. He should have expected it, and perhaps would have expected it if he hadn't been so intent on getting to his journey's end. The unremarkable man was carrying something. The box, dripping moisture on to the floor in heavy drops. At a nod from the pot-bellied man, he set it down on a table, heavily. As soon as he saw it, Robert knew that the game had changed. He tried to rebound from the shock and make his mind work faster than it had ever worked before. His first reaction was to call out a warning that they should treat it carefully, but he suppressed it and looked away from the box, back towards the pot-bellied man. He thought, *They've got it now, so they can kill Liberty and me, if they haven't killed her already.* He was calculating that if he got up from the chair he could stride across the room and aim a kick at the table that would dislodge the box and blow them all sky-high. Even if the messenger and the nondescript man tried to grab him, there'd be a struggle that would surely have the same effect. As he thought about it, he tried to keep completely still, so that Pot-belly wouldn't guess what was in his mind. The woman upstairs would die too, but she was part of it. The knowledge that the decisive next move could be his made his mind clear. He could do it at any time. Even if they closed in to kill him, he could make enough of a fight of it to do the job. Keep it in reserve, then. Assume that there was just the faintest chance, the merest sliver of a chance, that Liberty was still alive and play the game out.

'There are two things Professor Sobrero told me that you need to know before you start handling it,' he said. 'It's dangerously unstable. A shock can set it off.' He was surprised at how cool his voice sounded, and amused when the messenger and the nondescript man stepped smartly sideways, away from the table. The one thing in his favour might be their ignorance and fear. He knew precious little about the properties of pyroglycerine, but he'd have to gamble that they knew less.

'And the other?' Pot-belly asked.

'It's to do with precautions when you handle it. I want to see Liberty released before I tell you.'

For the first time, he saw a flicker of doubt in the round eyes. Pot-belly and the other two might try to beat the information out of him, but what if he lied to them? They needed his help, as men faced with a bad-tempered tiger needed an animal trainer. For some time, nobody said anything, then Pot-belly glanced at the messenger.

'Lock him up.'

Robert didn't resist when they took him down to the cellar and bolted the trap door over him. He sat on the floor with his back against the damp wall and heard the front door of the house open and close. Pot-belly was going for more instructions, he thought. So he wasn't the leader in whatever was happening, only a lieutenant. It was something to have put even a kink in their plans, but it would help if he had any idea what those plans were. In the meantime, all he could do was wait.

Nineteen

Another thing Tabby and I agreed about on our walk back was that we had to tell Amos about Cave's death as soon as possible. He was due to come round to Abel Yard later, but it couldn't wait. We crossed the park to Bayswater Road and went into the livery stables, standing aside for a couple of ladies and a groom riding out. Amos had just come in from a ride. He gave the reins of his horse to a groom and came over to us.

'Something up?' He saw from my face that this was serious and walked with me towards Rancie's box, talking as we went. Tabby stayed in the yard. 'There's been a man enquiring after you. Yesterday evening. Tallish, long dark hair. He's not at home with horses but reckoned he was interested in buying one. He said I'd been recommended to him by his friend, Mrs Carmichael. Then he wanted to know if I knew whether you were in town. If he'd been a friend he wouldn't have needed to ask me, would he?'

We went into Rancie's loosebox. She was there, rugged up. She'd been nosing at her hay net but turned when she saw me and gave that sound that's lower than a whinny, more like a horse purring. The sight and the smell of her were something from another world – what had been my world. I stroked her nose.

219

'Can you remember anything else about him?'

'First glance, he looked respectable enough – a lawyer's clerk, I'd have guessed – but underneath he was as nervy as a new colt, his eyes everywhere. Soft hat, black jacket, new-looking boots but cheap, badly tanned.'

'Yellowish boots?' The image of the poet came back into my mind. 'Amos, he was the man on the sloop. They're looking for me.'

'I thought that might be it. So I went . . .' A groom looked over the loose box door, wanting to know who should drive the phaeton for His Lordship. Amos sorted that out and turned back to me. 'I thought if he'd come here, he'd probably gone to your house as well. Turns out he had, but the maid had her instructions from Mrs Martley and just told him you were out of town.'

'Amos, the children . . .'

'Don't worry, we thought of that. Mrs Martley and I took them over to Mr and Mrs Brinkburn. Harry's asking after you but they're well. We made out to them it was a holiday.'

In my mind, I knew they'd be safe with Miles and Rosa, but I wouldn't feel it in my heart till I had them in my arms. 'What did you tell the Brinkburns?'

'That somebody had been hanging round your house – no details. But Mr Miles knows something's going on. I think we may have to tell the brothers after all. In fact . . .' He hesitated and bent down to check a buckle on the rug girth that didn't need checking. 'I reckon it may be about time we told Sergeant Bevan you got away.'

'We may have to in the end. Something else

has happened.' I told him about Cave's death and Felicity's brother.

'And you don't believe the brother had him killed?'

'No. But the people at the woodworker's shop will remember Maynard and ourselves enquiring for Cave's address. If Cave's body happens to be discovered, they'll go to the workshops and probably get a good description of all three of us. I didn't want to go to the police until we knew what was happening to Robert, but now . . .'

He turned away to straighten the rug. It hadn't been out by more than an inch or two. Amos was seriously disturbed about something.

'That's the other thing I was coming to tell you. I think he might be back.'

'Robert. When? Where?'

'I don't know where he is, if it is him. I've been keeping touch with the Dover coach drivers, buying them a drink now and again. One of them came to see me just before I went out on the ride. He was driving the coach that arrived from Dover yesterday evening. He reckons a man who looked very much like Mr Carmichael was with them as far as Dartford.'

'So he wasn't certain. Had he seen Robert before or was he just going on the description?' I was rocked sideways thinking of Robert so near.

'He'd seen him on the journey out. He said this gentleman had a beard—'

'Robert doesn't like beards.'

'But apart from that, he said he was the spitting image. He had some luggage with him that he was fussing over.'

'But you said Robert only had a bag when he left.'

'Then he must have picked some up. They've got good eyes, drivers. I'd say the odds are that it really was Mr Carmichael.'

'Why get off at Dartford? If he's back, why doesn't he come to me?' It was a useless cry because the answer was obvious. He couldn't.

Amos took both my hands, making the soothing sound he uses on nervous horses. 'Easy, easy. He's back, at least. Isn't that something?'

'But what has he come back to? It's not about the prison any more. We were wrong about that. Was anybody with him when your man thinks he saw him?'

'No. He was on his own, he said.'

'Can't we hope Cave's body isn't found and put off telling the police for two days at least? If Robert's back, surely we can find him. He might be trying to find a way to get to me.'

'Why two days?'

'Because whatever is going to happen, it will be in two days, the twenty-third of July. Friday. That's what I heard on the sloop. If we can only find Robert before then, we might still be able to keep him out of it.'

'Friday.' Amos considered. 'There won't be a lot else happening on Friday. The town'll be choked up with carriages from Piccadilly to Westminster.'

'Why?'

'The Queen's proroguing Parliament.' Then, seeing the expression on my face and thinking that I hadn't understood the technical term, he said, 'I mean, sending the MPs off on their holidays. But it's bigger than usual, because it will be in the new House of Lords for the first time. Everybody who can get a ticket will be there, with the ladies in enough diamonds to buy up Threadneedle Street. We've got our two dress chariots spoken for, and four of the lads turning footmen for the day.'

'Whatever they're planning, they're probably relying on that for a distraction. The police will be concentrating on what's going on at Westminster.'

'So we've got to give them a hint, at least. Will you let me talk to Bevan?'

'Perhaps. Let him know I've escaped, but don't tell him about Cave yet, and keep Robert out of it.' I'd been badly shaken by the appearance of the poet on our own territory.

Amos nodded. 'I'll see you and Tabby back home, then I'll go and look for him.'

Tabby was deep in conversation with one of the grooms. We collected her and made our way to the gates. We were within a few steps of them when a man came walking in. He wore a dark coat and black hat, but from the upright posture and a measured quality about the way he walked, he might as well have been in uniform. It took a lot to disconcert Amos, but I looked at his face and caught the shock before it froze into neutrality. He stepped forward.

'Good afternoon, Sergeant. I was just coming to see you.'

Bevan looked as grim as I'd ever seen him. It took him just a second to recognize my face inside the bonnet, then his voice matched his expression. 'Good afternoon, Mrs Carmichael. At liberty, I see.' I doubted if he'd intended the pun, and there was no humour in it.

Amos suggested that we should all go and sit down, and led the way to the tack room-cum-office. Bevan stood aside to let me go first, but I knew that was more from wanting to keep an eye on me than politeness. Tabby had melted away as usual. The tack room had two chairs – hard wooden ones. Again, Bevan waited for me to sit down with sarcastic politeness then took the second chair himself. Amos remained standing.

'So you were coming to see me, Mr Legge. Did you intend to accompany him, Mrs Carmichael? Were you ever kidnapped in the first place? I did wonder.'

'She was, right enough,' Amos said. Sergeant Bevan didn't take his eyes off me.

'I was drugged and imprisoned in a sloop on the Thames, just off Millbank, for ten days. I managed to escape a week ago.'

'And it didn't occur to you to report this inter-esting event to the police?'

'I wanted to find out what was happening first. I thought it was connected with an escape attempt from Millbank prison. I did try to take steps to tell the authorities about it, but I now think that wasn't the case.'

'Ah, yes, the escape attempt.' I wondered if, at his level, he knew about the part played by Mr Disraeli. Probably he did. I knew that Bevan had been involved in some delicate political situations in the past. 'So, nothing to do with it. What about the murder of Miss Felicity Maynard. Would it have had anything to do with that?'

'So she was murdered?'

'Yes. That head injury wouldn't have come from being thrown against Westminster Bridge. I'm asking myself if it's more than a coincidence that she was part of a household where you were having dinner just before you were taken from us. Or that she was killed at about the time you so luckily managed to escape.'

'It isn't a coincidence.' No point now in trying to hide this part of the story from him. 'Felicity had a half-brother who called himself Jonah Cave. He worked at the Parliament site as a woodcarver and he was seeing her in secret. He scared her. I'm nearly sure that this Jonah Cave was involved in abducting me, but I still don't know why.'

'And did he kill his half-sister?'

'No. Tabby was following him on the night she died, and he couldn't have. But she'd probably gone out to look for him when she was killed.'

'How do you know that?'

'From somebody closely connected with the Maynard family.' At some point, I'd probably have to throw Oliver Maynard to him, but not yet.

'You're not helping me very much, are you? Tell me, does your husband know that you've managed to escape?'

'My husband is travelling.'

'Indeed. He doesn't seem to have travelled very far. Would you be surprised to hear that he was crossing the Strand yesterday afternoon? Are you going to ask me how I know that?'

225

I said nothing, hardly daring to breathe, but he went on anyway.

'He gave a note to a crossing sweeper, with a half sovereign to deliver it. I'm sure there are perfectly honest and upright crossing sweepers in London who'd have done exactly that but, for better or worse, that man wasn't one of them. Instead of running off to deliver the note, he spent the half sovereign getting very drunk indeed – so drunk that he insulted two of our officers on the beat and ended up being arrested. In the normal course of events, they searched his pockets. It was a matter of sheer good luck that I happened to be at the station and recognized the name on the note.' He took a folded and scuffed-looking square of paper out of his pocket. I put out my hand for it, but he shook his head. 'Not for you, I'm afraid. It's addressed to one Amos Legge Esq., at the livery stables in Bayswater Road.'

He held it out and I could see the familiar writing, on cheap paper in pencil. For a moment, Amos didn't move, then he stepped forward to take it. Bevan shook his head again.

'It's police property. Evidence.'

'It's addressed to me,' Amos said.

'Evidence of what?' I said.

'That remains to be seen. For one thing, you seem to have managed to waste quite a lot of police time. It also sounds as if you've been concealing facts connected with a murder.'

'You've only just told us it was a murder and I've only recently found out the facts,' I said. But I couldn't even convince myself, because I was thinking about that other murder.

Amos tried again to persuade Bevan to hand over the note, but he put it back in his pocket.

'At least tell us what he says,' I pleaded. It had struck me that Robert thought I was still being held prisoner, or he'd have sent the note to me and not to Amos.

'Of course, we're not actually looking for Mr Carmichael,' Bevan said, ignoring the plea. 'There's no indication he's done anything wrong. Still, I can't help wondering where he is.' He paused, waiting for some comment from me.

'I don't know,' I said. 'I've only just found out he's back in London.'

'Back. So he's been away? Do you know where?'

'No.' It was the truth, but I could see he didn't believe me. For a moment, I'd had the impulse to tell him all I knew and have the police hunt for Robert, wherever he was and whatever he was doing, but if we didn't trust each other, what was the use? Still, one thing had to be said. 'Something's going to happen this Friday, two days away. The people who kidnapped me were talking about it.'

'What?'

'I don't know what, only that it must be something big.'

'In London?'

'I suppose so. I don't know.' I could see from his face that I wasn't impressing him and I couldn't be surprised. He turned to Amos.

'Mr Legge, has Mr Carmichael made any attempt to get in touch with you apart from this note?'

Amos shook his head.

'If he does, I'd appreciate it if you'd let me know, or preferably suggest that he comes to see me.'

'You said you're not looking for him,' I said.

'Not officially, but I should like to talk to him. And I'd like to talk to your girl, Tabby. I've had a description of a young woman observed around the Maynards' house who sounds very much like her. But I don't suppose you'd say anything, would you?'

He was right. I said nothing. He turned to go, raising his hat about a quarter of an inch.

'It's my note,' Amos said to his departing back.

I sensed that Amos was weighing up whether to leap on Bevan and wrestle the note from him. He could easily have done it. I shook my head. No point in getting arrested. We watched as Bevan went out through the gateway.

'The note would say where he is, or at least how we can get in touch with him,' Amos said. 'There'd have been no point otherwise. If we were to follow Bevan . . .'

'We'd have to follow half the London police force,' I said. 'If there's an address in that note, he'll already have sent men there.'

'And not found him, otherwise why would he be bothering us? We'll just have to hope that Mr Carmichael tries again.'

'If he can,' I said. I was half crazy with the idea that Robert was back in London somewhere and we had no idea how to find him.

Amos said he'd walk back with us to Abel Yard. We got to Adam's Mews with Tabby trailing behind us in that state of sullen fury that always followed any contact with the police. As Amos and I turned into the yard, I noticed that one of the lads who made some kind of living around the mews had stopped her and was talking urgently. She followed us upstairs to the parlour.

'A strange woman's been around here asking about you.'

My heart thumped. 'What did she look like?'

'Not young, black dress, hat with a veil. He said her forehead stuck out like this.' She mimed a bulge.

'Minerva.' I couldn't help shuddering as I said it. 'What did he tell her?'

'That he'd never heard of you, of course.'

I thanked the gods for the loyalty of Tabby's network, but felt terrified. With the poet at the stables and Minerva here, they were closing in. It was a week since I'd escaped from the sloop – something else must have happened. That something else was Robert's arrival back in London.

'You're coming back to the stables with me,' Amos said.

'I can't stay there.'

'Why not? In any case, if Mr Carmichael manages to get in touch with me again, you'll be there.'

'If I'd been here, I could have followed her,' Tabby said. 'I will, if she comes back.'

It made sense, as far as anything did. I put a few things together in a bag and walked with Amos back across the park. While he supervised the evening stables, I waited, sitting on a bale of straw in Rancie's box. When everybody else had gone, he cooked us bacon and eggs very neatly and skilfully on the range in the tack room and gave me his bed upstairs. He'd even found time to put on a fresh sheet and bolster cover. He'd be sleeping in the hayloft – he'd done it before many times, he said. All the time we were listening, for the gate opening, for footsteps in the yard that might be the poet or might be Robert. But there was nothing but the shifting hooves of horses and the rustlings of rats and cats in the straw. I dozed, more or less, but went on listening all night.

Twenty

Daylight was washing in slowly from downriver, along with the tide. The sun hadn't risen yet. The ride there in the rickety carriage behind the old horse had been entirely in the dark and at a walk because of what Robert had told them about the cargo. He calculated that the distance covered had been no more than a couple of miles at most. Three of them were travelling with him – Pot-belly, who was giving the orders, the messenger and a new one with long hair and new boots that squeaked. Pot-belly had a pistol in his jacket pocket and made sure Robert had seen it in the lamplight, but he didn't handle it like a man who intended to use it. Robert was being cooperative and had been since he had told them what he pretended to have learned from Professor Ascanio Sobrero in Turin.

'It's all too easy to set off. A sudden shock will do it. The problem is transferring it out of the bottle to wherever you intend to use it. The fumes are extremely toxic. They've lost one laboratory worker already and another has been very ill. That's the main drawback so far to using it as an explosive in the quarries.'

Two of them – Pot-belly and New-boots – had listened as intently as students in the hot, sour-beer-smelling room at the Compass, long after midnight. Pot-belly had asked, 'So how do you get over it, then?'

'The professor has produced breathing masks. They're very complicated things, with stiffened muslin and charcoal and some other ingredients I couldn't find out about. They seem to work if they're tied on carefully.' He'd never met the professor, never set foot in his laboratory, but as he spoke he was almost convincing himself.

'And you haven't brought one of them?'

'No.'

The two of them had looked at him, then at the box on the other side of the room. New-boots drew his chair further away from it.

'Looks like you're going to have to do it, then,' Pot-belly said.

They'd paid a price for his cooperation. He was holding it on his knees as he talked to them, the muslin soft under his sweating palm. Her petticoat was one of the outer ones she wore in summer, almost certainly the one she'd been wearing the night they went to dinner with the Maynards. He'd been sure it was hers as soon as he saw it, even without the confirmation of her initials stitched into the waistband for the laundry. It even smelled of her. It was stained and the hem was torn. He knew they could have taken it off her body. They claimed she was alive and well, that he'd see her soon. He had to pretend to believe them. So they got down to business. It had come as an unpleasant surprise to Pot-belly that the new explosive was liquid and not solid. It became clear that he was the technical expert and, like most experts, was more than ready to talk about his field.

'The point is we have to have something more

232

concentrated than gunpowder. With gunpowder you'd need a barrel of it, and we can't get a barrel in there. So when we heard about this new material in Turin, we had to have it. Trouble is we've made the arrangements for it and there's not much time to alter them. It's got to go in this.'

He nodded to New-boots. The man went to a corner of the room and came back with something heavy in his arms. He hoisted it on to the table where they were sitting. In the dim light, it looked like a roughly carved rectangular block of wood about two feet high. As Robert stared it began to take on the characteristics of a bear or a lion sitting on its haunches, open jaws and shaggy neck.

'Just the rough job this is, for testing,' Pot-belly said. He stood up and lifted the thing off its base, showing Robert that it was hollow inside. The base was the animal's clawed hind feet. A lion, then. 'But since it is a liquid, we'll have to use it in a bottle somehow. How big are the bottles it came in?'

Robert lifted the top off the box. All the ice had melted and most of the water had run away through a leak in the metal lining, leaving the two bottles of yellowish liquid exposed. Pot-belly looked down at them. 'Too wide, aren't they? So you're going to have to transfer it to another bottle before using.'

'Yes.'

'And you reckon that just one of those bottles is enough for a big explosion?'

'Yes.'

'So we can use the other one for testing, as soon as it gets light. We never wanted to leave it so near the time as this, but with you coming so late we've got no choice.'

'Where are you going to test it?'

'Somewhere a long way from anywhere, don't you worry. We'll find a bottle that's the right size and you can start transferring it.'

Robert tried hard to keep his voice level, knowing a lot depended on this. 'Wouldn't it be better to leave transferring it until we get to where we're testing it? The bottles it's in are safest for travelling.'

Pot-belly thought about it and nodded. 'Right you are. You can do it when we get there.'

In Robert's pocket on the journey was a long white silk scarf of the kind an elderly gentleman concerned about his chest might wear. It was the closest thing they could find to a mask, and Pot-belly said it would have to do.

The site they'd chosen for the test was alongside the river, probably where it took a loop southward between Chelsea and Chiswick, Robert thought, but as nearly without feature as a place could be – a flat field with a covering of low weeds and a straggling line of willows in the distance. New-boots helped him unload the carrying case, moving cautiously, and they took it two hundred yards or so from the carriage. Pot-belly put the carved lion down beside it and lifted off the hollow upper part.

'In the bottom here, that's the detonator – a small charge of gunpowder. From what you say, that will be more than enough to break the bottle and set it off. We've put a slow match on it, just a few inches, but it will be a lot more for the real thing. What you have to do is transfer the stuff to the other bottle, light the slow match, stand the bottle on the base and put the top on. Then you'll have plenty of time to get back to us before it goes off.'

Robert nodded.

'So give us a chance to get clear before you open the bottle, then start.' He handed Robert a flint lighter.

They walked back to the carriage. Robert wrapped the scarf carefully over his nose and mouth – he'd almost convinced himself – and had no need to pretend to be nervous. It was dangerous work, in any case. He lifted off the lid of the box and took out a bottle. It was sealed with red wax and, as they'd taken his pocket knife off him, he had to prise it away with his fingernails, keeping the bottle as level as possible. The cork under the wax came out quite easily. He put the bottle carefully on the ground while he settled the empty bottle from the inn beside it and raised his hand to the group by the carriage, signifying, he hoped, that he was about to begin the critical part of the operation. He poured, slowly and carefully. The new bottle was slimmer but taller, and the quantity just filled it. He opened up the wooden slide over the lion's paws and lit the slow match. There were about three inches of it. He remembered from somewhere that slow match burned at the rate of about a foot an hour, so there was plenty of time. Don't hurry. He stood the bottle on the base, slotted the rest of the lion over it and stood with his back to the party by the carriage, looking out over the leaden waters of the Thames. There were shouts for him to come back, to hurry. They weren't worried about him, of course, only the remaining bottle of the pyroglycerine. Perhaps it was in their minds that he was about to sabotage the whole thing and send up himself and both bottles in one almighty explosion. It was quite possible. He might have done so, too, except he'd decided to play the longer game. Unhurriedly, he put the empty bottle back in the case beside the full one, picked it up and carried it back to the carriage.

'What were you thinking of?' Pot-belly said, sounding shaken. 'You could have gone with it.'

'There's plenty of time,' Robert said. He sounded and felt totally calm. He was right too. It was another five minutes before the explosion happened.

It was louder than anything he'd ever heard, and rocked the carriage from two hundred yards away. For some time after it, he couldn't think of anything, stunned by the noise and the pattering of clods of earth raining down. New-boots was crouching with his arms over his head. They all stayed immobile for some time, then Pot-belly led the way across the torn earth to where the wooden lion had been. A crater large enough to swallow a four-horse carriage was all there was to see. At last, Pot-belly broke the silence.

'Satisfactory.'

On the journey in the carriage, it seemed as if witnessing the explosion together had made Robert a conspirator rather than a prisoner. They were still stunned by the force of it, but almost friendly. They didn't go back to the Compass but turned instead on to a narrow road that led to a landing stage by the river. They left him to carry the box from the carriage to the landing stage. A boat would come for them, Pot-belly said. While they were waiting, Robert lifted the lid to show them the empty bottle, the other still full of its pale yellow liquid. They didn't seem to want to inspect it too closely.

'Now for the real thing,' Pot-belly said.

Twenty-One

Tabby arrived back at Amos's yard around nine o'clock in the morning, when the place was getting busy. Amos had just ridden out with a mother and two children, one of them on a leading rein. He'd told me to stay in the tack room, but I was safe with Tabby so I went out to meet her, dodging round grooms and horses. Her eyes were dark-ringed from lack of sleep, but she was glowing with achievement and news.

'She did come back, the one you call Minerva. Went right into the yard and sat there on the mounting block, looking up at your windows. I was watching from my cabin. She got there soon after eight and stayed for nearly three hours. When it was well dark she gave up and left, so I followed her. All the way to Chelsea. There's a public house there called the Compass; doesn't look as if it gets much custom. It was all shut up, but she opened the front door with a key and went inside. The curtains were drawn downstairs so I couldn't see if there was anybody else in there, but there were no lights. There's a yard at the back of the place, so I kept watch from there. No sight or sound of anything all night, then just after it got light at around five o'clock, all hell broke loose.'

'What happened?'

'The police arrived, that's all – four of them

in a one-horse van. They knocked on the door until she opened up with just a coat over her, bare legs and no hat on, pushed their way in and searched the place.'

'Was Sergeant Bevan with them?'

'Nah. By the time she opened the door, half the neighbourhood was awake with the noise, so I just stood on the pavement and watched with the rest of them. She was giving them a mouthful – you could hear that from outside. She was just a respectable woman running a public house and they had no right and so on. Some of the neighbours were on her side or they just didn't like the police, because they were cheering her on and catcalling. Two of the policemen came out in the yard and you could see they were getting hot and bothered. They went round the yard, down into the cellars and upstairs, then they came out, got in their van and drove off, empty-handed. She slammed the door, the neighbours went away and that was it.'

Bevan might not have been there in person, but I was sure that he'd ordered the raid and it had been because of something in Robert's note. The thought that at last we had some clue to Robert made me so wound up that going straight to the Compass seemed the only thing to do.

I scribbled a message for Amos saying where we were going, and gave it to the head lad. Tabby had stopped behaving like a mother hen to me, thank goodness, and didn't even suggest waiting for a cab. We cut through the park to Knightsbridge, went down Sloane Street to the Chelsea Royal Hospital then past it to the Physic Garden by the river. I asked the gardener clipping a hedge if he knew of a public house called the Compass. He didn't, but called to another man, who thought he remembered it about half a mile back from the river, near the new houses. From the gardener's face, he was puzzled that we should be looking for such a place. We found it without too much trouble – a grimy, red-brick building with a faded compass sign over the door and grey curtains drawn across the windows. A man passing by with a donkey cart told us – unasked – that they only opened the place when it suited them and the public house up the road was a lot better. We walked past and stopped round a corner, out of sight of the windows of the house.

'There's the back way from the yard,' Tabby said. 'Unless you wanted to knock on the front door and see what happens.'

I didn't. The place looked so completely unremarkable it was hard to think that anything of significance had happened there. Even the police raid a few hours before seemed to have left no impression. We walked down the street and turned left, alongside a blank wall at the side of the house. An alleyway ran from the pavement to the back of the building. It was a wide one, probably meant for the delivery of beer barrels, but judging by the straw and torn newspapers littered along it, there'd been no recent traffic. It opened directly on to the back yard of the public house, with no gate. A few barrels stood along one side of the yard, looking as if they'd been there for some time, along with an old zinc bath tub. The ground had been mud but was now hard-baked, and a large dog kennel near the wall that no dog had inhabited for months or years leaned over at an angle. Two windows looked out on the yard from the ground floor of the building from either side of a shut door, but they were as closely curtained as the front.

'Behind the kennel will do,' Tabby said. 'We'll watch for a bit.'

The bleak surroundings gave very little cover. We checked that nobody was watching, then walked quickly across the yard and bent down so that the kennel was shielding us from anybody looking out of a window. Tabby settled herself at once with her back against the kennel and her knees drawn up. She was facing away from the house, but I knew her ears would catch the movement of a mouse. I put my back against the wall, so that I was looking out to the yard, and tried to copy her posture. I knew she'd wait for hours if necessary without moving. I doubted if I could. I didn't even know what we were waiting for, beyond the wild hope in my mind that the door would open and Robert would walk out. For an hour, at least, nothing happened, except that I shifted my position a few times, trying to get more comfortable. Tabby didn't bat an eyelash. I wondered what was in her mind in all the waiting and watching she did, or whether she had grasped the art of not thinking at all until it was needed. I knew every gap in the planks of the kennel, every knot in the wood. Litter had blown in between the back of it and the wall: a screwed-up piece of paper that looked as if it might have been an advertisement for a circus,

241

more straw, some rags. Except they weren't rags exactly, more like a dressmaker's off-cuts with straight edges – thick straight edges, so they'd been good quality material once. Nothing else about this place suggested straightness or quality. Idly, I reached out for one of the pieces, getting a frown from Tabby for fidgeting, then a sharper frown because I'd let out a gasp. I was holding a fragment of leather a few inches long, wider at one end than the other. Red leather. It was good quality dye, because it had hardly faded at all in spite of being left outside. My mind went back to something earlier – a formal occasion, my best blue silk, Robert's hand on my arm and, in my ears, Mr Disraeli's voice explaining that . . . Red benches, acres of them, all covered in the most rich and expensive red leather, women still working against the clock to finish them for royal inspection. Robert and I were being shown round the new chamber.

'House of Lords,' I whispered to Tabby. 'Somebody here worked on the House of Lords.'

She put a finger to her lips and shook her head. I'd have to explain to her later. I settled back but kept the piece of leather in my hand. More time passed. Suddenly Tabby twisted round so that she was looking out at the yard. She'd caught before I had the sound of a bolt being drawn back. A door scraped open. Tabby's eyes were following something I couldn't see at first, then a figure moved nearer the centre of the yard and I made out a child, male and barefoot, ten or eleven years old from his build, dressed only in a shirt. He had his back to me, and must have

242

been throwing bottles into the bathtub because there were crashes and a breaking of glass. Then he urinated against the opposite wall and turned so that I could see his face for the first time. The last time I'd seen that face, he'd been staring at me from the deck of the sloop before I dived. Minerva's assistant. This time, I managed to keep quiet as he went back towards the public house, disappearing from my view. The door scraped closed. I waited for a while, then caught Tabby's eye and jerked my head back towards the street. We went out of the yard and back along the alleyway.

'It's the same boy,' I said. I told her about trying to bribe him on the sloop, and about the leather.

'So is it just your Minerva in there with him?' she said.

'Unless somebody's come back since the police search.'

'Do we go in?'

If I'd thought Robert was inside I'd have said yes and never mind the consequences, but they surely wouldn't have moved him there now the police knew about the place. He might have been there once but he wasn't now.

'I think we need Amos,' I said. Tabby was an effective fighter but I wasn't back on my best form and it was possible that other members of the gang had arrived since the police raid. We went round the corner to the front of the house. It still looked completely shut and deserted. I'd have liked to suggest that one of us should stay on watch while the other went to meet Amos, but knew Tabby wouldn't leave me alone. I'd brought the offcut of red leather with me and, as we walked, I explained to her why I thought it mattered.

'That's at least two members of the gang who've been working on the Parliament site. Jonah Cave was a woodcarver and I'm guessing that Minerva may have been one of the women upholstering the Lords' benches.' I thought of those big, capable hands.

'So did they just happen to meet, or did they both get work there for a reason?'

A good question. If so, that suggested that something on the Parliament site had been the point of the plot all along. An idea began to stir in my mind. I'd thought we might meet Amos on the way, but when we got back to the stables he was waiting for us in the yard, looking grim. I told him about the Compass and suggested we should go back and search the place together, expecting instant agreement, but the grim look didn't shift.

'Something's been happening here. I got in from my ride and there was the maid come running from your house with a message. A man had been lurking round asking for Mr Carmichael, and cook had got him shut in the wood shed.'

My first panicked thought was for the children, until I remembered they were with Miles and Rosa. 'What did you do?'

'Went round and collected him, of course. I've got him shut up here now in the foaling box.'

'Is he the one with the new boots?'

'No, this one's a foreigner – from Italy, he says. When I hustled him round here he was trying to

244

tell me a story, but I said he should save it till I had time. I was coming to find you and Tabby. You shouldn't have gone off like that.'

I apologized and said we should speak to the man. Amos told me to go and wait in the fodder room, which at this time of day was the quietest place in the stables. Tabby came with me and we both perched ourselves on feed bins. A few minutes later, Amos came back with his captive. The young man sprang towards me as soon as they were through the door. Amos pulled him back by the arm and told him to behave.

'You are Madam Carmichael?' He looked no older than twenty or so and was unimpressive at first glance, a good foot shorter than Amos, thin and pale as paper, with large brown eyes shining out from hollowed sockets. His clothes were creased and stained and he was hatless, his dark, curly hair unwashed with a cobweb clinging to it, probably from our woodshed. It struck me that our cook, a robust woman, would have had no great problem in dealing with him. But for all that he had a kind of dignity about him. He stood straight and glared at me, eyebrows drawn together. Fury was burning off him. 'It is most urgent that I find Mr Carmichael.' The English was good, the accent strongly Italian.

'We should like to find him too,' I said.

'You know where he is, I believe.'

'I swear to you, I don't know. Just tell me what you want with him.'

'I've come all the way from Turin to find him. The woman at the house where he lives wouldn't let me in, so I found my way through the servants' entrance. Then another woman shut me up and this man handled me like a thief.' He glared at Amos. 'It's Robert Carmichael who is the thief, not I.'

'He's not a thief.' The protest was instinctive, but even as I made it I had to remind myself that I had no idea what he'd been doing. 'What's he supposed to have stolen?'

'Something very perilous. I've come to take it back.'

Amos and I looked at each other. I said to the young man, 'For a start, you'd better tell us who you are.'

I suppose any slight civility surprised him, after being locked in a shed then marched through Mayfair by Amos. He blinked, gave an automatic polite bow and introduced himself formally.

'My name is Antonio Ricci. I am a student of chemistry at the University of Turin; a student of Professor Ascanio Sobrero. His name means something to you?'

'Sobrero,' I repeated. The name had woken a faint echo in my memory, but I couldn't place it. 'I think my husband may have mentioned it. He spent time in Turin some years ago but I'm not sure he ever met the professor.'

'He was in Turin much more recently than that. Are you saying you didn't know?'

'No, I didn't know. The fact is, Mr Ricci, my husband has been missing for some time. We very much want to find him. It sounds as if you know more about where he might be than we do.' I watched his eyes. He was still on edge but some of his hostility was draining away. He looked hungry and desperately tired, as if only nervous energy held him together. 'You say you want to take back something he stole. What?'

He took a long breath. 'I shall have to explain to you what Professor Sobrero is doing. He is researching the effects of nitric acid on certain organic substances, such as sugar, lactose and glycerine. For some time, I have been assisting him. In one course of experiments, we added pure nitric acid to glycerol, then went further and added sulphuric acid. You follow me so far?'

I nodded. 'I'm no chemist, but that's clear enough.'

'Some of our compounds were explosive. We took careful precautions. But the results of this one were terrible. It exploded while the professor was handling it. Even a very small quantity set off a fire in our laboratory and burned the professor's face. He'll always have the scar. Entirely accidentally, the professor had invented the most powerful explosive ever known to man, far stronger than gunpowder. He called it pyroglycerine, though it can also be called nitro-glycerine. At first, his reaction was to keep it secret, knowing what great damage it could do, and for months we kept it to ourselves. But once something is invented it cannot be uninvented. We made more small quantities of it for our own research purposes. Also, it's in the professor's mind that a way might be found of tempering it, making it less volatile. In that case, it would be useful to quarrymen and roadbuilders. We couldn't keep it a secret. Scientists talk. How your husband found out about it, I don't know. Why he decided

247

to steal it, I don't know. When the professor found out that a quantity was missing, he was almost distracted. Because I speak English, I was the one among his students most able to do something. I promised him that I wouldn't rest until I had found Mr Carmichael and recovered the pyroglycerine.'

Silence. While Ricci was speaking, I'd sunk my head into my hands. I wished that we'd been right and that Robert had been engaged in some relatively innocent criminality like making financial provision for a fleeing criminal. I wished too that I could look Mr Ricci in the face and say confidently that of course my husband would never do any such thing. Amos spoke first, trying hard.

'Why do you say Mr Carmichael stole the stuff?'

Ricci twisted round in the chair to look at him. 'He had an accomplice – a laboratory worker named Marco. The fellow tried to make himself important, as if he were the professor's assistant, but he was only a washer of vessels. We found out almost at once that he'd taken it from the laboratory, bribed by Mr Carmichael. He never gave Marco his real name, but some people recognized him from the last time he'd been in Turin. By the time we found that out, he'd left. I was three days behind him.'

'And you followed him all the way to London?' I said.

'Yes. I never expected to have to come so far.'

'Because you thought you'd catch up with him first?'

Ricci shook his head. 'Because I thought I'd come across smoking ruins first.'

'What?'

He leaned forward in his chair, eyes holding mine. 'Pyroglycerine is very unstable. It's a colourless or yellowish, oily liquid, like melted fat, and looks quite innocent. But the slightest jolt of even a small quantity of it can set off a disastrous explosion. It's less unstable if it's kept very cold with ice packed round it, but even then, moving it is dangerous. Every crossroads I came to in pursuit of him, I expected to see the remains of a coach and bodies scattered round it. Every village I looked at the inn and was surprised to find it still standing. Every town I walked round looking for signs of an explosion. Nothing. Your husband has been a very lucky man. So far.'

A carriage rumbled over the cobbles in the stable yard. I pictured the cobbles all the way across Europe and had to stop myself shrinking into a protective ball, thinking of Robert and the most explosive substance known to man.

'How much was stolen?' My voice sounded a lot calmer than I felt.

'About as much as would fill two wine bottles.' His hand went to an empty feed bowl on the bin beside him. 'If this bowl here were half filled with pyroglycerine and I just pushed it like this . . . this room and possibly this whole place would be destroyed.'

He pushed the bowl and it clanged to the floor. I couldn't stop myself staring at it.

'So you should tell me where he is,' he said.

I wished I had a chance to talk to Amos alone.

We had a decision to make, and it depended on whether Ricci was telling the truth. I looked at the pale face and dusty hair, the sunken eyes. I believed him.

'Mr Ricci, I wish with all my heart that I could tell you. I haven't seen my husband for nearly three weeks. I believe he's now somewhere in London and we're trying to find out where. I wish as fervently as you do that the pyroglycerine were safe, back in the professor's laboratory, but it isn't and we have to do what we can.'

'Why did he steal it? What's he going to do with it?'

'He was forced to steal it. That's all I can tell you. He'll have passed it on to other people.'

I'd taken the decision to believe him, but that didn't mean I had to tell him everything. He stared at me, chin thrust out, wanting to quarrel.

'You must find him and these other people.'

Amos moved in closer, his hand touching Ricci's arm.

'I've told you, we're trying. We can't do more than we're doing,' I said.

We got him to believe us, but it took some time. In the end, his tiredness overcame him and he sagged, defeated, against the feed bin. Amos and I exchanged a look. If we simply allowed Ricci to go, goodness knows where he'd take his story. In any case, he'd probably want to stick close to us. Amos sighed.

'We'll keep him here for the moment. From the look of him, he needs to eat and sleep.'

He was probably offering horse rugs in the hayloft, but that would be more comfortable than many places Ricci would have slept on his journey. Ricci resisted at first but accepted in the end that his best chance of finding Robert was to stay close to us. He looked dazed now, having driven himself this far and found a dead end. Amos walked him out of the room, leaving me alone with Tabby. She picked up the feed bowl carefully, as if it really had contained explosive.

'So, is he mad?'

'No, I'm very much afraid he isn't.' I looked out of the window, across the yard to the busy Bayswater Road, dazed from the knowledge that somewhere out there in London was something that had never been there before – the most explosive substance known to man.

Twenty-Two

For a long time, neither Tabby nor I said anything. We'd arrived with the idea of collecting Amos and going back to the Compass, but that had been driven out of my head by Ricci. I tried to get my mind working, but for what seemed like a long time, it was no good. All it would produce were pictures of crossroads and coach wheels, and Robert with something in his hands that could destroy him and everything around him. Anger against him started to form. Why hadn't he refused? I wasn't worth that. Nobody was worth that. I wished I'd let them beat me to death before I signed those letters. Then something else came to me. I was back in the hold of the sloop, listening. *It's fixed now. The twenty-third of July, a Friday.*

'Tomorrow,' I said. Tabby looked at me. 'They put off the transportation because of it. Then I thought it would be a distraction from whatever they were going to do. It isn't. It's the thing itself.'

'What thing?'

I remembered that Tabby hadn't heard my conversation with Amos. 'Tomorrow they're proroguing . . . that's to say, they're officially dissolving Parliament before an election.' Tabby still looked puzzled. 'It's a great ceremony – the Queen, the Lords, the MPs. And it will be an

252

even bigger occasion than usual because it's in the new House of Lords for the first time. Everybody will be there.' Everybody, that is, of the few hundreds who ran the country or thought they were entitled to run the country. All the members of their noble families who could demand or beg a ticket in one of the grandest places built in England in the last few hundred years. 'November the fifth, all over again.'

'Guy Fawkes?' It was probably the only historical date Tabby knew.

'Guy Fawkes. And it's being planned by some of the people who've been building the place. Cave was a woodworker. Somebody from the Compass, probably Minerva, was working on upholstering the benches. Somebody knew about the sloops delivering stone to the wharf. They know the site and how to get in.'

'So what do we do?'

'I'll see Mr Disraeli again, tell him the whole story.'

'Are you going to tell him what the Italian fellow said about Mr Carmichael?'

I felt sick at the thought. 'I'll have to.'

Tabby and I went straight across the park to the Disraelis' house. Mr Disraeli was not at home and the butler didn't know where he might be found. He was obviously speaking the truth. I begged him to send a message to me at Abel Mews as soon as Mr Disraeli came in, saying it was of extreme urgency. He promised he would, but didn't know whether Mr Disraeli was expected home for dinner. Outside, on the pavement, I stopped and considered. I knew the right thing would be to go at once to Sergeant Bevan, but every instinct that I had was against it. I thought I could – just – manage to pass on Ricci's story to Disraeli, but couldn't imagine doing it under Bevan's cynical eyes. I compromised, telling myself if I hadn't heard from Disraeli by midnight, I'd go to Bevan. On the eve of the state occasion, he'd probably be working through the night. I looked at my watch. Six o'clock already.

Back at the stables, Amos said he'd left Ricci asleep in the hayloft, with strict instructions to the head groom that he wasn't to be allowed out of the yard. He still wasn't sure whether he believed Ricci, so my certainty that Robert really had brought pyroglycerine to London and it was intended for use at the House of Lords left him frankly disbelieving. I was almost glad of that, knowing he'd have wanted to go to Bevan at once. We'd had no chance until then to discuss our visit to the Compass. For once, he was too interested in what we'd found there to be angry that we'd gone without him.

'And the police found nothing?'

'Went away empty-handed,' Tabby said.

'I reckon Mr Carmichael's still there. They must have managed to hide him from the police somehow.'

'I'm not sure,' I said. 'The people on the sloop weren't the ringleaders. Somebody else was giving them orders. Robert's probably been taken somewhere else.' I couldn't let into my mind the probability that he was not even alive, that they'd killed him as soon as he'd delivered the explosive.

'In any case, we need to get in there and make sure,' Amos said. 'I'll collect a couple of friends of mine and break the door down if they won't let us in any other way.'

'No. For all we know, they could have the explosive in there.'

'So what, then?'

'I think Minerva would come out if she saw me,' I said. 'She must hate me for getting away from her. If I were to just walk up to the front door and knock . . .'

'No,' Amos said.

'Then we could get in at the back. Not a bad idea,' Tabby said.

'So Tabby and I will try it,' I said to Amos. 'We'll let you know how it goes.'

He argued more than he'd ever argued with me about anything, but when he saw that Tabby and I were determined he gave in, as I knew he would. It was after eight before we left the stables. We must have looked an odd trio walking down Sloane Street, Amos striding along in his riding boots beside me, still arguing, Tabby in her grey dress and urchin boots stomping behind us. I managed to distract him for some time by asking him about the arrangements for the ceremony the next day, which he knew in detail, as he did anything involving carriages.

'Twelve o'clock, they open the doors for ticket holders. There'll be carriages queuing up all the way along Whitehall. Ambassadors and what have you to be in position by one o'clock and MPs waiting in their chamber. The Queen leaves Buckingham Palace at twenty minutes to two.

There are five state carriages for the royal house-hold. The police will have cleared the streets by then so it shouldn't take them more than ten minutes to get to Parliament. Police all over the place, there'll be – no chance for anybody to do anything.'

I didn't try to convince him, saving my breath for when we got to the Compass.

At this time of the day, the many public houses we'd passed were doing a lively trade, but when we looked down the street at the Compass, it was as blank and closed as ever. We were standing at some distance from it, because although Tabby and I had seen no sign in the morning that anybody was keeping watch, we were more cautious now. Tabby, as usual, was looking for alleys and back entrances. She calculated that from where we were standing it would be possible to do a right angle and come out at the back entrance to the Compass. She suggested that she and Amos should wait in the yard while I went to the front door, but Amos wasn't having it. He insisted that they'd be closer to the street and the front entrance, by the side wall, no more than a dozen steps away from where I'd be. There was more risk that they'd be spotted but less chance that I'd be dragged inside before I could do anything. I agreed with him. Now we'd come to it, I was sweating with fear at the prospect of seeing Minerva again. Only the faint chance that Robert might be inside kept me to what we'd decided. It was harder because Amos was so very much against it. He'd still have preferred to shoulder charge the front door until it gave way, and I knew he'd try it if there was the slightest hitch. Tabby said I should give them ten minutes to get in position, and it was one of the longest ten minutes of my life. I waited round a corner, just out of sight of the Compass. At ten minutes exactly by the little round watch I keep in my pocket, I turned the corner and started walking down the street, quite slowly, with my bonnet pushed back to show my face clearly. I couldn't see if anybody was watching from a front window, but I imagined Minerva's jutting forehead pressed against the pane and her greedy, birdlike eyes on me. A few dozen yards from the Compass, I stepped to the edge of the pavement to give anybody inside a good view. The downstairs windows were still closely curtained. The upstairs ones, on either side of the Compass sign, looked blank. At the corner of the building by the entrance to the alley, I glimpsed the sleeve of a tweed jacket and hoped nobody else had. Amos was taking no chances. I turned and walked to the front door. There was no knocker on the faded brown wood, so I rapped hard with my knuckles and waited. No sound came from inside. I rapped again, harder and longer. Nothing. I waited several minutes, then Amos came to join me.

'Thought it wouldn't work. Stand back and . . .'

A piercing whistle came from the yard at the back. Tabby. We both rushed round, Amos in the lead, sure that she'd been set on, and found her standing by the open back door.

'Wasn't even bolted. Doesn't sound as if there's anybody in there.'

Amos, cheated of a chance to try brute strength,

insisted on going first. We followed him in through a scullery and cramped kitchen to the bar parlour. It was untidy, with chairs pushed back from tables and empty bottles on the counter, more than half dark with the curtains drawn. A door led to a passageway behind the closed front door with a small room on the other side that might have been intended as a snug but now looked as if it had served as a bedroom, with a dirty pallet on the floor, a table and chairs pushed back against the wall and plaster crumbling. Like the parlour, it was empty, but there was a smell to it – a human smell of piss and sweat that suggested it had recently been occupied. Stairs went up from the end of the passageway. Amos told us to stay downstairs and went up.

'Nobody.' His voice came down so we followed him. There were three rooms upstairs – two bedrooms and one storeroom with empty crates and boxes in it. The two bedrooms each had a pallet like the downstairs room. One of them, I was sure from the smell, had been a woman's. It's hard to describe why, but there is a difference, a sort of yeastiness under the sweat. Like the downstairs room, both felt and smelled as if they'd been occupied recently.

'Cleared out,' Tabby said. 'I suppose they would after the police came round. She was probably packing up when we were here this morning.'

If so, somebody would have seen them go. The rest of the street seemed respectable enough, though not prosperous, so people might talk to us, but first we had to find out anything we could from the Compass. I didn't trust the police to do the careful search we'd do, especially if they'd had Minerva nagging at them. We went back downstairs and drew back the curtains, letting the sunlight in. The parlour was as unpromising as it had looked at first glance, with nothing in it that didn't belong in a down-at-heel public house. The kitchen, it seemed, had been used recently. A saucepan on the small range had the dried-up remains of porridge in it, and the sight of it nearly made me sick. It looked much like what I'd been served on the sloop, but porridge is porridge, after all. The iron of the range was just warm to the touch but the fire would have stayed in for some time. In the corner of the scullery was a kind of nest, an old blanket and a bundle of rags that might have been a pillow. I supposed the boy would have slept there. So if we assumed that Minerva and the poet had a room each upstairs, that meant another person had slept in the downstairs snug. For some reason, I felt drawn to it, as if it could tell us something, although there was precious little to see. The pallet had a cover of striped ticking and was lumpy and stained. No pillow, no blanket. From the stains, many people had used it for many years, none of them fussy. A sprinkling of plaster dust had fallen on the edge nearest the wall and looked fresh. I stared at it for a while, thinking it odd but no more than that. Then my eyes went up to the wall and I saw why it had fallen. Two initials were scratched into the plaster, very plain and clear – an R and a C. I must have made some sort of sound because Tabby came in, asking what was up. She didn't share my certainty, but then writing never meant anything to her. The scratches were too deep for a fingernail to have made them. I turned up the edge of the pallet where it touched the wall and felt along it.

'What's this, then?' A signet ring with a square face, engraved with a sea nymph. Robert had bought it in Greece and wore it on the little finger of his left hand. It was quite tight and wouldn't come off easily. He'd left it there deliberately, believing that his note would get to Amos, believing that he and Tabby could come and search. I slipped it on my finger in place of my wedding ring and went to tell Amos. But it was all we found of Robert in the place, though we spent a long time looking in and behind everything, from the cellars to the attic where Tabby stamped above our heads, hopping from beam to beam. Minerva and the boy and everybody who'd ever been there had moved out with no sign of where they'd gone.

Tabby went out to the street to make enquiries and came back with the news that a covered cart had arrived while we'd been away and the woman and a boy had got into it – nobody with them and carrying nothing. Her informants hadn't taken any particular notice of the driver and, beyond the fact that it had gone off in the direction of the river, had no further information. The local feeling was that she'd been up to no good somehow and the police raid had made things too hot for her, but that was only guesswork, and nobody was interested enough in the Compass or its occupants to be curious. On the way out, I looked more closely at the bundled-up rags the boy had used as a pillow and noticed a few more scraps of red leather among them. Hoping that might at least prove a connection between the Compass and the House of Lords, I bundled the whole lot up to take with us. Tabby insisted on carrying it.

It was dark by the time we got back to Abel Yard, and there was no message from Disraeli's butler. Amos decided to go back to the stables to make sure that Ricci was safe. He supposed the man would be near demented because we hadn't found Robert or the explosive, but he'd have to put up with it. I walked round the corner and confirmed that Mr Disraeli was still away from home. He wasn't thought to be at the House of Commons and had probably dined privately with friends. By then, there were only fourteen hours to go before the doors of the House of Lords opened to a throng of ticket holders. I couldn't put it off any longer; I had to tell Sergeant Bevan the whole story. Tabby went with me most of the way, but I wasn't worried any more about my own safety because the worst was happening. All round me, by contrast, the west end of London was at its brightest at the end of a long summer evening. Most of the people in the great mansions and houses I passed would be attending the prorogation ceremony in the morning – robes, dresses and jewels already being laid out by valets and maids in the brightly lit upper floors while their owners drank coffee under the chandeliers gleaming from sitting rooms. Hundreds of grooms and coachmen in the mews at the back would be giving a final polish

261

to harness buckles and a last check to carriage horses already sleek under their rugs but due an extra grooming in the morning. Then, with the prorogation over, the MPs would have to scatter to their task of getting elected again while the luckier aristocrats had not long to go to the start of the grouse shooting season. None of them had the slightest suspicion of what I knew.

Bevan wasn't at his usual station and the duty constable there thought he'd be at Bow Street, so we had a long walk on past Covent Garden. The usual comments were called out to us that women on their own attract, but I was past caring. Tabby waited outside the police station. Inside, it was busy with drunk men, sullen women and lost dogs. A fight broke out between two men while I was waiting and they had to be pulled apart by constables. It was getting on for midnight by then. I'd told the duty officer that I needed to speak to Sergeant Bevan urgently on a matter of importance, but here everything and nothing was urgent. Most of another hour passed before a weary constable led me along a corridor to a small room with a door that looked as if somebody had kicked it several times. From the sound of drunk singing and cursing, it wasn't far from the police holding cells. Sergeant Bevan got to his feet when he saw me but took his time about it. He was in uniform, but it had a creased look and his complexion looked pale in the lamplight. The other man in the room was already standing. He was fiftyish, and dressed in civilian clothes. He had the look of a civil servant rather than a police officer. Sergeant Bevan didn't introduce him. We sat down. I was disconcerted by the presence of another man and felt like saying that this was for Bevan's ears only, but that would have been useless because it had gone beyond that. Keeping as calm as I could, and looking at him, not the other man, I told him almost everything – Robert's journey and return, Ricci, the pyroglycerine and my belief that it would be used when the Queen went to Parliament in the morning. Once, the other man coughed – a dry, disbelieving sound. At the end of it, neither of them said anything. The men in the holding cells had been joined by a tenor, drunk but still holding the note, and surprisingly tuneful.

'And where is Mr Carmichael now?' Bevan asked. I couldn't tell from his voice what he thought of the story.

'I don't know. In their hands – if he's still alive.' I sounded calm when I said it, like I was listening to somebody else entirely.

'In whose hands?'

'Whoever is planning this. All I know is that some of them are working at the Parliament building.'

From behind me, the other man spoke. His voice was smooth and precise. You could imagine him discussing Roman poets over port at an Oxford college. 'Do we know of pyroglycerine, Sergeant?'

'No, sir. But then, from Mrs Carmichael's account, it was developed overseas and very recently.'

'Along with the submarine flame-thrower, the rabid lapdog and the clockwork pineapple,' the man said. I turned to him, surprised. He smiled, almost friendly. 'Just three of the various ingenious ways intended to assassinate our sovereign. None of them, as it happens, with any existence outside the fevered imaginations of the people who reported them to the authorities. They all firmly believed in them.' I stared at him then back at Sergeant Bevan.

'Mrs Carmichael has a rather different record, sir,' Bevan said. I had the impression that he was taking a risk in contradicting this man. 'You may know of her by her maiden name, Liberty Lane.'

The other man nodded, but with an expression on his face that suggested he didn't much like what he knew about Liberty Lane. In my career, I'd done several things that were of great help to the authorities, but not always by methods they approved. 'So, we have a plot of which we don't know the nature, devised by men of whose identities we are ignorant, using an explosive substance of which even the Metropolitan Police are unaware. As it happens, this is not the first of Mrs Carmichael's ventures into explosives – purely by report, I hasten to add. Would I be right in thinking that you had a recent conversation on the subject with Mr Disraeli?' Then, seeing from my face that he'd hit it: 'Don't be concerned. Mr Disraeli never mentioned the name of his informant, but he has been known to associate with Liberty Lane, as we may call you for professional purposes.'

Bevan was looking puzzled. The man turned to him. 'You're aware of the Millbank escape attempt, of course, Sergeant? So, it seems, was Liberty Lane, only she believed it would be accomplished with an explosion, which was never the plan. I wonder what the reason is for this obsession with explosive substances?'

I realized there was no use trying to explain how we'd misunderstood. 'There's a man in London who can confirm what I've told you about the pyroglycerine,' I said. 'I could have him brought to you within an hour.'

Ricci would be only too glad to tell anyone about it. I think Bevan on his own would have taken me up on the offer, but the other man got in first. 'So often, these exaggerated ideas of assassination come from abroad. There may indeed be countries where men are planning to assassinate rulers they see as tyrants, but that is simply not the case here. We have a greatly loved young queen and a sound democracy. Such attempts as there have been against her life have been the feeble manifestations of lonely madmen, easily foiled. I believe you mean well, Mrs Carmichael, and I can only hope that whatever domestic difficulties have led to your current behaviour will be satisfactorily resolved.'

I couldn't understand what he meant. Then, slowly, it dawned on me that he thought Robert had left me and this was all some deranged attempt to get him back. The surprise of that made my protest less effective than it might have been. 'It isn't that. For goodness' sake, there is real danger tomorrow . . .'

It wouldn't have worked in any case. The man – I never knew his name – stood up and nodded to Sergeant Bevan. 'See that Mrs Carmichael is sent home in a cab.'

Bevan went down the corridor with me to the general office – not a long enough corridor to win an argument, though I did my best. He handed me over to the tired constable with instructions to call a cab which, this being Bow Street, arrived smartly at first whistle but not before Tabby, who arrived from nowhere and slid in beside me. Two o'clock struck raggedly from various clocks on the way back to Abel Yard. Amos was waiting in the parlour and he'd brought Ricci with him, who bounded to his feet as I came through the door, his eyes still sunken from tiredness but feverishly bright. I just shook my head. I'd have to explain to them somehow that the police weren't going to do anything, but now I just couldn't find the words.

Twenty-Three

They were in a sloop anchored in the Thames, somewhere off Chiswick. The small room was crowded – Robert, Pot-belly, New-boots and the woman. The messenger had been left on the river bank. A boy was there too, but he took up scarcely any room, curled in a corner. There were only two chairs. The woman planted herself in one of them and Pot-belly took the other, leaving Robert and New-boots squatting on the floor. Only a little daylight came through the porthole. A brown bottle stood on a rough table with a circle of cloudy glasses round it, and the smell of whisky filled the warm, overbreathed air. Pot-belly stood up and filled four glasses.

'To craftsmen.'

But the toast seemed to be directed to the other object on the table – a wooden lion much more finely carved than the one that had been destroyed in the explosion, varnished so that the golden colour of the oak shone. Robert said nothing and drank about half an inch of the whisky. It was raw stuff, burning into a stomach that had had no food in it for some time. He coughed.

'Is it getting to you?' Pot-belly said, sounding almost sympathetic.

Robert nodded.

'We let the scarf go off in the carriage by mistake so you'll have to do without it. There's probably a dish-clout somewhere.' He looked at the woman, who said nothing.

'When are we doing it?'

'Now. Just like last time, only whatever you do, don't light the slow match yet. We'll see to that later. We've put the stuff in the hold so you can do it in there. You pour it into the bottle like the last time and put it in our friend here.' He patted the lion on the head. 'Pity it's got to go. There's some nice workmanship in that.' He sounded genuinely regretful.

'When do I see Liberty?' It had become an incantation, although he didn't expect to see her again.

'You will afterwards, don't worry.' Pot-belly patted Robert's arm. It was as reassuring as the slap on a cow's rump by an assistant in an abattoir.

Soon after that, Pot-belly took him back down to the hold, carrying a lamp that he lodged at a safe distance in the corner. Robert carried the lion. It was surprisingly heavy. The light of the lamp played on it, casting a shadow of its snarling head on the wall of the hold. The box and an empty bottle were standing in the middle of the floor.

'Just like last time,' Pot-belly repeated. Any offer of a dish-clout seemed to have been forgotten.

'The fumes will be worse than out in the open,' Robert said.

He watched the indecision on Pot-belly's face and the slow victory of caution.

'I'll wait just outside the door,' Pot-belly said. 'Give a tap on it when you're finished.'

On his own, Robert moved slowly and carefully. He took the full bottle of liquid out of the carrying case, poured it very carefully into the other glass bottle then placed it inside the lion. He tapped on the door. Pot-belly opened it and came one step inside.

'Are you done?'

Robert nodded.

'Leave it there for the while. You can pick it up when the rowing boat comes.' He moved a step closer, looked at the lion and then the empty bottle. 'Be enough, will it?'

'You saw what happened last time.'

Pot-belly nodded. 'Wonderful stuff. You wouldn't think that much would do any harm, would you? Still, we saw what we saw.'

He picked up the lantern and led the way back to the living quarters. New-boots had poured himself another glass of whisky but the woman sat as upright as a statue, with her nearly full glass beside her. Robert sat down again on the floor with his back against the timbers that divided the living quarters from the hold, and let himself drift into a sleep. He woke to find that the other two men had gone, and heard noises from the deck. They must have pulled up the anchor because the sloop was moving slowly downriver. The woman was watching him.

'You saw her, didn't you?' he said. 'You saw Liberty.'

He didn't know why, but something in those cold eyes made him shiver as if a memory had come back to him, only it was somehow Liberty's memory, not his own. He felt that his mind was slipping away and he had to hold on to it. The woman didn't move or speak. Soon afterwards, Pot-belly came down from the deck. They were moving more rapidly now – either the pull of the tide was stronger or they'd managed to hoist a sail. Pot-belly sat in the vacant chair, looking down at Robert with an expression that might almost have been taken for kindness. Robert's exposure to the danger of the explosive seemed to have given him more status in Pot-belly's view, or perhaps he was simply the sacrificial animal. The man seemed both tired and keyed-up.

'Feeling bad?' he said.

Robert nodded.

'Not long now. We'll be anchoring again before long, then here's what happens. The rowing boat will come and we'll get into it. You'll be carrying the lion. On shore, we'll be met by someone. We stay with that person and do what he says – exactly what he says. If you make any attempt to talk to anybody, you know what will happen to her. You do know, don't you? Say it.'

'I know what will happen to her.' He could say it calmly.

'Good. Just maybe there'll be something out of it for you afterwards. Plenty for everybody – diamonds by the sackful like dried peas. You're making history, you should be proud. This is the biggest thing of its kind, ever. Biggest ever.'

His voice washed over Robert. Not long afterwards, Pot-belly went up on deck again, and the anchor must have gone down because the sloop was almost stationary, only shifting as the tide pulled at it. Not long afterwards, something bumped against the side and Pot-belly came back down to the cabin.

'Boat's here. Go and get it.'

He stood at the door to the hold while Robert went in and carefully picked up the lion. Pot-belly ushered him out on to the deck, and the morning light hit him so that he had to screw up his eyes. He opened them and saw on the north bank of the river, quite close, huge wooden stakes and platforms, a whole system of wharves. Behind them was a new grey tower, not completely built. Even as he watched, a Union Jack broke out on it, then another.

'Parliament,' he said. 'That's Parliament.'

Pot-belly gestured downwards towards the rowing boat. Robert clutched the lion to his chest with his left hand and arm, and used his right hand to let himself down the rope ladder and into the boat. Pot-belly and New-boots gave him plenty of time to settle before following him down, then sat as far from him as the small space in the rowing boat would allow. Pot-belly's face was glazed with sweat. The rower pushed off with an oar and turned towards the wharves.

Twenty-Four

Three o'clock in the morning. The four of us were in the parlour at Abel Yard, the fire unlit but two lamps burning, sending shadows shifting over the walls. Ricci was mostly pacing up and down, so his shadow was constantly shifting in shape and size, rearing up in the corner so that his thin body looked temporarily bearlike, looming over us. At first, he kept saying the same thing, over and over, that it was everything that Professor Sobrero had feared. And worse – the Queen would be killed and we'd all be hanged as accomplices, until Amos told him sharply to stop. After that, he went on pacing, twisting his hands together so violently that it looked as if he was trying to break his own fingers. Amos was sitting at the table, stubbornly working through what he knew about the cere-mony. Inevitably, his mind was fixed on what he understood best – the carriage procession from Buckingham Palace to the Houses of Parliament.

'It won't take them much more than ten minutes with the roads cleared for them. They could throw it in from the crowd anywhere – just throwing would do it from what Mr Ricci says – but if they want to be sure of killing her I reckon the most likely time is when she's getting out of the carriage at Parliament. The man who threw it would be grabbed on the spot, but it would be too late then.'

I went on saying what I'd said from the start – that whatever was going to happen would happen inside Parliament. We knew that craftsmen from the building team were involved and they'd have access anywhere. What their motive was for the assassination, I didn't know. The expense and complexity of the operation suggested a lot of money – possibly from abroad – but that was irrelevant now and all that mattered was trying to stop it. As soon as I got back from Bow Street I'd tried again to see Mr Disraeli, but the house was in darkness and knocking on the door produced no result. The first servants would be waking up in an hour or so and I'd try again then – force my way into his bedroom if necessary – but at that point the ceremony would be only hours away and Disraeli himself might not be able to get people to listen in time. There was just one other source of help I could think of – although it was clutching at straws – and that was Mr James. A leading foreman would have no powers at all over a state occasion, but at least he knew the parliamentary site. If I went to him and told him everything I knew, just possibly he'd be able to pass some warning up the chain of command. It was a faint hope, but then so was everything else.

Tabby was hunched on the rug by the cold fireplace, out of the way of Ricci's pacing feet. She looked up and caught my eye.

'That's why they killed the Maynard girl – because she knew about it?'

'I'm sure so, yes. Her half-brother might not have told her everything but he'd said enough to worry her. She was trying to get him away from whatever was happening and I think he wanted to get away. I wondered when I was talking to her friend why Felicity should have been so careful to keep the lion's feet carving safe. I think Jonah Cave had given it to her as evidence of some kind.'

The more I thought about it, the more it pointed to the House of Lords. It was true that all the buildings of the new Parliament were or would be crusted with woodcarving, but I'd been told more than once that by far the densest and most elaborate carving would be in the Lords, particularly around the throne. Suppose that Cave was part of a gang preparing a secret chamber that would go unnoticed among the rest of the elaboration, enough to contain a small but very effective amount of pyroglycerine? It was half in my mind to go and get the carving, but events were moving too fast.

'Once he knew Felicity was dead, it made up his mind for him,' I said. 'I think he told the people in the plot that he wanted no more to do with it, so they killed him.'

'Who? Your friend, Minerva?'

'I think she'd be quite capable of it. But there's somebody else giving them orders and we don't know who.'

Amos looked up from the table. 'You don't believe it's going to happen in the procession, do you?'

'I don't. Jonah Cave and almost certainly

274

Minerva were workers inside the site. That's not just a coincidence.'

'In that case, they couldn't have got it inside by now – just walked in with it.'

'Why not? There are materials going in and out all the time.' My thoughts went to the stone wharves at the back of the building site. A sloop putting in there would be unlikely to attract attention. They'd be taking a risk in using the boat again, but then audacity had been their style throughout. The explosive might be in place already, among the gilding and carving of the Lords' chamber, and the police wouldn't look because I was hysterical, vengeful against my husband, obsessed with explosives. It made me mad to think about it.

Tabby had something beside her on the rug and was running her fingers through it. At first, I thought she was stroking the cat, but it was only the bundle of rags we'd brought with us from the Compass that the boy had been using as a pillow. She'd sorted out some more thin slivers of red leather, like the ones we'd found in the yard. Along with them were the remains of an old moleskin waistcoat, pieces of faded chintz and oily rags. I turned them over, wondering without much hope if there might be something of Robert's there. Nothing. The lamplight caught a piece of soiled velvet in a colour I recognized. It was a panel of the dress I'd worn on the evening I'd been kidnapped. I picked it up then stared at something small and bright underneath it. My hand touched something stiffer, more resistant than the rags. When I picked it up, I was holding a rectangular pouch. It wasn't as dirty as the other things in the bundle; the colours were still fresh. Thickly clustered embroidery of rosebuds and forget-me-nots, the sort of thing a girl with too much time on her hands might work on to create a tobacco pouch for a young man who probably wouldn't appreciate it. I must have said something, or at least made a sound, because they were all looking at me. Even Ricci had stopped his pacing.

'It's the one I gave Mr James.'

Tabby knew at once what I was talking about, but I had to explain to Amos.

'So what was it doing there?' he said.

I'd thought my mind was as dark as it could be, but now a deeper blackness came over it and I pictured the good, painstaking man. Mr James had saved my life and I'd repaid him by having him murdered. He'd seemed not to be very interested in what I'd said to him, but he must have started making his own investigations and they'd led him to the Compass. The gang there would have made sure he never walked out of it. At some point, the pouch had fallen out of his pocket and the boy had gathered it up. I explained this to Amos as best I could and he said it wasn't my fault, though I knew it was. He'd never known Mr James. I thought of the man running his fingers over the carving, his quiet pleasure in his work. He'd have hated the idea that anybody in his team was planning destruction. My plan that I might go to Mr James and get him to do something was destroyed. Surely he'd have been missed at his workplace. I wondered if he'd been reported missing and if the police were looking for him. If so, that might be a way of getting the police to investigate what had happened at the Compass, only there was no time for such an indirect way.

As my mind cleared enough to start thinking again, I decided that, in spite of the loss of Mr James, Tabby and I should still go to the building site, because everything so far had centred on it. Amos, meanwhile, had a decision to make, with two of his carriages ordered for minor lordly families who'd be attending the prorogation ceremony. In a couple of hours, he should be in his stable yard helping to prepare them. Did he cancel the bookings and explain to enraged clients that he feared something was going to happen, or let them go ahead with no warning of possible danger? It seemed a small thing compared to what we were facing, but letting down two influential clients on such an important day could finish his business. In the end, he decided to let them go ahead, on the grounds that the clients were not important enough to be anywhere near the Queen's large party so would escape whatever was going to happen, if it did. I thought that in his heart Amos did not entirely believe that the attempt would happen, but was too loyal to say so. When it became clear that Tabby and I were determined to go to the parliamentary site, he said he'd meet us at the gates there at nine o'clock and we'd compare notes. He left as soon as it got light.

Soon after he left, I judged that servants would be stirring in the Disraeli household. I decided to take Ricci with me because he'd be more eloquent than I could be on the subject of pyroglycerine. He looked a pretty wild object, still in his creased and stained travelling clothes, his face white and drawn, and I don't suppose I was very much better, though I combed my hair and slammed on a bonnet. I took us round to the tradesmen's door, knowing nobody would answer the front door so early, and banged on it until it was opened by the boot boy with a patent leather shoe in one hand, looking angry and scared. He looked even more scared when I told him it was imperative that I should speak to Mr Disraeli at once and he should wake up the butler or housekeeper. He stood there stuttering protests, then tried to shut the door. I leaned my shoulder against it. He was only a small lad and went flying backwards. Ricci picked him up from the floor while I followed him in and shut the door behind us, keeping my back to it. The boy looked up at Ricci, who was still holding him, and let out a yell that brought a maid running, probably from the kitchen regions. She wasn't much older than the boot boy and her eyes were still bleary with sleep. There were ash smears on her skirt and a smear of blacking on her cheek. I repeated to her my need to speak to Mr Disraeli, and the demand that she should wake the housekeeper. Showing some spirit, she said she'd call the police. I kept my back against the door. I heard a sudden yell from Ricci and curses in Italian. The boot boy had bitten him on the wrist and made a break for it, along the corridor and presumably back to the scullery. Ricci ran after him, goodness knows

278

why, and must have fallen over something, because there was a noise of crashing metal and another yell. The maid opened her mouth and let out a scream that could probably be heard on the far side of Park Lane, then another. I let her scream because the noise was doing what I wanted. Doors opened two floors up, and a woman's voice called down asking what was happening.

'Thieves!' the maid screamed.

Several pairs of feet came padding down the back stairs. A man in a shirt, breeches and bare feet appeared from along the corridor, followed closely by a young woman in corset and petticoats, her hair loose. They closed on me.

'There's one of them in the kitchen,' the first maid gasped. The man ran in that direction and the maid in petticoats grabbed hold of my arm. I tried to tell her that it was all right, that I only wanted to speak to her master, but she clung like a burr and I didn't struggle. She was still clinging to me when the housekeeper arrived, in dressing gown and slippers, but with her air of authority firmly in place. I'd seen her on a few visits to the house.

'I'm Liberty Lane.' It only occurred to me afterwards how the old name came back to me in anything like a fight. 'We've met. I've dined here.' I pushed my bonnet back with my free hand to let her see my face. It obviously was not reassuring. 'I need to speak to Mr Disraeli most urgently.'

'Mr Disraeli is going to be very occupied today. He is not receiving visitors.' Then, in a less formal voice, 'Besides, it's five o'clock in the morning.'

Trying to keep my voice calm, I said it didn't matter what the time was – he needed to hear what I had to tell him at once. Then a woman's voice sounded from the next floor.

'What is it? What's going on?'

It was Disraeli's wife, Mary Anne. For some reason, she'd never liked me.

'It's a Liberty Lane, ma'am. I'm attempting to explain to her that she can't see Mr Disraeli.'

I called up desperately, 'Please, please ask him to see me. It's a matter of national emergency.'

'We have those all the time. Now go away and . . .' She broke off. From what I knew of Mary Anne, there was only one person in the world who could stop her talking, and my hopes rose. He couldn't have failed to hear the noise from downstairs. For a minute, there was silence, then Mary Anne's voice again, telling the house-keeper to come up and see her. The housekeeper glanced down ruefully at her slippers and dressing gown and went, leaving the maid still clinging to my arm. Ricci came back from the kitchen area, his whole face a question mark, with a cut over his left eye. Soon after that, an apparition appeared.

I doubt if Disraeli had ever visited the servants' area of his house before. He, too, was wearing a dressing gown and slippers, but he looked as glamorous and exotic as a genie in a pantomime, the gown in what seemed to be red-and-gold antique damask, the slippers red velvet, embroidered with crests. His black hair was in fine disorder and his cheeks unshaven, dark stubble contributing to the severity of his frown.

'Mrs Carmichael, is there a reason for this disturbance?'

'The best of reasons. Something's going to happen today, in a few hours. Please listen to us.'

He glanced at Ricci. I introduced him, adding simply that he was a student of chemistry from Turin. Disraeli stared at him, then at me, and made up his mind, still frowning. 'Come with me.'

He led the way through the servants' door into the hallway, then to a small salon. It was dim, with the blinds still down over the windows and yesterday's roses shedding petals on the carpet. Without waiting to sit down, I told him everything, up to and including my belief that a foreman from the parliamentary site had also been murdered. Ricci described the theft of the pyroglycerine and his pursuit of it as effectively as he'd told it to me. Disraeli turned from him to me.

'And it was your husband that brought it to this country?'

'Yes.'

'So where is he now?'

'In their hands – if he's still alive.' It was the first time I'd said it out loud.

'And the police wouldn't listen to you?'

'They listened, but they won't do anything. There was a gentleman there from the Home Office, I think. He didn't believe me.'

He walked to the window, tweaked at the side of one of the blinds and looked out. 'If you're right – if there's even a strong possibility that you are right – then the sensible thing would be to call off today's whole event and let it be known that Her Majesty has taken a chill.'

'Yes.' My heart pounded at the size of the decision, but mostly from relief.

'But that won't happen. I can tell you that in advance. The Queen is – well, if it were any other lady, I might say stubborn, but let's say resolute. She totally refuses to believe that any of her subjects wishes to harm her. If all her ministers and MPs were to inform her that there was likely to be an assassin with the most powerful explosive in the world somewhere along the route or in the chamber and beg her not to attend, she'd insist on going ahead as planned. That's a fact of the case, and there's nothing I or anybody else in the kingdom can do about it.'

'You could at least get them to search the Lords' chamber and put a guard on the wharves where they bring in the stone.'

'I'll do what I can, but if the Home Office refuses to believe you, that's a big weight against which to push. What did this gentleman in the police station look like?'

I described the man and he nodded. 'Yes, I know him. He's in the Home Office and pretty senior.' Disraeli was usually so certain of his own powers that it was unsettling to see him so nearly at a loss. He repeated that he'd do what he could and would personally check the Lords' chamber before it was opened to ticket holders at midday, but the place was so complex with all its carvings and Gothic ornaments that I knew it would take a large company of men to search it properly. He asked what I intended to do.

'Get into the building site, at least. I want to

282

know if anybody has missed Mr James and done anything about it.'

In case it would be more difficult to get inside the site on a day of such ceremonial activities, I asked him to write me a pass, for myself and two companions. Something had to be done with Ricci, so we might as well take him with us. Disraeli went upstairs for a pen and paper, and soon came down with a few lines in his authoritative handwriting. He warned me that it wouldn't get us into the Lords for the ceremony. Duchesses had been battling for tickets for months past. It was enough, I said. It wasn't anywhere near enough, but it was all I would get.

Twenty-Five

It was half past six by the time Ricci and I left Disraeli's house, by the back door again. Tabby was waiting outside for us.

'Can he do anything?'

'Not much.'

But then, she'd never expected anything. Mayfair already had an atmosphere to it that suggested something special about the day – more carriages on the streets, more servants out on the pavement. This was the last big event of the season and, in the tall houses alongside the park, the powerful and the wealthy would soon be stirring, sipping coffee and getting ready for a long day in velvet and jewels or decorations and knee breeches. I had to resist the temptation to shout that they should stay in their beds and be safe, but getting arrested as a lunatic wouldn't make matters any better, though I didn't see how they could be much worse. At the bottom of Park Lane, I took us through Green Park to Buckingham Palace. Somewhere inside that slabby stone building, little Vicky was probably awake already. We could hear horses stamping and carriage wheels grinding from inside the mews. We turned across the front of the palace and along Pall Mall, following the route the Queen's procession would take. Already, people were beginning to gather, and more police constables than usual were patrolling. We went across the empty expanse of Trafalgar Square with Nelson marooned high on his new column, desperately far from any sight of the sea, and down Whitehall with flags out on the buildings to Parliament Square. It was past seven o'clock now and more crowds were gathering. Food and drink sellers were circulating with barrows and there were even a few early-rising pickpockets. I saw Tabby signalling discreetly to a couple of them, probably warning them to let us alone. The two unfinished towers on the parliamentary site had flags flying from the scaffolding. I used Disraeli's pass at the main gates because two police constables were on duty, but I think they might have let us in anyway. They seemed quite relaxed and unworried. Even if Disraeli did manage to stir somebody to action, it was too early to have any effect yet. At this end of the site, we were nearer the incomplete Commons chamber and the clock tower than the Lords, and the working day seemed to be starting more or less normally. We made straight for the stone wharves, getting a few curious glances along the way, but nobody tried to stop us. The wharves stood empty – there were no sloops in and only a rowing boat tied up to one of the vertical timbers. Nobody was on guard. The nearest workmen were several hundred yards away and had their backs to us. The river was busy with sailing barges and steamers, none of them making for the stone wharves. Three boats were anchored out from the bank on our side of the river – one quite large and two that seemed to resemble slightly the one where I was imprisoned, but I hadn't taken enough note of it to be sure. Nobody was visible on any of them.

'They've probably already landed it,' I said. It would have made sense to do it by darkness. Tabby and Ricci were looking at me, waiting for directions. I said they should stay at the wharves, watch out for anybody landing and take whatever steps they thought necessary to stop them. I'd go to the woodcarvers' area and try to find anybody who knew about Mr James. When I got there, the huts were deserted. Either it was too early for the woodcarvers to come on duty or they were all at the Vauxhall Bridge workshops. I tried to remember the name of the man who'd helped Mr James pull me out of the river. Evans. I had no idea where he worked on the site. I went back to a busier area and asked some men sifting sand. It seemed that there were even more Evanses on the site than Jameses, and unless I knew his department they couldn't help.

'Welsh and religious,' I said, almost despairing.

Their faces cleared. 'You'll need to ask the Sackbuts. They're chapel, and if he's Welsh he's bound to be.'

The Sackbuts turned out to be scaffolders working on the clock tower. One of them came swinging down a series of ladders and did indeed know a man who sounded like my Mr Evans. He worked in the drawing office and Mr Sackbut escorted me over to it, worried for my safety over uneven ground, clutching at my elbow now and then if he thought I looked like falling. At the drawing office, Mr Evans looked alarmed to see me, but I guessed that was on account of the teasing he knew he'd get from the other men who were bent over their desks, pretending not to look at the rare appearance of a woman. He took me outside to talk to me. When I asked if he'd seen Mr James recently, he shook his head.

'Not since Wednesday. But then, I don't think he comes here every day. He could have been at the Vauxhall Bridge workshops.'

His manner was still tense. I had to remind myself that he knew me only as a failed suicide. It might have been in his mind, too, that I had romantic intentions towards Mr James.

'I'm very much afraid something may have happened to him,' I said. 'Do you know if he has a family?'

I could see that the question confirmed his suspicions. 'If there'd been an accident we'd all have heard. I'm afraid I don't know him well, only to pass the time of day with now and then.'

'You were near the wharves with him.'

'I like looking at the river. Soothing, it is, before a day's hard work. I get in early sometimes, and I suppose he does too. But he struck me as a quiet man, does his job and keeps himself to himself.'

If I'd told him outright that I feared Mr James were dead, I was sure he would only have taken it for more hysteria. It seemed wrong that a man could disappear and nobody miss him. Mr James had done well, discovering the group at the Compass. Too well. Without knowing it, Evans had killed my faint hope that there might be a police search for him going on.

'Did he ever happen to mention to you a

woodcarver named Jonah Cave? I think he may have been looking for him.'

He frowned, trying to remember. 'I don't recall him looking for him. But I do remember seeing them together.'

'When?'

The urgency of my question rattled him. 'Three or four weeks ago, it would have been. I happened to be walking past with one of the inspectors. A group of men had come down from the workshops and were talking to him. I heard one of them being called "Whalebait". It struck me as an unusual name for a man, so I asked one of them and he said it was really Jonah. Walked with a bit of a limp, he did.'

'That's the man. And he was with Mr James? Mr James knew him?'

'Well, he must have, mustn't he? He was there with the rest of them.'

I thought back to my conversation with Mr James. I hadn't given him Cave's name, but the description had been quite good and the limp should have identified him, yet he'd denied knowing him. Or had he quite? I thought back to the conversation. *I'm sorry I can't help you.* Not exactly a denial, but if he'd known the man I was talking about, why not say so?

Mr Evans said he must get back to his desk and was turning to go. Unpromising though it was, I had to try on him the appeal I'd hoped to make to Mr James.

'Mr Evans, I know you'll find it hard to believe, but something serious is happening. I have good reason to think that some people have brought a very powerful explosive into this site and intend to use it at the House of Lords ceremony.'

His look now was frankly scared, but not in the way I wanted. He was scared of me. He shook his head, turned and went at a fast walk back to the safety of the drawing office.

I was still holding Disraeli's note and, in spite of what he said, I hoped it might get me into the Lords' chamber. I picked my way across the site towards a side entrance and found a mass of people – workmen, officials, men in top hats, police officers. Although there were still five hours to go to the ceremony and three before the first of the invited spectators arrived, the building was already a magnet. I wanted to shout a warning to them all, but the reaction of everybody, from Mr Evans to the high official from the Home Office, told me it would be a waste of time. Worse, it would probably lead to me being locked up as a madwoman, even less able to influence events. If only I could get into the chamber. With the memory of the piece of wood carving that Jonah Cave had given to Felicity, I might be able to spot something out of place. It was a faint hope but the only one I had left. I walked up as boldly as I could and presented my pass to the official on the door. He hardly glanced at it before shaking his head.

'Official invitations only, ma'am.'

It was past nine o'clock. I made my way back to the main gates and found Amos and Ricci waiting, but not Tabby. Amos was dressed formally in breeches, waistcoat, brown jacket and best boots, but with a low-crowned hat instead of his usual top hat with the cockade. Half his mind was still on his two carriages that would be collecting their fairly distinguished clients in a few hours, worrying if he'd done the wrong thing by not warning the drivers.

'Where's Tabby?' I said.

Ricci looked apologetic. 'I lost her. We were down at the wharves together and suddenly she wasn't there. I don't know where she went.'

Ricci naturally wouldn't have known about Tabby's almost uncanny ability to melt away. It was in my mind that she might simply have got bored with his company but, more likely, she'd seen somebody to follow. It was worrying, but by now almost every thought in my mind was focused on getting inside the Lords' chamber. Tabby would have to wait because an idea had come to me, desperate but just possible with luck.

'Go back inside and try to find her,' I said to Ricci. 'If she's in any sort of trouble, do whatever you can. Amos, will you come with me as far as Knightsbridge?'

He agreed at once. We watched as Ricci went unwillingly back inside the gates. As we walked across St James's Park, going as fast as we could through the gathering crowds, I told him what I was hoping.

'Will she, do you think?'

'Probably not, but I can't think of any other way.'

We stopped outside the bright new stone facade of Lord Brinkburns' London house and wished each other luck. There seemed to be nothing else to say. He watched as I went up the steps and rang the bell, then turned as the front door opened and walked away towards Hyde Park. The butler didn't recognize me at first in my old clothes, although he'd seen me many times. Perhaps he knew I was supposed to be missing because he stood staring at me, as close as I'd ever seen to a butler at a loss what to do. I asked him in as normal manner as possible if Lady Brinkburn was at home.

'Her . . . Her Ladyship is upstairs, ma'am.'

'Then perhaps you'll kindly show me up to her.'

He asked me to excuse him while he let Her Ladyship know I was here, and I watched him as he made his dignified way up the wide stairs – carefully, not hurrying. It was several minutes before he came down, his face as expressionless as he could manage.

'Her Ladyship will see you, ma'am.'

I followed him upstairs, the carpet soft under my feet. He showed me into Her Ladyship's dressing room and withdrew, closing the door behind him.

'Liberty!' Julia was on her feet, her face incredulous. She was wearing a blue satin dressing gown and velvet slippers, her hair done up in a turban. Behind her, on a dressmaker's dummy, was a blue dress with elaborate embroidery. Her maid was arranging brushes on the dressing table. 'You've been . . . We thought you were . . . Where have you been?'

'It's a long story.' I glanced at the maid.

'Betty, will you leave us, please. I'll ring when I want you.'

Julia and I were friends as well as sisters-in-law. In fact, I liked her better than I liked her husband, Stephen, Lord Brinkburn. But I couldn't tell her everything. For one thing, there wasn't time. For another, I still hesitated to tell the family about Robert. So I described my escape, leaving out the fact that it had been more than a week ago, my belief that an attack on the Queen was planned in the House of Lords and my attempts to get anybody in authority to listen. Luckily, she knew quite a lot about things I'd been involved with in the past and at least didn't look at me as if I'd lost my mind. Understandably, it took some time for her to take in what I was saying.

'Where's Robert?' she said.

'I don't know. The fact is I need to be inside the House of Lords. You're going?' The elaborate dress on the stand would have answered the question in itself. Julia was not extravagant and would only have spent so much for a royal occasion.

She nodded. 'Along with all the rest of the peers' wives. Obligatory.'

'Could I go in your place?'

She considered for a moment. 'Heaven knows, I don't want to go. I've a headache already at the thought of sitting for hours shut up in this heat dressed like a waxwork.' She bent her head, considered some more, then looked up at me. 'All right. I don't know what's happening and I don't suppose you've told me everything. But I trust you, and if you think it's necessary, I'll do it. Only we have to hurry because the carriage is coming round in an hour.'

Her maid, Betty, had to be told, because

apparently the task of changing me from my unwashed and unkempt state into a lady fit for the royal presence was more than Julia and I could handle by ourselves. Betty was totally loyal, she said, and she'd tell her only that her sister-in-law had agreed to take her place because of the headache. In fact, Betty seemed to find the whole thing amusing and treated it like a dressing-up game. She sent down to the kitchen for jugs of hot water and organized things in a bathroom across the corridor that already had piped cold water. The bath she prepared, warm and scented, would have been a luxury at any other time, but now I stayed in it only long enough to get clean, resenting the minutes ticking by. Then I wore Julia's silk underwear, cool against my skin, and Julia's dressing gown. Betty did my hair. There was no time to wash and dry it, but at least that made it easier to put up. In the course of all this, I registered that Julia's husband was already at the House of Lords on some committee business. If he'd been at home, I don't think she'd have dared do it.

Julia and Betty fitted the dress on me. It felt as heavy as armour from the stiff lining and all the embroidery. Since I'm thinner than Julia, it needed taking in and stitching, and Betty was as light-fingered as a fairy at that. The shoes that matched it were too short for me but possible when I scrunched up my toes. Julia and Betty looked at me critically.

'You'll do,' Julia said. 'Now the jewels.'

Carefully, Betty lifted a silk cloth from a cushion on a small table. It was like sun on an

293

ice palace – a cold blaze of light reflected at many angles. On it were a necklace of diamonds, square cut and heavy, with a tear-shaped pendant, two matching bracelets and a tiara.

'We keep them in the bank and I only wear them once in a blue moon,' Julia said. 'But on a day like today, it will be all guns blazing. Most of the jewellery collections in the kingdom will be on show. These will be no more than daisy chains in comparison.'

'I can't wear these.' The dress was bad enough. Carrying Julia's ancestral diamonds into whatever might happen was too much.

'You'll be naked without them.'

'Naked, then. But nobody will be looking at me.' In any case, I hoped not.

'The tiara, at least. Without a tiara, everybody will be looking at you, like it or not.'

So I let them fix it in my hair. At least it was a simple design, as tiaras go. Julia and Betty took one last look at me and were satisfied. Carriage wheels came to a halt below the window.

'Don't worry about the coachman,' Julia said. 'He's so shy he never even looks up at me. I don't suppose he'll notice, and if he does it's no business of his.' As I was going out of the door, she ran after me, put an arm carefully round my shoulders so as not to crush the dress, and kissed me on the cheek. 'I hope . . . Whatever it is, good luck.'

Betty came downstairs with me and saw me into the carriage. If it had been Julia, she'd have travelled to Westminster with her to arrange the dress when she got down, but I didn't need

294

her. Creases in the dress were the least of my worries.

It took an age to get there. The driver chose to go by Piccadilly, probably hoping to avoid even greater hold-ups nearer the palace, but as it was we struck such a press of carriages near the top of Whitehall that we couldn't move for nearly half an hour. It was past midday. If it hadn't been for the dress and shoes, I'd have chosen to get out and walk. As it was, I fretted for every minute that passed and opened the window right down to listen. All I could hear was normal traffic sounds of horses' hooves fidgeting, a harness jingling as a carriage shifted a few inches, and coachmen cursing occasionally in voices more subdued than usual because their employers were on board. At least nothing had happened yet, but then I didn't expect it out here. Even if Amos were right and an attack would be made on the Queen's procession, that was nearly two hours away. I supposed Amos was somewhere there, striding among the mass of carriages, looking for anything out of the way, but I didn't expect to see him. A tortoise could have overtaken us as we crawled down Whitehall and at last rounded the corner into Parliament Square. Crowds were deep on the pavement now, flags waving. At long last, we drew up outside the Victoria Tower and the footman got down from the back to open the door and let down the step. I joined the queue of gentlemen in knee breeches, stockings and decorations, and ladies even more richly dressed than I was. Julia's official invitation was clutched in my hand. The official at the door hardly glanced at it before I was carried in on the slow tide of velvet, ermine and trailing trains, ostrich feathers waving and diamonds flashing, to the huge red-and-gold cavern of the House of Lords.

Twenty-Six

An usher showed me up to my place, or rather Julia's, in the gallery. For the first moment, as I looked down, the sheer magnificence of the place struck me. I'd seen it before, but not like this. Even at midday, the gas lights were blazing, glinting on gilt and bronze everywhere, highlighting the polish on the leather benches. The next thing that struck me was the sheer amount of woodcarving on the thrones, on the canopy over the thrones and a long stretch beside them, the walls, the ends of the benches and the door surrounds. It looked as if a great cavern of stalactites and stalagmites had been transformed to wood. Every inch of it was fretted and carved into swirling shapes, angels, heraldic beasts, shields, foliage. It would take a whole army of people hours to search it properly. With nearly two hours to go to the arrival of the royal party, the benches in the main part of the chamber were already half full, most of them with ladies. Their lordships would generally be arriving later. The dresses, jewels and coiffures were like the grandest of nights at the opera, only more so. The heat must have been in the seventies, and some of the ladies were already red in the face, fanning themselves. Corsets would be tight under those embroidered dresses, and it would be hours before they found any relief. Scents of rose, gardenia and perspiration floated up on the hot air. Being up above it in the gallery was no use for my purposes, so as soon as the usher had gone I went down to the floor of the house. Luckily, quite a few of the ladies were milling round, chatting to acquaintances or admiring the carvings. Some of the uniformed attendants were gathering groups of ladies round them as they explained various details. I was about to attach myself to one of the groups, hoping to ask a question or two, when I recognized one of my former clients. We were on friendly terms, but the last thing I wanted was to be recognized, and there were likely to be quite a few ladies in the assembly who knew me. I backed away and wandered over to the shallow red carpeted steps that led up to the throne for little Vicky. Two attendants stood at the foot of the steps, obviously to discourage anybody from impertinently approaching the throne. I stared as closely as I could at a great gilded coat of arms above it, the carved panels with heraldic symbols alongside it. There were lions there – dozens of them – but mostly in half relief, and none with feet like the carving that Jonah Cave had given Felicity.

'Splendid, isn't it, ma'am?' one of the attendants said, like a zoo keeper exhibiting his beasts.

'Very splendid. I suppose there's been a lot of last-minute work done here to get ready for the opening.'

He shook his head. 'No, ma'am – they've been using the chamber for some time. A few repairs here and there, of course, if things got damaged, but mostly finished in good time.'

'Repairs? Where?'

But he couldn't be exact about it, because he and the other attendant were on loan for the occasion from the temporary committee buildings. I stayed for some time, walking round the bottom of the steps and back again, looking up until swirls of gilt swam and merged in my eyes. Behind me, the chamber was filling rapidly. The front benches, at right angles to the throne, were reserved for the wives of senior peers, and many of those had now taken their seats. When I turned, my already strained eyes were dazzled by a blaze of jewellery such as I'd never seen before in my life. When Julia had said that her own quite considerable diamonds would be only daisy chains in comparison, I hadn't believed her, but she'd been right. Bright rectangles of diamonds, square-cut emeralds, constellations of the bluest sapphires and rubies the size of pigeon eggs gleamed on chests, throats and wrists all along the line, so it seemed that the wearers of them were a defensive force totally armoured in precious stones. All the vaults and safes in London must have been emptied of their contents for these few hours. Some of the wearers of them were looking at me – not in a particularly interested way but as a distraction. It was almost too hot now for the effort of speaking to neighbours, and in any case these senior peeresses, most of them elderly, had probably got through all they wanted to say to each other long since. It was clear that under their disinterested but unswerving stares I'd get no closer to the throne. I was almost certain now that Felicity's piece of carving didn't

299

belong there, but that left thousands of pieces still to search and it was a quarter past one. In three-quarters of an hour, the Queen, notoriously punctual, would have arrived. I asked an attendant which way she'd come in and he said along the royal gallery, coming out at a doorway next to the throne. I checked round the doorway and found nothing like those lion feet. When I turned back to the chamber, I saw a peeress on the end of the second row opposite, who knew me all too well. She'd once employed my services. It had been a complicated case that had turned out very much not to her credit, and she blamed me because I hadn't been prepared to lie for her. Naturally, she hadn't paid me either. She'd recognize me, guess that I wasn't supposed to be there and probably use her quite considerable rank to have me thrown out. I turned so that I had my back to her and squeezed my way along the front benches on the other side, brushing against a dense hedge of silk and velvet skirts, treading on toes only slightly protected by satin shoes. I heard hisses of protest. Perhaps the charitable assumed I'd been overcome by the heat. I was past caring. The end of the row was blocked by about half-a-dozen younger ladies, talking and giggling. The scent of gardenia was particularly strong here. I waited as patiently as I could for them to see me and let me through, but the gossip was too good for them to notice. As I waited, I gradually became aware of something not quite right. Ahead of me, I heard giggles and saw gardenias. Just behind me were the massed ranks of senior peeresses, then the throne and its attendants at the far end of the chamber. I wasn't looking for the explosive lion at this end because I assumed that, if it was intended to kill the Queen, it would be closer to her. The thing not quite right was a smell. At first, with all the other scents around, I was hardly aware of it, because it was so small and modest in comparison – the smell you get from a candlewick when you've just lit it, before the wax starts melting. It wasn't a big, expensive candle either, just one of the ordinary ones you buy by the bundle at the grocer's. But there'd be no cheap kitchen candles in these surroundings, and in any case the lighting was gas. The smell – the merest whisper of a smell – was coming from close at hand. Something small was burning. At first, with my mind on explosions, I didn't understand the significance of it, thinking a fire had broken out but nobody was looking or panicking. By chance, standing where I was standing, I was the only person aware of it. I turned round, looked down and saw the lion.

A hefty wooden partition closed off the end of the benches, going down in steps, with an heraldic animal perched on every step. One of them was a lion, and the animal's feet were exactly the twins of the ones now among the wreaths on Felicity's grave. I must have made some sound because the ladies turned round and looked at me, open-mouthed. I pushed them out of the way and went for the lion. A line just above its feet, where the curve of the bent leg began, showed they were separate from the rest of the carving. I'd almost got my hands on it when I tripped on a step and fell to my knees.

301

'It's the heat,' somebody said. 'We should get her into the air.'

An attendant hurried up. 'If I might give you a hand, ma'am . . .'

'There's a slow match burning inside there and that lion's full of explosive,' I said, getting myself up. 'I suggest you move people away.'

They drew back like the sea in an earthquake. As they went, I heard my old client say 'It's that Liberty Lane woman' in tones that suggested blowing up most of the aristocracy was exactly what I might be expected to do. The smell of burning wick was strong now. Since nobody else was doing anything, I walked up to the lion, hooked my fingers round its feet and pulled. They slid out as easily as any properly made drawer should, and I was looking at the tiny red glow at the end of a piece of slow match. It was surrounded by a fine grey ash and there were about four inches of it left. The unlit end of it ran up to a small cotton bag glued to the side of the drawer. I pinched out the red glow almost as easily as you'd extinguish a candle flame. Then there was shouting and a couple of attendants laid hold of me. One of them grabbed the paws with the slow match out of my hands.

'Don't worry about that,' I said. 'That's just the fuse. The rest of it is where the explosive is – only for goodness' sake, move it carefully.'

But they hustled me out, through a side door and into a courtyard. When we got there, I turned and saw a police constable following us. He was carrying the carved lion with only moderate care, as a careless child might carry a doll. It was tipped slightly sidewards.

'Keep it upright,' I said. 'It could explode at any moment.'

'Not with the fuse taken out,' one of the attendants said. They seemed, for the moment, at a loss to know what to do with me.

'It's not gunpowder. It can go off on its own accord.' I wished I had Ricci there to explain.

The police constable stood the footless lion on the ground and lifted it, revealing a bottle inside. I'd never seen pyroglycerine before and looked at it curiously. It was a yellow liquid, quite thin. Mr Ricci had said it was greasy but it didn't look it. Not that I had a very good view, because the policeman and attendants were standing either side of me, not quite holding my arms but making it clear that I shouldn't try to walk away. My mind had started moving again and I thought that if somebody had intended to assassinate the Queen, it was a very ineffective place to put the explosive, quite a distance from the throne. The main sufferers would have been the rows of bejewelled senior peeresses. Then I understood. We all jumped as a gunshot sounded from outside, but it turned out that it was only the first of the formal salute marking the arrival of little Vicky. It jolted the police constable into a decision.

'I'm going to find the sergeant,' he said. 'You two keep her here.'

'I don't need to be kept anywhere,' I said. 'I'm the one who found it. If it hadn't been for me, there'd be a great hole in the House of Lords.'

But they took no notice, and the constable went off at a fast walk.

'You should be looking for the man who put it there,' I said. 'At least, the one who organized it. He's a foreman in the woodworking section, and his name is Mr James.'

It had come to me quite suddenly after I found out that he'd lied to me about not knowing Jonah Cave. There could be two reasons for the tobacco pouch being at the Compass: one, that it had been taken from him, and the second that he just happened to leave it there when visiting Minerva and the others. I thought back to my first acquaintance with Mr James, when he'd pulled me out of the river. Only he hadn't. In fact, he'd almost done quite the reverse. I remembered clinging on to the pole while Mr James had tried to sink me down into the water. I'd assumed it was clumsiness, but it had been anything but that. He'd recognized me as the woman they'd kidnapped and guessed I'd escaped from the sloop. Only the arrival on the scene of Mr Evans had stopped him drowning me. It hadn't occurred to me until a few minutes before to ask myself what a foreman was doing on the wharves so early in the morning, long before his workers arrived. He was expecting Felicity Maynard, come to look for her brother. That morning I'd arrived, not Felicity, but the next day she'd come as expected. He'd bludgeoned her, probably with one of the many bits of stone lying to hand, and thrown her body in the river. Then, knowing Jonah Cave had betrayed the plot, he'd killed him as well.

Not surprisingly, the attendants didn't react at

all to what I'd told them. A rumbling came from the direction of the Lords' chamber, not loud but clearly audible to us in the courtyard. Nothing explosive, just the sound made by a large number of ladies and gentlemen rising to their feet. They must have reassembled quickly after the shock, but most of them didn't realize quite what had happened, except that there'd been a disturbance, soon handled. Little Vicky would be coming in to take her seat on the throne, looking out over the ranks of jewelled and decorated chests and tiara-clasped heads. She might have been in no danger from the explosion, but it would have been a different matter for the peeresses. The constable came back, and with him a uniformed sergeant. He was walking fast, top hat in hand, looking far more worried than the police constable.

He saw me and stopped dead. 'Liberty Lane. I thought it would be.'

'Good afternoon, Sergeant Bevan.'

I started trying to tell him about Mr James, but I'd got no more than a few words out before a commotion started outside. It came from the far side of the courtyard, towards the river: a man shouting, then a woman's voice shouting to some-body to stop. Tabby's voice. I broke away from the attendants and went running towards the noise, flagstones underfoot, through a door, then bare earth. I heard heavy feet behind me and hoped fleetingly that they'd left somebody guarding the bottle of pyroglycerine. I'd had several seconds' start on them and was running as fast as I'd ever run in my life. I felt Julia's tiara work loose, put up a hand to save it, then

305

thought, *Why worry?* and let it fly away. The hoists on the wharves were in sight, but the running steps were coming closer. I ran on and came to the landward end of one of the wharves. A thin figure was standing at the far end, looking as if it wanted to spread its arms and fly out over the river. Tabby. I ran towards her. The steps followed, drumming on the planks. As I came near Tabby, she turned to me, her face screwed up with tension.

'They're getting away.'

I almost overbalanced and she caught me before I went in the river again. I looked over her shoulder and saw a rowing boat already at some distance from the bank, with one person in it as well as a man rowing strongly. It was making for a sloop moored a little way out from the bank. The sloop's sail was partially hoisted and it was straining at its anchor rope, wanting to go with the tide. The man had his back to us.

'He was waiting,' Tabby said. 'We thought he'd been murdered but he was here, waiting.'

The men caught up with us, Bevan leading the constable by a short head.

'Stop.'

He yelled it out to the boat, I suppose more for the sake of saying it than any expectation he'd be obeyed. The only result was that the man with his back to us turned, and I glimpsed briefly the neat beard and impassive face of Mr James before he turned towards the sloop again. It was only then that I noticed something else in the water. Somebody was swimming after the rowing boat, fast and strongly but not fast enough to catch it,

306

and the water between him and the boat was widening.

'Come back!' Bevan shouted, at the swimmer rather than the rowing boat this time. The swimmer lifted his head out of the water and looked back but didn't turn. Then I saw his face.

'Robert.'

He looked up again, and this time the expression on his face was sheer puzzlement, as if I'd landed from the moon. Then he turned and began swimming back. He had to fight hard against the tide to get to a flight of iron steps down from the end of the wharf, and my lungs rasped with every straining breath he took. Bevan and I were both at the top of the ladder, fighting to help him up. When Robert's arms clasped round me and his head came down wet and heavy on my shoulder, at least Bevan had the decency to stand aside. For a few seconds. Over Robert's bent head, I saw the rowing boat reach the sloop, then Mr James climbing the rope ladder. I didn't care.

'Mr Carmichael,' Bevan said, 'have you any knowledge about the placing of an explosive substance in the House of Lords?'

Robert straightened up and focused on him. In the last few minutes, the attendant from the Lords had arrived, carrying the bottle with its yellow liquid, still far too casually for my liking.

'That? Oh, yes, I put it in there. The others were scared of it.' He didn't have much breath left but his voice sounded nearly normal, almost amused. He walked an unsteady couple of steps over to the attendant and, before anybody could stop him, took the bottle out of his hands and stood there, holding it. Bevan and the constable went tense.

'Mr Carmichael, I should warn you . . .' Bevan began.

But Robert took no notice. His eyes on Bevan, he eased the cork out of the bottle, upended it and poured the liquid inside in a steady stream on to the planks of the wharf. A familiar odour drifted round us. The attendant, who'd screwed up his eyes, opened them and gasped.

'Piss,' Robert said to Bevan. 'The best I could do in the circumstances.'

I supposed we were under arrest, though Bevan didn't say so. As he escorted us out of the gates of the building site, the Queen and her procession of carriages were just driving away and the air was full of cheering. We got a closed carriage to Bow Street.

Twenty-Seven

'It was the jewels,' Robert said. 'They never wanted to kill the Queen, just steal the jewels.'

It was in the early hours of Saturday morning, probably with the light just breaking outside but no indication of it here, in the big, tidy room in Bow Street with the gas lamps burning. At the end, while waiting for the explosion in a shed on the building site, New-boots and Pot-belly had talked about the thing to Robert and even promised him a diamond or two from the haul, though he was sure they really intended to kill him before they sailed away. The biggest jewel robbery in the history of the world, they told him, and they might have been right. The theft of the jewels of even one aristocratic family would have been a big event, but the despoiling of almost every serious collection in the country at one blow would have been unique in criminal history. The fact that they'd be stripping them off dead and broken bodies in the confusion following the explosion didn't seem to disturb them one bit, Robert said. It was all part of the game.

Bevan nodded. 'Quite unrepentant, the two of them. They even taunted me that we've no proof against them, though that's not quite true, with Mr Carmichael's possible testimony.'

Pot-belly and New-boots had both been arrested on the site, confused and leaderless after the lack

309

of an explosion and the knowledge that Mr James had sailed away without them. They'd talked.

'Not quite true? It's not true at all,' I said. 'There's my testimony about the kidnapping, too.' The man Robert thought of as New-boots was my poet and I'd happily give evidence against him. As for Mr James and Minerva, the police were waiting for news of their arrest at any moment. There'd been a delay before a steam launch was despatched down the river after the sloop – some business with a new boiler – but Bevan had been confident they'd catch up before it reached the estuary.

'You're assuming that Mr Carmichael would be in the witness box and not the dock with them,' Bevan said.

'That's nonsense, and you know it,' I said. I hoped I sounded more confident than I felt. 'He risked his life, making that substitution for the pyroglycerine.'

Robert had told us how he'd used his minute with his back turned to the others to pour out the second bottle of nitroglycerine and replace it with the only liquid available.

'I risked your life, too,' Robert said, looking at me as if Bevan weren't there. 'I thought that if you were still alive, you were in their hands. I thought when they knew I'd tricked them, they'd . . .'

He'd carried the deadly stuff across Europe for me then, when it came to it, knew that he couldn't help them use it against human beings, not at any risk. I understood that. I hoped, in time, I'd be able to convince him of it. The harsh gas light

310

made his cheeks and eye sockets look shadowed and hollow. I moved my chair closer and took his hand. Bevan at least made no move to stop me. Robert's fingers closed on mine.

'And he was risking his life all over again, trying to stop Mr James getting away,' I said. I guessed, though, that Robert had been swimming so desperately after the rowing boat because of the faint hope that it would lead him to me. 'So it turns out that all of this was for Kidson.'

'Kidson. Kidson. Kidson.' Bevan was looking deathly tired, too. He thumped his hand down on the table with every repetition. 'The escape plot wasn't the end of it. He'd even prepared this for if it went wrong and he really was transported. It was to be the biggest jewel robbery on earth, with most of the proceeds waiting for him in whatever country he liked when his transportation was over. A real jewel robbery instead of the made-up one he was convicted for.'

'And Mr James was corrupted?'

'I think Mr James was one of those people Kidson kept on his payroll in case they were needed,' Bevan said. 'There are probably dozens if not hundreds like him – foremen at public works, fairly senior civil servants, probably police officers too, though I'll deny ever having said that, waiting until called.'

'And when you catch him, you'll put him on trial for killing Felicity Maynard and Jonah Cave?'

Bevan gave me a long look. 'Probably, if we can prove it.'

'Probably!'

311

'I think he killed them too. When we catch up with him he might even admit it, or one of the others might give evidence against him. But proving it in court will be an uphill struggle, and Kidson's organization is probably still quite capable of providing effective lawyers.' He paused. 'There is another consideration.' The silence drew out.

'Why do I know that you're going to use the word embarrassment?' I said.

He gave a twisted smile. 'Was I? Possibly, yes. The fact is that even with Kidson in prison, his organization proved capable of placing a very powerful explosive in a place that might possibly have killed the Queen and would certainly have killed the ladies of some of the most powerful families in the land.'

'But it wasn't explosive,' I said.

'They didn't know that, and incidentally, you didn't know it when you pulled out the fuse. That is another factor. At some point, an expert would have to stand up in court and give evidence as to what exactly was hidden in that carving. When he has to say that it was . . . well . . .'

'Threatening the most powerful families in the land with a bottle of piss,' I said.

Bevan went red.

'Yes, I do see how that might cause embarrassment.'

He recovered quickly. 'If they go on trial for attempting to cause an explosion, Mr Carmichael will be in the dock with them. Who brought the explosive from Italy in the first place?'

'And who risked his life to see that they didn't

use it?' I said. Robert was saying nothing, just looking at me, his face unreadable. I knew he felt guilty, mainly because he thought he'd risked my life in doing what he did, so wouldn't defend himself.

'It's not my decision,' Bevan said. 'But I have to say, I think there's a strong likelihood that the House of Lords business will never come to court.' That anonymous man from the Home Office wasn't there this time, yet somehow I could see his shadow looming over Bevan.

They let us go at around seven o'clock on Saturday morning, with people out walking on the pavements and carts in the streets. Once we were clear of the police station, Tabby appeared from around a corner, Ricci with her. Ricci practically flew at Robert. What had he done with the pyroglycerine? Why did the police let him go? Since Robert had no idea of Ricci's existence until that point, I had to do some explaining. Wearily and politely, Robert answered his questions. All he could do for Ricci was to explain that both bottles would have gone up in the trial explosion by the Thames, and express his deepest regret for the theft. Not surprisingly, that didn't satisfy Ricci, but he did agree to come back with us and hear the story. The four of us walked slowly together to Abel Yard while Robert told it. Amos was waiting in the yard, and his face when he saw Robert switched from disbelief to joy, then to a world of questions.

'Tabby will tell you,' I said, and hugged him. I was almost too tired to speak. We left them there with Ricci, promising to come back. Robert and I paused at the gates into the mews, looking out on the comings and goings of an early Saturday morning.

'Home?' he said.

'Home.'

So we started walking to our house, not far away. So many explanations to give, so many apologies to be made, but together.

We made them – the apologies and explanations, and most of them were accepted. Even Amos was a little hurt, though he tried to conceal it, about not being there at the end. Ricci left for Italy with a long letter from Robert to Professor Sobrero, not excusing but explaining. Later, Robert and I would go to Turin together and apologize in person. And Mr James and Minerva? They got away. The steamboat with the police on it didn't catch up with the sloop until it had turned up the east coast out of the estuary. Neither of them was on board by then, and the crew of two and a boy, going about their stone-carrying business, denied all knowledge of them. Julia's tiara came back. One of the workmen found it on the Saturday morning after the Lords ceremony by the path, a little dusty and out of shape, and very honestly handed it in. I suppose it rated as the high class of litter you might expect after a state occasion. Work at the building site went on as normal. Nobody expected it to be finished for years.